CURING DEATH

MARK ROSENBERG M.D.

Rosemark Press

I dedicate this book to all those who are fighting to hold on to life. Do your best to stay with us. Regardless of the outcome, be at peace, knowing that this life is not the end.

PREFACE

I started writing this novel in the year 2000, while I was the Assistant Chief of Emergency Medicine at my local hospital. I began by writing a synopsis of the story you're about to read. But because of my heavy workload, I didn't have time to complete the manuscript. Into the drawer it went.

In 2004, my mother presented to me in the emergency department complaining of chest pain. I ordered a CT scan and eventually diagnosed her with metastatic lung cancer to liver, spleen, bilateral adrenal glands, and left hip. I learned that chemotherapy might give her up to six months to live, compared to four-to-six months if we chose supportive care only. My mother chose to do some alternative therapies, and she lived eleven months, ten of those with a reasonable quality of life.

My interest in understanding cancer grew ever stronger after my mother passed. I started researching avidly online, and then completed some in-vitro studies that further piqued my curiosity. I began treating cancer patients with my own version of "integrative therapies." While I have never been satisfied with my accomplishments, I have improved the quality of life for many of my patients, and significantly extended their survival time.

Years later, I started a pharmaceutical company, with the goal to target cancer stem cells. We eventually merged with a Harvard spin-out and hope to begin human trials in 2024. More recently, my team and I have been at work on an extracorporeal filtration device to eliminate tumor clusters from the bloodstream. These clusters are responsible for the metastatic seeding process: the spread of cancer throughout the body. It is my hypothesis that if we can keep these clusters to zero by filtering them out as often as needed, we can significantly extend survival, and perhaps convert a systemic disease back into a local disease.

In 2022, I decided to re-read my novel synopsis and this time, the timing clicked. This novel is the manifestation of my creativity, my masterpiece. The same heart, mind, and soul that allows me to study and attempt to understand cancer, has granted me the inspiration to write this science-fiction fantasy.

My primary objective in writing this novel was to entertain myself and other readers. My secondary objective is to perhaps inspire some scientists to think outside of the box. I believe we can make far greater strides in our treatment of cancer and other terminal diseases than we have to date.

As I wrote this book, I laughed, and I cried. Most of the emergency department visits in this book are based on my actual experiences. I hope my novel brings you the same enjoyment I experienced while writing it.

All my best,

Mark Rosenberg, M.D.

CHAPTER 1

"**G**et me a needle and a chest tube."

Dr. Mike Royce keeps his eyes trained on the boy wheezing and sputtering on the gurney. Blood pools from a gunshot wound, slick and viscous across his dark brown chest. One look and Royce knows the teenager—his shoulders slight like a child's—has a collapsed lung.

Another gang incident, Royce thinks, as the seconds tick by. It's only 9:45 p.m., and gang-related trauma has been barreling through the emergency department. Tonight, he's already treated two stabbings and a gunshot wound to the pelvis, the results of three separate gang fights across town. Gang injuries and fatalities were common in his ER, especially on these suffocating Albuquerque nights.

Sweat collects on Royce's brow, and perspiration trickles down his spine like a steady drip of a faucet. His gloved hands carefully roam the boy's chest, feeling for the bullet wound. Royce opens his mouth to ask for assistance when a hand mops his forehead dry with a sterile cloth. He doesn't need to turn his gaze to know who stepped in; Nurse Alesha Simmons is always there right when he needs her. Royce nods a thank you, but his favorite nurse has already slipped back into the busy dance of the ER.

"If I don't get a needle in his chest immediately, he's not going to make it!" Royce feels a surge of irritation rising like a small fire in his throat. He has neither the time nor the patience for anyone who can't keep up with him. As he turns his attention back to his patient, he catches a glimpse of Alesha across the exam room. She shoots him a measured look that says *watch yourself* as she steps aside for the new nurse on the floor to deliver the needle to Royce's waiting hands.

Royce stands over the boy, steadies himself, then plunges the needle into the injured chest, all the way to the hub. Air rushes out through the needle, and Royce holds his breath, eyes unblinking. He watches the boy's labored breathing ease, heart rate decrease, and blood pressure normalize.

"Chest tube," he says as he prepares to make a three-centimeter incision between the boy's ribs. The novice nurse, learning fast, is at his elbow, ready with the tube. As Royce prepares to place the tube in the patient's chest, the trauma room doors slam open with a thundercrack.

For a single, frozen instant, Royce struggles to understand what's happening. A swarm of hooded figures surge into the ER. The young nurse beside him screams, breaking his paralyzed trance as the room melts into chaos.

The hooded boys charge toward the gurney, pointed guns glinting under the surgical lights. Still screaming, the young nurse crumples to the floor—Royce can't tell if she's been shot or if she's collapsed in terror—as pops snap from pistols.

"Security!" Royce shouts. He backs himself up against the gurney to shield his patient and spots Alesha across the room, crouched against the wall, her trembling arm reaching for the phone. Rage rises to meet his panic as he realizes the terrible, lethal failure that's already happened. It's standard protocol for the hospital to be locked down when there's an active shooter in the area. Now there are six—no, eight—gun-wielding gang members here to finish the job they started with nothing stopping them.

Royce stares into the black holes of twin muzzles as two boys march toward him, their target behind Royce. Royce lifts his arms, palms out—a doomed attempt to stop them, but what can he do— as gunshots crackle behind him. Royce's hands instinctively fly to his ears. He turns to see his patient's head and torso riddled with bullets. The smell of burning metal hits his nose, filling his lungs with an acrid, sulfurous burn.

"Security!" Royce tries to yell a second time. But he can't hear anything, can't tell if his mouth is forming words or if any sound is escaping his body at all.

The two boys in front of him are as still as statues, guns raised and pointed at Royce's heart. He holds up his hands again, this time in surrender. Memories of his lifetime play inside his head: listening to his mother sing from the backseat of his father's beloved Cadillac, then making frantic, elated love to his high school girlfriend, then lifting his medical school diploma in glee, then doubling over in pain at the loss of his first patient. The movie playing in his head cuts off as a bullet rips into his chest.

Like an oil slick lit by a match, a roiling fire spreads throughout his body. A heavy fog rises around him, clouding his vision, and he reels backward, collapsing onto the floor. His hands fly to his chest, his fingers sinking into the blood pooling and dripping down his torso.

As the gang members flee, Royce sees feet scrambling toward him, hears the clang of instrument tables being overturned and the ring of sirens in the distance. The other ER doc on duty is at his side, shouting guttural commands that sound like they're coming from far away. Royce's chest pulses and spasms as he struggles to take a breath. He blinks frantically as darkness closes in.

Suddenly, he bolts upright to the sound of his own bloodcurdling scream. Gone is the frenzied panic and chaos of the ER. The room is pitch black and silent. Royce is drenched in sweat; he feels it seeping down his face and back, his T-shirt clinging to his clammy skin. His hand flies to his chest as his eyes dart around the room. Disoriented still, his heart is racing until, it dawns on him; he's in his bedroom. He touches the cool, familiar linen sheets beneath him.

A nightmare? The shot, the screams, the feel of the blood and the smell of the smoke—it was so vivid, so unerringly real, like no other dream he'd ever experienced.

Trembling and weak-kneed, Royce leaves the bed and stumbles to his dresser. In the dream, he'd been wearing his lucky T-shirt under his scrubs, like he often did during his ER shifts. He'd had the shirt since he was eighteen. Since then, he'd survived dozens of accidents, including falls, cuts, bruises, a motorcycle fall, tumbling from a rock twenty feet high, and a slip of a knife—cutting an apple, of all things. During each mishap, Royce had been wearing his shirt, and while wearing it in the ER, he rarely lost a patient. Mike Royce isn't a superstitious man, but he knows that his shirt is a powerful talisman.

He slowly pulls his second dresser drawer open. The dream

still gripping his psyche, he almost can't bear to look. But it's there, folded in a neat square. He shakes the shirt loose and holds it up by the shoulders. It looks the same as it did yesterday and the day before that, faded and worn, seams crooked from all the times he's patched it up.

He runs his hands across the thin cotton. Sure enough, there's no hole at the heart.

It really was just a dream.

Towel wrapped around his waist, Royce stares into his reflection in the mirror. Beads of sweat collect against his temples, his thick, dark hair still damp from a shower that did little to calm his rattled nerves. As Royce meets his own gaze, he leans in closer to the mirror. He inspects the subtle lines extending from the corners of his eyes and pulls the skin taut on both sides. Sighing, he drops his hands. Royce is lean and well-muscled, his frame carved from a stringent, five-day-a-week workout regimen and a meticulous diet. But age is creeping in, accelerated by the emotional and physical strain of his work.

Anything that can be loved so strongly can be hated just as intensely. That's exactly how Dr. Mike Royce is starting to feel about his relationship with emergency medicine. In 2013, he completed his residency training in emergency medicine. At the time, he was certain he could do this forever. His passion for medicine felt boundless. In the years since, he's grown into a superb clinician. His technical skills are extraordinary. When the ER is verging out of control, that's when Royce performs at his best, functioning with the speed and accuracy that few other emergency physicians can attain.

Now, after more than ten years on the front lines, he's struggling with a burnout that he'd never anticipated. Despite a disciplined attention to his own health that borders on obsession, his body suffers under the grind of long, physically demanding ER shifts and too little sleep. But more than anything, death is becoming harder and harder to take. For all his technical prowess as a physician, Royce prides himself equally on the deep compassion that he extends to his patients. He's emotionally tortured by the human tragedy that he encounters daily in the emergency room, and every patient lost fuels an anger that he finds increasingly hard to quell.

His twelve-hour shifts often leave him feeling depleted, irritable, and hopeless. He knows that the only way he'll be able to stick it out is to reduce the number of shifts. Sometimes he thinks about retiring from medicine altogether. At only thirty-eight years old, he can't ignore the voice that infiltrates his head: *You can't sustain this.*

Death has found its way into his dreams before, but never his own death, and never with such terrifying realism. Royce can't stop running his hands across his torso, his chest feeling tight and wracked by phantom pain. He has devoted his existence to a pair of passions that are intertwined: his career in medicine, and the pursuit of eternal youth. He eats the cleanest food, devotes hours a day to vigorous exercise, and fuels his system with a precise routine of nutritional supplements. In his free time, he consumes scientific studies on the aging process, reading vociferously about the pathways that lead to aging, disease, and eventual death of the body.

Alongside his ER duties, he's been developing his own research project about the intersection of past medical history, family history, and lifestyle factors in aging and disease. In a matter of weeks, he'll go before the hospital board to request funding, the culmination of months of hard work assembling a research team, designing a study and research protocols. For Royce, pushing back against the aging process—and more so, working against the clock that is life—has become an obsession.

But it never feels like enough.

The limitations of anti-aging and longevity science make him want to scream and tear his hair out. Diet, exercise, sleep, mental health, preventative care, and early intervention are all valuable, of course, but they only go so far. Royce lives a model existence, from eating a pristine diet to following a precise exercise routine. As a doctor, he has access to the latest and best information. Still, he's aware of his body changing, slowing down, growing more vulnerable. He can't help but feel that this morning's dream was a harbinger of what's to come for him. Not a shot to the chest, but a rogue cell that turns cancerous, a weak-walled blood vessel that bursts, a runaway protein in his brain that steals his cognition.

And what about his patients? If Royce—with his abundant resources, his scientific knowledge, and his unusual discipline and drive—can't forestall aging, how can his patients ever hope to? The futility of it all gnaws at him. And every death makes him desperate to do more.

Royce had felt himself at a breaking point near the end of a night shift. It was nearing three a.m., and Royce was on his way to the break room when the ambulance bay doors swung open. Two EMTs rushed a man into room one. From down the hall, Royce saw the volume of blood on the sheets. He dropped his water bottle and protein bar, ready to assess the patient.

"Car accident," one of the ER nurses informed Royce as he approached the gurney. "Significant lacerations on the left side."

The man was unconscious and unresponsive. Abrasions to his head indicated a possible brain injury that needed immediate assessment.

"Get him in the CT scanner ASAP. Let's scan his head, chest, abdomen, and pelvis," Royce ordered as he moved to the phone and called radiology.

As he dialed the extension, one of the nurses called out, "Dr. Royce!"

He turned to see the patient convulsing. In less than a minute, the monitor flatlined, one long and loud beep that echoed throughout the halls. A haunting sound that no one working in the ER ever becomes numb to. Walking away, Royce punched the door beside him. He didn't know how much longer he could stand to do this day in and day out when he couldn't control the outcome.

He whispered to himself, "I'm going to stop this."

"What's that, Dr. Royce?" one of the ER nurses asked solemnly, breaking the collective silence that they'd been in since the monitor flatlined.

He met the nurse's eyes and shook his head, saying, "No, nothing." His gaze landed on the patient's bloody, lifeless body.

What good did it do to focus on anti-aging, when it, at best, delayed the inevitable? When it did little for the people who were already sick or injured? Mike Royce had never been accused of aiming low, and what he really wanted to know was this: could the brakes be pulled on death itself?

. . .

Royce leans in close to the mirror. His reflection greets him with a look of defiance. The man's death yesterday and his own death in a dream that felt more real than most of his waking life have pushed him to this point. He can no longer look away from the question that circles constantly in his mind: *Is death inevitable?*

CHAPTER 2

Slavish to his routine, Royce slips on his lucky T-shirt and heads to the gym before his shift, unsettled by the waves of anxiety that course through him like aftershocks from his nightmare. For years, Royce's obsession with optimizing his mind and body has helped him avoid thinking about his own death. There's no hole in his chest, but he feels wounded and shaken.

After a light warm-up run around the indoor track, he heads to the weight room. A typical workout routine for Royce takes two hours. He goes through his chest and back routine, hitting the bench press, pushing himself until he's breathing hard and drenched in sweat. Moving his body through this familiar routine is helping to restore his sense of control and calm. But he knows it's only temporary; he'll be on duty at the hospital later.

Halfway through his first rep of bicep curls, he realizes that he's lifting his typical fifty-pound dumbbells with unusual ease. Certain he's picked up a lighter pair by mistake, he's surprised to see the number fifty stamped on each side. He puts them back and selects a pair of sixty-pound weights. Royce has no idea how it's possible, but these feel easier than the lighter ones.

Never one to shy away from a challenge, Royce grabs the seventy-five-pounders, a weight that only yesterday would have been tough for him to lift through a single rep. When his forearms rise with ease, he's shocked. His surprise and confusion grow when he's able to complete a full set, then another, then a third. He sits down on an empty weight bench and pulls a long draw from his water bottle, puzzled and proud. *How was that possible?* He's feeling energized, not depleted, after extending himself well beyond his previous personal best. Several years ago, when he was training intensely, he could barely have made it through these sets, and now he's doing it with ease. *Where is this strength coming from?* Had the dream, horrible as it was, somehow purged something from his mind, some existential anxiety that had been dragging him down?

Royce laughs at this dime-store self-analysis. Always on the lookout for the latest, cutting-edge research about ways to boost cellular rejuvenation, he is constantly tweaking his supplement routine. He rationalizes that the new combination of amino acids he switched to last month is probably the source of this newfound physical prowess.

Royce hops up from the bench and grabs a pair of dumbbells. His ego brimming, he half-tosses the weights upward in his hands as he's dropping them back down to their rack. One of the dumbbells slips from his hand. He lurches to the right to avoid the weight crashing down on his foot. But he can't move fast enough; it grazes his left side, knocking the wind out of him. He drops to his knees, doubled over, his vision going blurry as pain radiates through his ribcage.

"Mike? Are you okay?" One of the trainers rushes over and kneels next to him.

Royce is unable to breathe out a response; the pain in his rib is searing.

The trainer calls out to the front desk. "Raquel, call an ambulance."

Royce lifts himself to his feet and extends his hand to grasp the trainer's muscled arm, saying, "No, Bill, I'm okay." He lifts up his now-ripped T-shirt and gingerly touches his throbbing side. He tries to take a deeper breath and shudders. It hurts, but it could be worse. He's pretty sure the rib isn't cracked.

The trainer looks skeptical. "Are you sure? I can get someone to drive you to the hospital."

"Seriously, Billy," Royce says. "I'm on my way to work from here. I'll get it looked at."

In the locker room, Royce gingerly removes his shirt, wincing as he lifts his arm over his head. He threads his finger through the latest tear and pulls the ripped sides together, closing the gap. He'll stitch it tonight after his shift. His lucky shirt came through for him again, helping him make it through another accident— two, if he counts the dream he can't seem to shake.

"You're lucky, Mike." Dr. Adele Washington steps back from the screen so Royce can see his X-ray. "It's bruised, but not broken. Got a little carried away being a fitness bro?" His ER colleague offers him a wry smile.

Royce shrugs sheepishly, at a rare loss for words. He wonders again what came over him with those weights. He'd felt an almost superhuman strength. He still feels the outsize energy running through his bloodstream. As he dangles his legs off the gurney, he strains to sit up straight with his wounded side.

"I'll call PT and get you on their schedule this week. A few weeks of therapy and you should be all set."

"I don't think I need—"

"Don't go there, Mike." Dr. Washington puts up a firm hand. "You're not going to be that doctor, you hear me? Go home and rest and do your physical therapy like a good patient."

Royce reluctantly agrees to PT but insists on working his shift tonight as scheduled.

"I don't recommend it, Mike," says Dr. Washington. No joking around now; she's employing her full-on cautionary physician tone. She rolls her eyes, her clasped hands spreading apart like a pair of exasperated wings taking flight. "But I know better than to waste my time arguing with you. Be sure to ice it for twenty or so every few hours. And for god's sake, don't blow off PT, okay?"

"I promise." Royce zips up his sweatshirt. "Thanks, Adele."

"No problem, happy to help. Just don't expect me to pick up your slack today." Her eyes crinkle as she breaks into a playful smile.

Royce laughs. "Like I'd ever."

She's halfway out the door when she stops and gives him a look of thoughtful concern. "You sure you're okay, Mike?" She sounds like she's asking about more than his bruised rib.

"I feel good." Royce lifts his arms and swivels his torso, doing his best to mask the ribbon of pain shooting through his chest.

Oddly, he means it. His side hurts, and he's frustrated with his carelessness. He'll have to scale back his workouts for a while. But he's still humming with energy. Maybe coming so close to death—even in a dream—kicked something primal loose inside of him, putting him in touch with the privilege of living and getting to do what he loves. He feels a striking vitality coursing through his body, tickling his every cell. For the first time in longer than he cares to admit, Royce can't wait to get to work. Whatever this is, he's going to ride this energy wave for as long as it lasts.

The ER is as hectic and grueling as usual. It's a steady trickle of minor accidents and non-life-threatening illness punctuated by major traumas that hit in ceaseless waves: heart attacks and head traumas and seizures and strokes, victims of car wrecks and victims of violence, cut or beaten or shot. Despite his throbbing ribcage, Royce cruises through most of his shift. He barely needs a break, though under Dr. Washington's disapproving gaze he makes sure to periodically retreat to the staff lounge with a fresh ice pack. He catches himself a couple of times whistling and humming as he moves swiftly between exam rooms. He hasn't felt this good, this alive, in months. He feels like he's home again after a long absence, thriving in the ER, the place that means the most to him.

After ten hours, reality hits. Royce starts to slow down. Fatigue creeps in and the pain in his side hikes. He's about to retreat to his small office to update charts when Alesha calls to him from down the corridor.

"Dr. Royce! Exam room one—we need you."

Dropping the stack of charts on the charge nurse's desk, he pivots and strides down the hall. Royce opens the door to find a pleasant-looking, older gentleman reclining on the gurney, wearing an easy smile. A kind-eyed woman—his wife, Royce assumes—anxiously strokes his arm. Royce greets the couple with a smile as he flips open the man's chart. After a quick scan, Royce lifts his eyes for another look at the patient. You'd think seventy-year-old Harry Samuelson was relaxing with a cup of tea on his front porch, not experiencing very low blood pressure, the result of his main blood vessel, the abdominal aorta, rupturing.

Harry Samuelson returns Royce's look of knowing surprise with a measured, knowing look of his own.

"I'm going to die soon," Harry says. He sounds as he looks: the picture of calm. Patients aren't typically this composed, this enlightened, under the harsh glare of ER lights, when their lives are in jeopardy. Royce feels unsettled, maybe even threatened, by the man's deep sense of peace in the face of death.

"Harry, please stop," his wife says, sounding desperate and tired. "You're making me so nervous." She turns to Royce. "Please tell him he's full of beans, doctor." She's trying to keep things light, but Royce sees the panic in her eyes when she asks, "What does he need?"

"We're going to take good care of you, Mr. Samuelson." Dr. Royce makes sure to include the man's frantic wife in his compassionate gaze. Alesha, amid adjusting Harry's blood pressure cuff, places her hand briefly on Mrs. Samuelson's quaking shoulders.

Harry looks Royce steadily in the eyes but doesn't respond. He continues to sit tranquilly in his bed, an even deeper look of peace washing over him as his wife, tears welling, leans in and grasps both his hands in her own.

It's uncanny, and Royce has seen it before. Somehow, even when it's not anticipated by the physician, patients frequently know when their time has come. Most aren't as sanguine about it as the patient in front of him, but the knowing is often there. He hopes this isn't the case with Samuelson, but the man's deep composure has him rattled and concerned. He looks at Harry and his wife, Harry the picture of tranquility and her a weeping, anxious mess.

Dr. Royce excuses himself to phone the surgeon on call. A wave of fatigue washes over him, and he leans against the wall as he's being patched through to the hospital's top cardiothoracic surgeon, Dr. Bradley Roberts.

"What've you got, Mike?"

"Brad, I have a seventy-year-old male with a ruptured abdominal aorta. His blood pressure is dropping. How quickly can you be here?" Royce rubs his aching side, his waves of fatigue now alternating with a rising sense of alarm.

"I'm ten minutes away," the surgeon says. He starts to say something else when Alesha comes up behind Royce.

"What?" Royce whispers, pulling the phone away from his ear.

"You're needed in room two."

Royce makes a fist around the phone cord. "I'm not the only physician on duty, Alesha," he hisses.

He watches Alesha's eyes widen and immediately regrets his tone. It's not like Royce to snap at her, of all people, and he's not in the habit of trying to dump cases onto other doctors. If Royce had his way, he'd be the one to handle every patient who came through the doors on his shift. The stress of this strange day is catching up with him.

Royce exhales and pulls the phone back to his ear. "See you in ten, Brad—if you can make it eight, so the better. I'm worried about this one."

Alesha hands him the chart for the patient in exam two and he scans it quickly as he enters the room. He swallows hard as the lump in his throat swells. There is a twenty-week-old fetus hanging partway out of a young girl's vagina. Royce's face twists as he watches the fetus gasp for air. He takes a deep breath to regain his composure. One look tells him this fetus won't be in this world long. Because of the immaturity of the lungs, a fetus is generally not viable until at least twenty-four weeks of age. A surge of powerlessness rises inside of him; he tries to push it down, but it is stubborn and buoyant.

Alesha moves immediately to the girl's shoulders, draping her upper body across the girl's own to quiet her panicked writhing. Royce snaps on his gloves and moves between the girl's legs, putting his hands under the tiny body as a nurse behind him wheels in an incubator. The fetus slips into his hands, its weight barely registering on Royce's palms. The girl screams, a sound Royce knows well as a dreadful cocktail of pain, fear, and grief. Royce cuts the umbilical cord.

As he lifts the frail body into the incubator, a pair of eyelids flutter and for an instant, Royce's eyes meet two dark pools. His breath catches in his throat; it's as though a hand is gripping his heart. He performs a short exam, which tells him all he needs to know about the fetus's chances of survival. Royce's eyes meet Alesha's before Royce quickly turns away from her tears, trying to avert his own. He'll call neonatology down to the floor, but he knows they won't be able to save this life. He motions to the nurse, who steps in to wrap the fragile body and transfer the male fetus to the girl's arms for the short while that remains.

Royce follows Alesha out to the hallway. She peels off toward exam one for a check on Samuelson, and Royce goes back again to the phone. Leaning against the wall once more, he speaks briefly with the neonatologist. He hangs up and puts his hands on his head. There's nothing to do but wait. A familiar helpless rage begins to simmer inside him. His side aches.

"Dr. Royce!" Alesha calls to him from down the hall.

He rushes back to room one, the intensity in her voice telling him to hurry. He passes Mrs. Samuelson, who has been ushered from her husband's room, weeping as she walks in a tight circle, hands flapping with nothing to hold. With a cry, she reaches out for Royce, who has nothing to give her at this moment. The most he can do for her is get to her husband as fast as he can.

He steps inside to see a dark and widening pool of blood exsanguinating on the gurney beneath Harry. There must be five liters, maybe more. The man's aneurysm has likely eroded into his bowel. Dr. Royce rushes to Harry's side, and as he's about to lift the light blanket off the man's thin frame, the monitor goes into one long beep. Time stops, and all eyes watch the flatline.

Mrs. Samuelson bursts into the room, her sobs drowning out the mechanical tone. She rushes to his lifeless body and buries her face in his chest, tears leaking into the fabric of his hospital gown. She fumbles to regain a hold on hands that can no longer return her grasp.

"Harry, no—Harry—please, Harry, come back!"

Alesha attempts to pull Mrs. Samuelson out of the room for a second time now. "Please, ma'am, move back so the doctor can—"

"I love you, Harry!" Mrs. Samuelson yells as she's pulled away from her husband's body and toward the door. "Don't forget our deal!"

Suddenly, a single ventricular complex blip comes across the monitor. Royce and Alesha both stop in their tracks and stare at the screen. For one instant that feels like a lifetime, Royce holds his breath as he waits for a second blip. Air rushes from his lungs as the monitor reverts to a flatline.

Royce looks at Alesha and raises his eyebrows. She returns a similar expression. Alesha's arm is still draped across Mrs. Samuelson's shoulder, the pair standing stone-still in the middle of the room. The woman doesn't look surprised. For the first time since they've arrived at the hospital, she looks calm and composed. Royce can't make sense of it.

In a quiet voice, he asks, "You said something about a deal, Mrs. Samuelson. What was that about?"

Harry's wife leans her head back and closes her eyes, as if traveling back in time to a memory. A smile overtakes her face before she says, "We always said that whoever dies first has to promise to watch over the other." Her eyes drift back to her husband's body, and she reaches her hands out to the empty space of the room. "I heard you, Harry. I feel you. I *see* you." Silent tears still stream down her face, but she looks at peace.

Dr. Royce looks into Harry's eyes. They seem impenetrable, flat, and opaque. It dawns on him that he can no longer look *into* Harry's eyes the way he could just prior to Harry's death. He can now only look *at* them. Dr. Royce feels the rush and the weight of a great epiphany. He has gazed into the eyes of the living, the dying, and the dead countless times, yet only now does he recognize what he's seeing.

When he looks into the eyes of the living, he senses an infinite depth, an energy behind the eyes that has no boundaries. When a patient dies, it seems like a wall comes down behind the eyes that replaces that energy. Is this what people mean when they say the eyes truly are windows to the soul? Royce has never been preoccupied with the idea of a soul. So consumed by pulling bodies away from death, so obsessed with finding the perfect formula to stave off illness and disease, he's dismissed thoughts of the soul as fuzzy and irrelevant, unquantifiable, and therefore not of interest or use to him as a man of science. But he can't deny what he saw—what he felt—as he watched the life disappear from Harry Samuelson's eyes.

The final two hours of this shift have felt like a lifetime. Two lives, one at each end of the spectrum. Two sets of eyes that Mike Royce had been the last person to see animated with life. Two deaths he could do nothing to prevent. He couldn't stop them, but were they truly inevitable? Or had science not yet found the tools to avert them?

His left side throbs. He feels ragged and empty, the energy that earlier surged through him depleted, drained by the powerlessness he feels. He can no longer abide it, death itself and his impotence in the face of it.

CHAPTER 3

After a long, hot shower at home that does little to wash him free of the day's painful emotional residue, Royce stands in front of the foggy mirror. He wipes at it with his hand to clear the fog and applies shaving cream. With a frown, he notes the ever-increasing number of gray hairs in his previously jet-black stubble. He touches the razor to his face, then lowers it to the sink and lets his hands fall to the cool, damp marble. He stares deeply into his own eyes. It's an uncomfortable exercise, one Royce can't remember ever doing before. He searches his own gaze, stretching to see a self that exists beyond the corporeal body he lavishes with care. *Is it possible?*

He thinks about Harry Samuelson's peaceful, intelligent eyes, brimming with energy even as his body eroded within. He thinks about the tiny, underdeveloped eyes of the twenty-week-old fetus, fighting to flutter open and take in a brief glimpse of the world.

· · ·

For all the years he's been practicing medicine, each heart-wrenching case takes up permanent residence somewhere in Royce's mind. The weight of the losses is driving him out of a career he loves. The loss of two patients today, at opposite poles of life, hit him with equal torment and frustration. And his constant proximity to death has done nothing to bring him peace about his own eventual demise. He's chilled at the thought of the blackness he imagines awaiting him.

Royce gives his head a rough shake, as if to empty his thoughts. He's got to blow off some steam and put this strange day behind him. At least the pain of his bruised rib has subsided.

"I need to get out," he mumbles to himself. What he really needs is a drink and some company. The company of a good friend, and the company of beautiful women.

With that thought, he feels his cells tickle to life, a rush of energy spreading through him. Dr. Royce is keenly aware of his ability to captivate the opposite sex. Women love Mike Royce. He is, empirically, attractive. That's not ego talking; he works tirelessly at his body, and his fit good looks are the result. And he knows it doesn't hurt that he's a doctor. He and his fellow physician friends occasionally joke about the halo effect of having an MD when it comes to romancing women. Beyond looks or professional cachet, Royce has a preternatural skill for connecting with women on an emotional level.

He has always thought of that ability as being one facet of his larger gift, which is his flair for making any person feel loved, nearly instantaneously. How many times had he heard patients tell him that he's the most caring doctor they'd ever met, after he had spent less than five minutes with them? He had never given much thought to how he'd come to possess this ability. It was always just there. From his earliest rounds as an eager, inexperienced intern, he knew his patients could genuinely feel his empathy and caring nature. And he was certain it wasn't so much what he would say that seemed to touch them; rather, it was the way he would look in their eyes while he spoke.

There they are. The eyes, again. He just wants to stop thinking about it all for a while. About souls and dying and how little he knows despite years of hard work and endless study. But his rigorous mind has seized this subject and will not let go.

Dr. Royce phones his buddy and fellow ER doc, Manny Walters.

"Hey, you up for hitting the town?" Royce asks as he tucks his dress shirt, neatly pressed, into a pair of custom-tailored jeans. He already knows the answer. Manny never lets him down.

"I'm in. Be there at ten," Manny says and hangs up without another word. There's no need to make plans. Royce and Manny have a well-established routine: they meet at the same exclusive, members-only social club in Nob Hill for a couple of drinks and a lot of mingling with women. Manny and Royce have the same idea about what makes for a good night out. For them, it's more about seeking female companionship rather than sitting around and gabbing with friends. Royce spends what little free time he has out romancing women in an endless series of rendezvous. Some turn into dates. A select few turn into relationships. But they never last long because Dr. Royce is looking for the perfect mate. He is on a relentless, methodical, as yet fruitless search for the woman who can match him, physically and intellectually. Royce grabs his keys and is out the door. He's not sure if he's ever needed a night out so badly.

He hands his keys to the valet and walks into the club, feeling the rhythmic drumming of the music from the dance floor before he hears it. His spirits soar. This is just what he needs tonight. The lights are low, the club is packed, and Royce finds Manny without even trying. His friend is sitting at their usual table with a beer waiting for him.

Manny shakes Royce's hand and gestures for him to sit. Royce downs the beer Manny had waiting for him in two large gulps.

Manny raises his eyebrows. "Tough day?"

"You could say that." Royce wipes his mouth with the back of his hand. "I'm gonna get us a couple more."

He heads for the bar, pushing his way through the masses of people dancing, sweating, unleashing their worries and their burdens in a sensual frenzy of movement. Royce is desperate to lose himself in the thick of it all.

A pair of lagers in hand, Royce returns to find Manny flirting with a reed-thin woman in her twenties. He slides Manny's beer under his friend's arm and sits back, stretching his legs underneath the small table. Usually, nights like these feel endless with possibility and light as air. Tonight, the endless possibilities on Royce's mind feel uncomfortably heavy. Compartmentalizing is something that he's learned to do well to survive the emotional gauntlet of his work. So why can't he shake loose the thought of Harry Samuelson and the tiny eyes of the fetus he held in his arms earlier?

"Cheers, buddy." Manny breaks Royce's trance with a clink to his lager.

"That didn't last long." Royce watches the waifish woman slip into the crowd.

"She's an investment advisor. Wouldn't stop talking about setting me up in one of her funds. The minute she heard about my student loans she was outta here." Manny shrugs. "Can't get blood from a stone, babe."

Royce utters a distracted laugh and drains the last of his beer.

Manny's eyes widen. "What's up with you tonight? You're usually good for two beers all night."

Royce looks at his friend for a long moment then takes the leap. "Do you believe souls exist?"

Manny laughs. "Dude, I didn't know what to expect from you, but I did not expect that. You must have had some day."

"Definitely a ringer."

Manny's eyes soften and he nods. A fellow ER traveler, he knows how bad it can get.

"Okay, well, I'm not religious. Got more than my share of that growing up. The organized, dogmatic routine didn't suit me. But I'm pretty comfortable saying I can't rule it out. Feels above my pay grade, you know?"

"Don't you want to know?" Royce leans across the table. "I mean, really know, with certainty, whether we have a life force that lives beyond our body? Imagine what we could do with that knowledge."

"Do with it? What would change if we knew? We still wouldn't know what comes after death. Until we get there."

"But what if we could change it all, stop the *after* from coming?"

Manny lets out a low whistle before saying, "Must've been a whopper of a day." He takes a swig of beer and eyes a pair of women as they clasp hands and skip toward the dance floor.

"Look, I'm a simple man, Mike. I'm a mechanic in the big cosmic game of life. It's my job to patch them up as best I can, keep them running for a while longer. And when I can't, it hurts, for sure. But I leave the metaphysical stuff to the philosophers, priests, and rabbis."

Dr. Royce flushes with embarrassment. He worries that he sounds delusional. He knows that he's different from Manny and his other colleagues. Every one of them feels the pain and defeat of losing a patient. But to Royce, death feels like a failure. A failure of the body, and also a failure of the human imagination, a failure of science to step in and solve our most universal existential problem. Maybe the beer is clouding his thinking, but in this moment, he believes he can be the person to stop death in its tracks. It sounds impossibly grand, even ludicrous, to his own ears.

"Let's get out there," he says, looking at the dance floor. Manny looks relieved and hops up to follow the pair of women who skipped by their table. Royce stands slowly, assessing the dance floor, looking for his opening move. His eyes track to the left and settle on a redheaded woman in a flowing maxi dress, sipping on her cocktail straw and swaying her hips as she scans the crowd. Royce gestures toward the dance floor. She nods, and they meet halfway, hips already moving in sync. They dance close, not touching yet, bodies feeling each other out, twisting and shaking close, then away, then close again. His side feels no pain. The woman's long hair streams across her face as she swings her hips and shoulders. Royce can't see her eyes.

As she sways her hips to move closer to his, she raises her arms and whips her head from side to side, hair flying. Her mouth spreads into a sensual smile as her eyelids close. She's beauty in motion, but all Royce can think about is catching her gaze, being able to look straight into her eyes. Without realizing it, he stops dancing. He's standing perfectly still. Watching, waiting for her eyes to open. He wonders, *If the soul exists, is it animated or otherwise powered by that boundless energy that dwells behind the eyes?*

. . .

It takes a few more beats of the music for the woman to realize she's dancing alone. She brushes her hair from her face and gives him a puzzled look as she drifts away in search of another nameless dance partner. Royce snaps back to reality. *What is wrong with me*, he wonders. He should be enjoying the moment, not letting himself be consumed by questions he cannot answer. Manny is right. His job as a physician is to repair the body. And in his research, he can work to build a better machine, to keep the body running longer and better. That's more than enough. Except for Royce, it isn't enough. Not nearly enough. Not anymore.

He takes a break from the dance floor and strolls up to the bar for another beer. He's officially over his self-imposed alcohol limit for the night, but he doesn't care. Taking a pull from the ice-cold bottle, he spots a woman looking right at him. As he looks back, Royce makes a conscious effort to project loving thoughts through his gaze. He's used to projecting compassion and even a love of sorts toward his patients and to their grieving loved ones. That's never required particular effort or thought on his part. But now, he feels as if his thoughts are almost tangible, able to be moved outward as if on a wave of energy, toward whatever target he chooses. He smiles, laughing to himself that he has achieved the perfect mixture of telepathy and alcohol.

Royce feels almost convinced, in his mildly intoxicated state, that not only does the soul live behind the eyes, he can access another person's soul and connect it to his own through his thoughts and his gaze. He continues to look intently at the woman and watches as her face transforms. Her smile, at first flirtatious, becomes wide and genuine, her lips parted in a kind of peaceful glee. Her eyes soften and widen and begin to search his own with a look of hopeful ardor. She appears captivated and overwhelmed, as if she's been taken by surprise at the arrival of a most cherished friend or lover. Royce rocks back on his heels. Is it the beer, his mood, his thoughts, or his energy that's truly communicating with her? Even if it is the alcohol, at this moment, he feels that he has the ability to directly communicate with her soul. Royce takes the dozen steps needed to reach the woman without breaking eye contact. Her eyes seem to shimmer.

"I'm Beverly," she says.

"Beverly, can I buy you a drink?"

Dr. Royce says a quick goodbye to Manny, who's still occupied with the same two women he'd followed to the dance floor. He takes Beverly's hand and leads her out of the club. Her cheek grazes his shoulder affectionately as they wait for the valet to bring Royce's Audi.

"My apartment is on Copper Avenue," she says softly as he opens the passenger door.

They loosely hold hands as they stand side by side while the elevator climbs to her breezy, top floor studio. Royce lifts Beverly's chin gently between his thumb and forefinger and turns her head toward him.

"I want to look at you," he says. Her eyes widen in delight. She takes in a sharp breath, filled with anticipation. Inside, Beverly grabs him a beer and quickly mixes herself a cocktail. Royce admires the large-scale abstracts that line the walls. Beverly walks up behind him and passes him the beer, resting her hand briefly on his hip.

"Who's the artist?" he asks.

"I am." Beverly holds up her hands, stretching her long, unadorned fingers. "This manicure is hiding painter's hands."

"You're very talented," Royce says, meaning it. She doesn't blush.

"Ah, you know you're good, I can see that," Royce teases.

"I work hard at it." The belated blush rises across Beverly's cheeks as Royce finds her gaze once more. "I'm glad you like them."

Her bed is a cool tangle of linen sheets, and the skin on Royce's neck prickles with anticipation as he leans into the bounty of soft pillows. Beverly stands at the foot of her bed and slowly removes her dress, taking her time to let one shoulder strap fall before moving on to the next. Royce cannot look away from her body, lithe and muscular. Thoughts of the soul, and of death—old, young, his own—have been banished at last as his body's desires take full hold of him. Beverly lowers her long, naked frame over him, her strong arms keeping her aloft as her face meets his. She reaches his lips with soft, languid kisses; Royce responds with a kiss that's urgent and seeking. He moves his hands across her body as he's done with countless women, marking her breasts, her stomach, her mound with his experienced touch. She touches him similarly. But Royce is impatient, needy, ready to meet his goal. His head is buried in her shoulder, and he's writhing inside her, rising to his climax, when she lifts her head and demands his eyes once more.

"Where has all your charm gone?" Her voice is a harsh whisper.

As his body releases, the thought lands in his mind like a deadweight. At the moment they touched, he relinquished his loving thoughts and the intentions of his gaze. He had conquered his prey; there was nothing left for him to seek or to see. Royce feels his mood turn dark. He had used Beverly, first as an experiment and then as a warm, welcome body. He had used himself, too, playing a role that many men play, but one that was foreign to him.

He slides out of her bed and reaches for his clothes, his side stabbing again. Beverly gives him a withering glare, a combination of disbelief and contempt as she watches him prepare to leave.

"You really are some kind of asshole," she mutters, as she hikes the sheet over her body. *Of course she doesn't want me to look at her anymore*, he thinks.

"You're right," he says, avoiding her eyes as he slips on his loafers. "And I'm sorry. You didn't deserve this."

Royce grabs his phone and wallet from the nightstand.

"You know, you don't have to leave," Beverly says. There's a slice of desperation in her voice now. "We could have another drink. Try again?"

Royce stops and turns back to the gorgeous, lonely woman lying on the bed. He wants to tell her to expect more and better from her lovers. He wants to raise the strobe light of his compassion again and leave her feeling healed. But he doesn't have it in him.

There's only one person he wants to talk to right now.

CHAPTER 4

"What the hell, Mike? You can't sleep it off at home?"

Alesha stands in her doorway, pulling her long blonde hair up into a messy bun, looking less than thrilled to be awakened at midnight. Royce feels a fleeting stab of guilt. He knows she's on shift at the hospital at seven in the morning.

"I'm not drunk. Okay, maybe I'm a little drunk," Royce says with a smile he's counting on to charm her awake and grant him entry to her house.

Alesha shoots him a look that says, unmistakably: *If you're looking for sex, buddy, think again.*

"No—seriously—Alesha, I really need to talk."

She sighs and opens the door wide with a tired sweep of her arm.

After five years of working together, there's no other colleague Royce trusts more when things are spiraling in the emergency room. As a nurse, her skills are exceptional. And she seems to know, always, what Royce needs—and what he's thinking—almost before he knows it himself. But their history runs far deeper than their professional relationship.

Before they were colleagues, Alesha was his patient. Six years ago, Alesha arrived at Royce's ER with an intense headache and slurred speech. Royce had been the one to diagnose her with a subarachnoid hemorrhage, a massive brain bleed. He recalls in Technicolor detail the moment he watched the lovely and unusual woman he'd just treated being wheeled away to the operating room to have her aneurysm clipped. It was one of the only times he could remember feeling real nerves when he was on duty. Royce cared deeply about all his patients. But for reasons he still doesn't understand, he'd become instantly and unusually invested in Alesha's recovery. Seeing her wheeled away to surgery, he'd found himself worrying about her more like a loved one than a patient.

Nobody, including Royce and the neurosurgeon on her case, expected Alesha to survive, at least not without significant brain damage. But she'd surprised everyone and defied all medical odds. Within three days of her surgery, Alesha had returned to full function with no neurological deficits. It made no rational sense and frankly, was bizarre. Even tonight, as he stands at her doorstep watching her rub sleep out of her eyes, he's reminded that her very presence is miraculous. He catches himself in that thought. *Miraculous.* That's a word Alesha might use, but never him—not before today, anyway. Today, it seems, his mind is determined to go places it has never gone before.

Alesha has always been candid about her curiosity for the spiritual. She'd studied at Pacific College of Oriental Medicine in San Diego. The school offered a hefty dose of Western medicine, leading her to nursing school to earn her living. She bridged two worlds in a way that Royce himself struggled to understand, functioning at the top of her game as a nurse practicing conventional medicine while staying curious and wide open to a belief that the mysteries of human existence and experience could not be explained by science alone.

Mike Royce didn't speak the language of miracles and spirituality. Science was his arbiter and guide in every aspect of his life. Yet here he was, consumed by thoughts of a soul leaving the body.

"Tea?" Alesha asks as she walks lightly to the kitchen to turn on the kettle, not waiting for Royce to answer. They have a rhythm between them that doesn't require words. At work, they are dance partners who rarely miss a step in the complicated tango of emergency medicine, and the more intense things get on the floor, the better they execute as a pair. Outside of work, their rapport shifts to a close and trusting intimacy that exists whether or not they're spending time in each other's beds. After Alesha's recovery, they became romantically involved. But they have been inconsistent with each other over the years, sometimes on, sometimes off, never exclusive. Friends before all else, they gave each other space to pursue other people romantically. Though Royce often felt a longing from Alesha that he couldn't fulfill.

It wasn't that Alesha wasn't attractive or intelligent; she was both, and then some. He often sensed that Alesha wanted more from him, a different level of commitment, a more sustained and deeper emotional connection, a more constant companionship and romance. There were times when Royce thought he wanted the same thing. And then there were times when the thought made him squirm. He respected the hell out of Alesha and cared for her in a way that felt like love, as least as much as Royce understood what love feels like between two complicated, independent adults.

. . .

Royce wanders into the living room. Alesha's place is so different from his own modern loft, decorated with a minimalist eye and a penchant for highly curated, expensive art. Beyond his study, which is dense with volumes of medical research and organized with his typical precision, Royce maintains a home intentionally free of clutter. A select few objets d'art take up space on surfaces, and he keeps few mementos from his early life beyond a couple of framed photographs of him with his mom and of Royce himself on adventures around the world: his trip up El Capitan, crossing the finish line at his first Ironman, cycling trips through Morocco and the South of France. For Royce, clean lines and blank spaces are the visual expression of his disciplined life and need to think and focus. Alesha's home is a perfect expression of her warmth, her curiosity, her nurture. Lined with layered rugs, bright pillows strewn on couches and chairs, stacks of novels and self-help books at every end table, and a gallery of art made by her nieces and nephews, Alesha's home sings with color and texture.

Royce settles himself on a yellow linen couch draped with bright, tasseled throw blankets. Alesha hands him a steaming cup of tea and sits opposite him on the couch, legs folded and knees at her chin. She rests her mug on her slender legs and looks at him expectantly.

Where does he begin? Royce opens his mouth to talk about the Henry Samuelson and the twenty-week-old fetus. He also wants to talk about the feeling he had at the club of communicating life-force to life-force, through the eyes, but can't get the words out. Even with Alesha, whom he trusts more than anyone, he doesn't know how to broach the subject. It feels illicit, even dangerous, for Royce, a man of science, to dig too deeply into these tangled thoughts about the soul.

Alesha gives him a puzzled look. She's unaccustomed to seeing Royce at a loss for words.

One step at a time, he thinks.

She smiles at him, a silent gesture of encouragement.

"So, you know I'm getting ready to present my research project to the board."

He sees disappointment cross Alesha's eyes, as she realizes this late-night conversation is about work. She nods and waits for him to continue.

"What would you say if I told you I'm thinking about switching gears and going in a different direction with the project?"

Alesha lets out a laugh. "I'd say that doesn't sound like you at all."

Royce smiles in agreement. He's definitely playing outside his comfort zone today in just about every way imaginable.

"So, here's the thing." Royce pauses for a breath and collects his thoughts. "I want to research death. Specifically, I want to run a study that looks at whether death is predetermined before it occurs."

Alesha straightens up and leans forward, her eyes unblinking. If she's surprised, she's not showing it. But he's got her attention.

She nods. "Go on."

Royce sets his tea down on the antique oak coffee table and rubs his hands together. He's feeling the adrenaline rush that he gets when his mind locks into an idea and starts to spin it together, like an airplane gathering speed to take flight.

"Well, I want to get a group of subjects together. Ones diagnosed with a terminal illness." He shrugs. "Cancer, we'll say."

Alesha nods again, deep in thought. Royce watches as she

crosses her arms over her chest, as if to protect herself from the word. Cancer is far more than a professional concern for Alesha. She was diagnosed with stage one breast cancer in her early twenties. She caught it early and was several years into remission when she and Royce met. Still, the emotional scars of her cancer bout seem deeper to Royce than the fright she experienced with the aneurysm that brought her to Royce's ER.

Eager for her input, he presses on. "I want to run tests to see if we can determine the moment when—or if—their death becomes inevitable, no matter what interventions are undertaken. Additionally, I want to see if there are common denominators. Is there a pattern or a sequence of events that can allow us to recognize the moment of inevitability before it takes place?"

Alesha looks at him steadily. He knows she's not a poker player. But she should be. She's not giving anything away when she says, "There's more, isn't there." It's a statement, not a question. She knows him well.

Royce takes a sip of tea and swallows hard. "If we can pinpoint —no, if we can *predict*—the point when death becomes inevitable, is there a way to change it or reverse it?" He lets out a sigh that makes his whole body ripple, barely noticing that the pain of his bruised rib has quieted. He's stated his intentions. He's said it out loud.

Alesha gazes at the ceiling, tapping her finger to her chin. He's about to explode with anticipation when she finally looks back at him. "You know, illness is its own energy. Why couldn't it be changed?"

Royce wants to take her in his arms and hug her, so strong is his joy at having her pick up the ball and run with his big, radical idea. And he would do just that. But her thought is too arresting. His mind begins to spin again.

"Talk more," he says, waggling his hand to speed her along. He wants to hear more from her, and he needs her to keep talking so his own mind can synthesize the thoughts that are taking shape in his mind.

"Have you ever thought of cancer as a wave with its own frequency?" she asks.

Royce pauses for a moment. "No, I never have, actually." He looks at her, still thinking about it. "But all cells—all matter—generate frequencies."

"I've been doing a lot of reading lately, and a lot of thinking, about the energy of life. Cancer, and all diseases, are an elemental part of being alive. I wonder, is its energy something we can identify and track somehow?" Alesha still has her arms wrapped tightly around her chest.

Royce has no framework, no spiritual practice or belief system, to comprehend the soul. He struggles to even accept it, much less define it or understand it. He feels dizzy even thinking in terms of souls; it's so far from the terrain on which he's built his life. But energy is another matter. Energy can be measured, its patterns and conversions observed and predicted.

Alesha continues, unaware of the excitement brewing inside Royce. "And dogs can detect those frequencies, including cancer," she says. "They snuggle up to their sick companions and treat the disease with their own vibes. And they seem to catch it coincident with their masters. Sometimes they die soon afterward." She pauses, having an internal debate about whether to continue. "I felt a shift—I knew something had changed—months before my cancer was diagnosed, before I was symptomatic at all. That sense saved my life."

It appears as though a cloud passes over Alesha's eyes. She's faced death twice already and come through each time. Royce sometimes wonders how much her eagerness to explore all realms of spirituality, and to bring them into the practice of medicine, is a fight against the cold fear of dying, against the fear of diseases that can't be cured.

Thoughts coalesce in his mind. "Yes, that is odd," he says.

Alesha continues talking about animals and the terminally ill, and the bonds that deepen through illness. But Royce can barely hear her. His whole body is pulsing now, as his thoughts slide into order.

He's going to track the journey of that proof-of-life energy he watched disappear from Harry Samuelson's eyes. And he's going to figure out a way to stop it before it converts into whatever form unleashes it from the human body.

He looks at Alesha, her hands flying, perched on her knees as she talks about the journey toward death. He loves her with abandon and wonders why he never tells her so. Something has always held their relationship back, even though they have both confessed to feeling destined to be together. Destined was Alesha's way of describing it. Royce didn't think of it like that, but he knows that he feels tied to Alesha in a way that's different from any other woman he's ever known. They're less than partners, more than friends, and family in all the ways that matter.

They're also opposites in nearly every way. Alesha likes long walks with no purpose or destination as well as free-ranging conversations with no direction. Royce needs a goal for everything, from his workouts to his trips through the supermarket. Royce enjoys visiting museums to see the great works; Alesha likes to watch children make art, delighting in the spontaneous artistic compositions of nature, like the pattern of raindrops on a pond.

Royce cares about facts. He believes that that no connection is useful unless it's replicable—causal at best, or at least correlated. Alesha doesn't believe in the primacy of facts; to her, coincidences are valid references.

Royce believes death is a bodily failure—one he is now determined to disrupt. Even without talking to Alesha about his own uncomfortable questions about the soul, he knows Alesha believes that death released an essential form of energy from the body, "freed to join the flow of intelligent energy that glues our universe together," as she'd once described. Royce remembers rolling his eyes when she'd described death that way. That earned him a quick, playful slap on the gut. He often doesn't agree with her, sometimes struggling to understand how she makes connections out of what seems to him like thin air. But she always makes him think, pushing him beyond his obsession with facts and data to look at problems from different angles. They have a rhythm to their intellectual sparring that sometimes feels to Royce like being inside a piece of beautiful music.

Alesha asks, "Do you believe outer space is a void?"

"Matterless? I don't know, but it's full of fields of subatomic radiation."

"Actually, I've just read a theory that it's full of virtual particles in self-annihilating pairs of energy too subtle to measure, not observable on the cosmic operating table . . ."

"Hawking's radiation, a universal stew that brews matter to organize life, then dematerializes it into black holes," Royce interrupts.

". . . when dark energy, another mystery, pushes the cycle outward again. Imagine the privilege of our lives existing despite all that randomness, even chaos," Alesha muses out loud, her eyes taking on a dreamy, faraway look.

"A speck of matter-in-conflict for a spark of time," Royce says.

"Weird. Always creative-destruction, the opposites joined like one."

Just as they were. They share an unspoken sadness about their odd, star-crossed pairing.

Alesha gazes into Royce's eyes.

"What is it?" he says.

"We're paired but at odds," she says, her eye contact not wavering.

He nods, understanding what she means.

"We're complements, like yin and yang," she continues.

Royce scratches his chin, not much for the philosophical. "Or magnets maybe. Attracting, repelling—"

She laughs. "Exactly."

Their differences sometimes put them in conflict, and Royce has his doubts about whether they could ever find enough common ground to have the romantic partnership that both of them want in life. But about one thing, he is certain.

"Would you join my research team?"

She doesn't hesitate. "I'd love to. Plus, you'll need somebody on your team who isn't afraid to say no to you," she says with a mischievous grin. "Seriously, though, this is pretty radical stuff."

"That's why I need you there with me. I need someone who doesn't think like I do and who will challenge me. Plus, I need your conscience. And there's nobody I trust more."

Alesha's grin spreads wider, her cheeks bright with pleasure.

Royce returns her smile. "We're going to ruffle some feathers, you know."

"When do we start?"

CHAPTER 5

Royce shifts uncomfortably in his chair, shaking the stiffness from his shoulders. Riding high from his conversation with Alesha, he sat down three days ago to begin the redesign of his research project. It felt like an impossibly steep hill to climb, to reconfigure his entire project in time to present to the board for funding, as scheduled. There was also the matter of convincing the conservative, profit-obsessed hospital board of directors to fund a study that sought to find the means to halt death. But that was another looming mountain to conquer in the near distance. First, he had to reframe the study itself and then get his research team on board.

All his life, Royce has been a realist. An ambitious, tenacious striver, but a practical man at his core. On paper, he knows it makes zero sense to pivot his research in this new and uncharted direction. Controversial doesn't come close to capturing how provocative, even heretical, this investigation might be seen by the higher-ups in the hospital administration and by many of his colleagues. He's aware of the risks to his reputation; what he's about to do is basically the textbook definition of career suicide. What surprises him is how little he cares.

Over the past seventy-two hours, he's stunned himself with his productivity in transforming his study protocols. He's amazed at how naturally his study can be re-directed from an exploration of the factors that affect longevity to a search for the point where death becomes irreversible. It's almost as though he'd known, without knowing, that his work would ultimately lead here. The first phase of his original study had two parts. The prospective arm of the study had been intended to collect historical data and a long list of metrics in healthy patients to identify factors that correlated to the onset of disease. Now, that prospective study would assess the histories and real-time health trajectories of patients who had recently been diagnosed with terminal illnesses.

The study's retrospective arm originally had been designed to analyze deceased patients' charts, and interview their loved ones, to identify correlations with lifespan. Now their retrospective investigation would mine these data pools for clues about the point when disease truly became terminal. Currently, patients are categorized as terminal when physicians believe they can no longer be cured. It's a prediction that's based on clinical evidence, including a patient's response to treatment, the progression of their disease, and the patient's overall physiological condition. But never, not even from the most experienced, brilliant physician, is the classification of terminal anything more than an educated, informed guess. Royce's research would seek out specific data to help identify when a "terminal" illness became truly and irreversibly terminal in patients who'd already completed their journey to death.

There is a dizzying amount of work needed to redesign the study's detailed parts, including its methodology for gathering data and the computer models that will analyze that data. Royce will need his team to work fiendishly to make that happen before the board meeting. But he sees clearly how. And the deeper he digs into the details, the less crazy it all seems. Over the past few days, locked in his apartment, all but chained to his desk, Royce has become certain that this path he's put himself on isn't the path of a crazy dreamer, but that of the ultimate realist. He accepts that death exists, but he no longer accepts the premise that it is inevitable. And once the premise of inevitable death is rejected, the most practical, reasonable response is to stop it. Anything less is a dereliction of his duty as a physician.

Without pulling his face away from his laptop, he reaches for his coffee cup and takes a big swallow. With a jerk of his head, he half-coughs, half-spits out the liquid, spraying the contents of his desk. That isn't coffee; it's whiskey. Royce looks at the glass in his hand; not a mug, but a double-walled crystal tumbler. He looks at the wall of windows that line his loft and is startled by his own disheveled reflection. Beyond his three-day stubble, rumpled sweats and uncombed hair, the lights of downtown Albuquerque twinkle in a panorama against a pitch-black sky.

What the fuck? Royce looks at his watch. Two-forty-five a.m. How long had he been sitting here? Royce surveys the long teak dining table where he's been camped out for the past seventy-two hours, barely breaking his concentration to retrieve his takeout delivery orders from the door. The elegant wood slab is buried in towers of binders, textbooks, and loose stacks of research journals, but otherwise is clutter-free and clean. No leftover sushi, no green juice cups, no empty salad containers from the macrobiotic café around the corner.

He slaps himself gingerly on the cheeks as if to rouse himself from a trance. Royce is confused. Had Georgina been here? His housekeeper came twice a week for a thorough deep clean and to water the plants that surely wouldn't survive in his care alone. Had she swept through without him noticing?

Royce walks to the potted Mission olive tree next to the wet bar. He touches the soil with his fingertips. It's damp. He shakes his head, marveling at the sustained depths of his concentration. Not even as a medical student with the energy of a twentysomething had he been able to work at this kind of fevered pitch for so many hours. Had he slept since Friday? He cannot remember leaving the table.

He stands and stretches his arms overhead, the muscles of his long frame releasing their tightness. He walks toward the balcony doors to take in some of the cool night air but turns around mid-step. His work pulls at him like a magnet. He reviews the outline he's made for his research team, mapping out how they'll reconfigure the study protocols. He's satisfied that he's taken the work as far as he can go alone. He's marked the trail. Now he needs to convince this team to follow him into the woods.

But first, he needs sleep.

At last, Royce can tear himself away from the table. He pours himself a tall glass of alkaline water from the ionizer and pads slowly to the dark bedroom. He pulls back the light comforter and feels himself plunging into a deep sleep before he's fully prone.

In his dream, he's four or five years old, on a trip with his mother to the beach in Corpus Christi. He's afraid of the water, the pushing and pulling waves, the froth that sizzles on the hot sand, the dark place he sees swimmers' bodies disappear into as they wade farther out. He knows his mother wants him to swim, but he can't make himself step out beyond his ankles, can't stop racing away from the waves as they rush toward him.

"Do you want my help?" his mother asks. He nods, relieved to have her full attention and her protection at the water's edge. She picks him up and carries him in her strong arms several paces out. Royce scrunches his knees high to keep the waves from lapping his toes.

"Your best is enough," she whispers in his ear. And then she tosses him forward into the water to find his way through and out.

* * *

"Thank you all for coming in." Dr. Royce greets the members of his research team as they shuffle into the conference room. He watches their eyes light up when they see the lunch he arranged for their meeting: Tex Mex flautas, jicama salad, and thick slices of mango and pineapple sprinkled with Tajin.

"Sweet," says Rudy, one of the computer engineers, as he piles food on a plate. "I'm going to pretend I didn't just eat leftover birthday cake in the lounge."

"Hey, Dr. Royce, I heard you took it on the chest the other day," says Eric, another engineer.

Royce freezes, stunned. He instantly flashes back to his ER gunshot dream.

Rudy knots his brows in concern. "You okay, doc?"

"How did you know?" Royce breathes in a hoarse, rattled whisper.

"About your rib? Billy's my trainer. He asked me how you were doing."

Royce briefly shuts his eyes and shakes his head to clear the cobwebs still lingering from his marathon, sleepless work session. "Oh, right, sure. I'm fine. It was a dumb move."

Royce waits until the six scientists have filled their plates and are seated around the conference table, chatting between bites.

Still no sign of Alesha. He probably should have called her after their late-night talk. Instead, consumed by his work, he'd managed only to send her a quick text over the weekend letting her know the time and place for today's meeting. Had she changed her mind about coming on board with the project? Royce feels a flicker of anxiety at the thought. He needs Alesha with him on this scientific journey. He can't quite explain it, but he can't imagine doing it without her at his side. He checks his phone. No message to say she'd be late. Scrolling back, the most recent text exchange between them was from a couple of weeks ago. He can't find the message he's sure that he sent her on Saturday. *Damn, I might've really fucked up.*

Just then, the heavy conference room door creaks open and Alesha slips in, mouthing a silent apology and sliding into an empty chair at the table.

Royce feels the muscles in his chest relax. He closes his eyes and draws a long breath, taking a moment to center himself.

"Folks, as you know, we're coming up on our—my—big meeting with the board." Royce feels nervous, unsure about how to deliver the news to his team, who've worked hard for months designing the research protocols he is now about to change. In a flash of insight, he thinks about how he delivers difficult information to patients and feels himself shift into that familiar mode of compassion and directness.

"I have some important news to share. Our study is making a change in direction. I know this may catch you off guard. Please know that your work—all of your work—has been stellar, and this change has nothing to do with the quality of the work we've accomplished so far."

Royce catalogues the looks of surprise and alarm that light up the faces around the table.

"Rest assured; I want everyone on board for this new direction."

"What is that direction?" The question comes from Dr. Margo Holloway, an ER resident.

"We are going to investigate whether there is a moment when death becomes inevitable." He pauses, glancing at each of his team members. They look uniformly stunned and confused.

"I don't understand," says Lucy, a research assistant. "Death *is* inevitable."

Royce nods. "Agreed. But we know basically nothing about when the inevitability of death arises, when it becomes fixed and irreversible in a *living* person—if it does at all."

"Okay, but that's what we do as physicians," Lucy says, her voice rising. "We diagnose, we treat, we do all we can to push back death until it becomes inevitable."

Before Royce can respond, Rudy jumps in. "Luce, I think you're using *inevitable* when you mean *unavoidable*. Like, say you have a stroke patient who survives the event and but never recovers and dies. Another patient—same age, same basic level of health, same type of stroke—makes a full recovery. So, what was happening in that first patient's body—or in their mind, or with the care they got, or other circumstances of their case—that made recovery impossible? Is that right, Dr. Royce?"

Royce smiles. It's a thrill—and a promising sign—to see his at least one member of his team leap into this discussion.

"You're on the right track. There are countless conditions that can kill—and something will eventually cause each of us to die," Royce says. "Irrespective of the particular ailment, are there factors —physiological, psychological, other—that, when present, corre-late with fatal outcomes?"

Lucy closes her eyes and nods. "Okay, so it sounds like we're going to look at death as we would a disease, creating a profile of 'symptoms,'" she says, waggling her fingers for air quotes, "that tell us death is present."

"Oh, that's interesting," murmurs the other research assistant.

Royce leaps up from his seat. "Yes, yes, yes." He's suddenly filled with an intense vigor. "We want to know: is there an identifiable turning point when death becomes pre-ordained in a living patient?"

Clark, the third engineer, who's been silent throughout, raises his hand. "Wait, so we're going to create a whole new study protocol for this in just a couple of weeks?"

Royce nods. "Granted, it's a tall order. But I've spent the past few days reviewing our methodology and mapping out our revisions." He pulls out copies of his notes to distribute. "I'm telling you; this can be done. We can re-focus our existing protocols to our new investigative objectives."

Together, they review Royce's notes on revisions to the first phase of the study. All terminally ill patients will be closely monitored on a monthly basis, including complete blood count, comprehensive metabolic panel, urinalysis, clotting studies, autoimmune studies, endocrine function, heavy metals, and inflammatory cytokines. Vital signs, height, weight, body fat, and lung function testing will also be monitored monthly. A CT scan of the head, chest, abdomen, and pelvis will be performed upon entrance into the study, and then directly post-mortem.

Collection of historical data is a notoriously time consuming and difficult process. "Over the next couple of weeks, we'll need to make decisions about what information we ought to obtain, from demographic data to how often patients pray," says Royce.

The retrospective evaluation of the recently deceased patients will include a historical query for the patients' families as well as the review of hospital charts for historical and laboratory data. Royce has sketched out a rough draft of the query and the methodology for reviewing charts and labs.

"You did all this since Friday?" asks Dr. Rick Davies, the team's radiologist, scanning through the thick outline.

Royce nods, feeling strangely self-conscious. He, too, doesn't know quite how he managed it.

"Obviously the lab results are critical," Royce says, returning his attention to the group. "But we're going to need to glean as much historical data as possible from each patient. As the patient progresses through the illness and eventually dies, the computer program will need to analyze which historical and or laboratory data correlate with a longer or shorter life span."

Lucy makes an "hmm" sound as Rudy scratches his head.

"For the retrospective study, we will review charts and interview families of recently deceased patients," Royce continues. "This historical data will also be analyzed for a possible correlation with lifespan."

"I think we need these protocols designed to allow some flexibility as we go," Alesha says. "Nobody's ever done a study like this before, as far as we know." She pauses to smile in Royce's direction before continuing, "And we may need to make some adjustments once we get underway."

"There's also a real possibility we might not be able to make any connections with the data." Lucy looks skeptical.

"That's true," Royce says. "But there's only one way to find out."

Royce catches Alesha looking at him expectantly, waiting for him to drop the rest of the news.

He clears his throat. "If we do discover statistically significant correlations, that raises another question. If death is preordained, and we can recognize that it is imminent well before the patient becomes ill, can we intervene, and thereby forestall—or terminate —the act of dying?"

Rudy lets out a long whistle. Dr. Holloway gasps. The rest of the team is silent and slack jawed. Alesha gazes calmly at Royce, as if to say, *hold steady*. She is the only person in the room who knew what was coming.

Royce is met with a few wary glances but eventually everyone in the room is wearing a smile—the possibility that they could be involved in changing the face of medicine sets in, and the room is charged with excitement.

"I'm open to discussion about this. I want to hear everyone's thoughts. This is new territory, and we need to move forward as a team," Royce says. Even as he speaks, he recognizes that he's not being fully honest. He's genuinely interested in hearing people's thoughts. But he's not, in fact, open to discussion about the direction the study will take. Anyone who isn't on board can jump ship, but he's moving ahead no matter what.

"This sounds a lot like playing God to me." Dr. Holloway's face radiates disdain.

"Whoa, wait a minute," says Eric. "Are you saying there are places that science can't go? I'm not down with that."

"I absolutely think there are limits to where science should go," Dr. Holloway shoots back. "I became a doctor to save people's lives, not fuck around with them. Death is a natural part of the lifecycle. Trying to stop it altogether feels wrong to me."

Alesha jumps in. "Margo, I hear you, and I share some of your reservations." She avoids Royce's penetrating stare as she continues. "You don't have to believe in God to feel there is an order to life in our world. And what Dr. Royce is proposing is a challenge to that order as we know it."

Dr. Holloway nods rapidly. "Yes, so why would we—"

Alesha puts up her hand. "I wasn't finished," she says gently. She takes a moment to meet Royce's gaze before she continues, and he feels a rush of affection for her. "This study challenges what we all consider to be the course of life, there's no question. But we're not at the mercy of the results, whatever they may be. We don't know if we're going to find anything, much less how our discoveries might be used to save lives or relieve suffering without violating the natural order."

"Agreed," says Rudy, another engineer. "This could be groundbreaking."

Dr. Holloway picks up her copy of the outline and tosses it in Royce's direction. "I knew you were an egotist, but you've really outdone yourself this time. I can't be part of this." She walks out before Royce can thank her for being honest. If she'd stayed with such intense reservations held unspoken, she could have caused real damage to the study's integrity and progress.

He turns to the group. "What about y'all? There's no shame in leaving this project. But if you're out, now's the time to say so."

* * *

Royce pulls a beer from the fridge and runs the icy bottle across his forehead before snapping off the cap. He takes an icepack from the freezer and holds it gingerly against his still-tender rib. He's bone tired, but relieved to be one step closer in making his study a reality. He's moving forward with most of his team intact.

After Dr. Holloway left, the computer engineers and research assistants all committed to staying. They have a lot of work in front of them to get ready to request funding, much less to enact the study itself. And he senses fear and unease among some of the team, despite their proffers of support. He feels as though he's bringing this research to fruition through sheer force of will, a will that comes from a place so deep inside him, he hadn't known it existed until now. Tapping into this source is simultaneously exhausting and exhilarating, and Royce feels himself increasingly swinging between these two extremes without much time spent in the middle.

From inside his pocket, his phone pings. Royce almost ignores the beep signaling a new message. He's not on call tonight. Is there anything, from anyone, that can't wait until after he drinks a beer in silence and gets some rest? But he can't not look.

It's an email from the ER admin, with his schedule for the upcoming month. *Shit.* He forgot to reach out to request a reduction in shifts from his usual eighteen per month to twelve. He's got to reduce his clinical workload to focus on the research. Now he's going to have to wait another month.

He opens the attachment and gives it a quick glance as he takes a long swig of his beer.

Is that a mistake? He sets his beer down and leans close to the phone, rubbing his eyes. No, he's reading correctly. He's scheduled for twelve shifts this month, not eighteen. *That's bizarre*, he thinks. Had he talked to admin and now doesn't remember? Even in his obsessive state of mind, he's surely capable of remembering that conversation. He has no idea how this decision was made, but he's not about to argue. If he brings the issue to someone's attention, he'll wind up back on the schedule for eighteen. Someone's oversight is his lucky break.

CHAPTER 6

"**D**amn it." Royce pulls the long, thin line of silk from his neck. How is it that the same hands that can flawlessly suture a wound or intubate a writhing patient have so much trouble tying a tie? His fingers feel uncharacteristically thick and uncooperative. He lifts his chin to try again, taking stock of himself in the full-length mirror in his walk-in closet. A single breasted, two-button suit, gray with a subtle stripe. Slim fit, with a navy grenadine silk tie. A coordinated pocket square that almost made the cut now lays discarded on his dresser. It looked too pushy and ostentatious, and he doesn't want to appear like he's trying too hard. Never one to neglect his appearance, Royce has obsessed over every component of today's outfit. Conservative, reliable, and sharp but not flashy; a silent, sartorial communique of trust and confidence. Is it possible to communicate all that with a suit and tie? He hopes so.

Today is a landmark day. In a couple of hours, he'll stand before the hospital board of directors and ask them to fund his research. He and his team worked nonstop the past two weeks to update their study protocols, ensuring it matches their new objectives. There were times when Royce sensed the concerns among the group that he was pushing too far. But Alesha was always there to step in and bridge divides to keep them all on common ground. Now it's up to Royce to sell this study to the board.

Obsessing about his attire gives Royce a break from rehearsing his presentation, which he's been doing since before dawn. He is prepared to explain in detail the data-gathering methods and the analytical tools they'll use to investigate whether death is preordained in the living. He feels like he once did as a medical student, when he'd reached the end of a frenzied study session preparing for an exam: he could feel the knowledge locked down in his mind, and he knew he could field any medical or technical question that the board lobbed his way. He also knows that the success of his project will not depend on how well he explains and defends the technical details of his research protocols. To give him the go-ahead—and the funds—to pursue this research, the members of the board will need to believe in the integrity and necessity of his project. They'll also need to believe his study can be a source of profit for the hospital. But that's the easy part. It's not hard to see how the fruits of his research could eventually fatten their wallets.

Royce knows it's not about getting them to set aside their concerns. He's got to spark their curiosity and their compassion at the same time. He needs them to want the answer to these questions about death and learn about the capacity to ward it off. After all the labor that's brought him to this point, he's not sure if he's up to this next task. He's been in a spiral of insecurity all morning long.

. . .

"Your best is enough."

At the sound of his mother's voice, Royce freezes and whips his head around. The bedroom is empty.

"Mom?" Royce walks to the large, open living area of his loft. "Mom?"

Your best is enough was what his mother always used to say to him whenever he was nervous as a child. Before every big exam, every soccer tryout and track competition, he would withdraw at some point to stew in his anticipation. Inevitably, she would find him wherever he had tucked himself away, from their backyard treehouse to his book-filled bedroom, and whisper those words into his ear. The day before he took his medical board exam, a note with these four words had arrived at his small on-campus apartment. Mom, reminding him that his hard work would pay off.

Just now, he'd heard those words again. No surprise that they might echo in his mind on this morning, of all mornings. But it hadn't been an echo. He'd heard them in her actual voice. Unmistakably, as though she was standing behind him like she had when he was a nervous, determined, pole-thin teenager on the eve of a calculus exam.

But of course, she's not here. She's at home in Sandia Heights, a quiet suburb outside Albuquerque, probably pulling up weeds in her voluminous garden or playing her fifteenth round of rummy with her neighbors. She'll have a laugh when he tells her about how she visited him this morning. He makes a mental note to call her after the board meeting, and without another trip to the mirror, grabs his keys and phone. He drapes his suitcoat over his arm. There's a hot sun blasting outside. He pauses at the bowl of apples Georgina must've set out for him on the kitchen island and almost reaches for one before thinking better of it. He'll eat after the meeting. Hunger keeps him sharp.

* * *

Royce stands at one end of the long, sleek table. To his left are seats reserved for the members of the hospital board, and to his right, seats for the chairs of most of the medical departments. He's about to be flanked by the money minders and the most experienced medical professionals at Albuquerque Medical Center. Collectively, they hold the purse string that will determine whether his study will proceed.

"How did you manage to stay dry?" Royce is startled from his thoughts by the executive assistant to the board president, a twentysomething man in a sharp suit whose arms are currently laden with soggy overcoats.

"Excuse me?" Royce doesn't understand the question.

"I'd ask to take your coat," the assistant says, "but you haven't got a drop on you."

Royce stares at the dripping raincoats draped over the young man's forearms. He turns around to see thick sheets of rain hitting the conference room windows at a noisy angle. That came on fast.

As the board members pour themselves coffee, make awkward small talk, and settle into their seats, Royce takes a few moments to get his bearings with the group he's about to pitch his big, bold proposal. He knows most of them a little, and only a couple of them well. Among those are his boss, Greg Sanchez, the chief of emergency medicine, who gives him a supportive nod as he balances a towering plate of fruit and a full cup of coffee on his tablet, making his way to the table. Royce hasn't told Sanchez what he's about to do; his boss has no idea of the dramatic shift in his study's focus. Royce wanted to, but he couldn't take the risk that Sanchez would try to interfere. Not for the first time, he wonders if he'll have a job at the end of the day. But he thinks the ER chief could be an important ally today. He's not a friend or even a mentor, but he's a decent guy and a pretty great, no-bullshit doctor, one who Royce has watched grapple with the gut-twisting rage at the limits of their ability to keep people alive, even in a major metro hospital with access to the latest technology. If Sanchez can get over his bruised ego at being blindsided today—a big if, Royce admits to himself—he could imagine his boss coming around quick in support of the project.

Royce makes note of some of the other department heads filtering in. Cardiology and orthopedics, those two guys are the real old guard, docs who've been practicing medicine since Royce was in diapers. He's not feeling great about his chances with either of them, but maybe one of them will surprise him. The head of oncology is a different story. Melinda Dillon is a star in the hospital and in her field, part of the younger vanguard of physicians at Albuquerque Medical Center who have risen to positions of power in the years since Royce has been practicing here. He finds her funny and senses she's open to unorthodox ideas. And as an oncologist, she's travelled the journey to death with too many patients to count.

Royce holds back a laugh as he glances at Allan Schmidt, chief of neurology, who's already tapping his pen on his crossed leg as though the meeting is running late before it's even begun. He's got no time for anything but his own department. Royce is pretty sure he'd vote in support of human cloning if it got him out of this meeting. The head of radiology, haughty and standoffish—*Who even knows? I can't figure that guy out*—Royce thinks. And he wonders about the chief of pathology, Marian Hsu, with her thoughtful demeanor and her intimate, granular, constant acquaintance with the post-mortem.

He's less familiar with the bean counters who are lining up on the other side of the table. He watches as Evelyn Price practically floats through the door, shifting the energy in the room with her presence. Elegant, imposing, Price is supremely in command of the board and the hospital. At Albuquerque Medical, there are fiefdoms but no real power spheres—there's Evelyn P. Everyone else is playing in a little sandbox, from what Royce understands. They've been introduced a few times at hospital functions, and if he'd been the type to be intimidated, she'd have done that to him. Instead, he found her impressive, whip-smart, a master in command. And he sensed a similarity between them. If he could get her support, he'd walk out of this room with his research funded.

Bodies drop into seats as Evelyn Price takes her place at the head of the table, facing Dr. Royce. Their eyes meet for a moment. Royce catches a flicker of interest in otherwise inscrutable, verdant green pools.

The board moves quickly through their call to order, followed by several housekeeping items. Royce's proposal review is first on the agenda.

"Dr. Royce, welcome," says Price. "I understand we're to hear from you on a proposal for research funding. I don't see your materials in our board packet." She flicks an impatient finger through a stack of papers.

Royce clears his throat. "Yes, ma'am. I'm distributing it right now." He's gone to exceptional lengths to keep the subject of his research under wraps until this meeting. Royce taps his phone. Up and down the table, tablets and cellphones ping with delivery notifications as his proposal, "Is Death 'Curable'?: A Search for the

Moment of Preordainment in Dying" arrives in inboxes around the room.

Royce watches their faces as they open the document. He keeps one eye trained on Price, who greets the study title with a short, harsh intake of breath and a sharp look in his direction. Sharp and angry or sharp and interested, Royce can't tell.

"Is this a joke?" The chief of cardiology is red-faced and angry.

"I assure you, it is not," Royce says. "With your support, I intend to search for the moment that signals death's irreversibility. And when I identify that tipping point—and the factors associated with it—I will investigate how to stop it from happening."

The room erupts in a rumble of surprise and alarm. Price holds up a hand. "Okay, okay. Dr. Royce, you've made quite an entrance here today." She furrows her eyebrows slightly. "Why don't you walk us through this unusual proposal."

Royce nods and reaches down for his notes. His hands come up empty. He tries not to panic as his fingers scramble around the table. Where could they have gone? He'd been leafing through them just a few minutes ago. They must've fallen under the table. Looks like he'll be doing this from memory. He stands to address the room.

"I hear your surprise and alarm, and I understand it," Royce begins as he looks around the room. Greg Sanchez is red in the face and staring at his shoes. A few of the bean counters have their arms crossed tightly at their chests, looking puffed up and defensive. Royce has time to note that several of the other non-physician board members look shocked, yet intrigued.

"I am a physician. I took an oath to 'apply, for the benefit of the sick, all measures that are required' . . .'" Royce sees the oncologist, Dr. Dillon, shifting uncomfortably in her seat. The impatient head of neurology is sitting uncharacteristically still, with a pained expression on his frozen face. A flicker of despair flares inside Royce. It feels like he's lost them before he's even begun.

He trudges on. "As a physician, it is my obligation to learn everything I can about death in order to—" *This isn't working,* he thinks, as desperation rises like bile in his throat.

Royce stops and drops his hands to the table, leaning forward like a cat on the prowl as he scans the faces at the table. "I am not okay with my patients dying. It tears me up to my core, again and again. Every time I lose someone, I die a small death myself, and I watch their loved ones suffer even greater pain and torture.

"How can this be the status quo? How are we okay with not exploring every corner of the scientific universe to better understand death, in hopes of stopping it whenever we can, for however long we can?"

His boss, Dr. Sanchez, lifts his head and the two men make eye contact. Royce sees his own pain and frustration reflected in the older man's eyes. In the next instant, he becomes aware of seeing beyond that shared pain, to a shared humanity that is pure in its compassion, empathy, and understanding. He sees, in Dr. Sanchez's eyes, hope. He knows, in that moment, that Sanchez *wants* to be convinced of the righteousness of this study. The power of their connection in this moment nearly knocks Royce off his feet. In a split second, he realizes that it won't be his words that win today. If he can reach these people at the core of their humanity, if he can connect with their souls—that word feels alien in his mind, but he doesn't know what other word to use—he will walk out with their approval.

"Imagine the life-saving innovations that would never have been discovered if scientists stayed safely inside existing boundaries and conventions. Why has death itself been exempt from that kind of brave interrogation? It's time for that to change. And I —we—are uniquely positioned to do so."

As he continues to pitch his study, Royce trains his eyes first on the individuals he thinks are most receptive to his project. He starts with the physicians. With Dr. Sanchez now raptly listening, Royce seeks an intentional connection with Dr. Dillon; Dr. Hsu, a surprisingly emotional chief of radiology; and several of the board members who met his fumbling introductory remarks with intrigue.

He walks the crowd of bigwigs through the protocols for the prospective and retrospective arms of his study, how he and his team will gather real-time and historical data on terminal patients and analyze it to seek out correlations with their passage from life to death. With each person in turn, he recognizes a moment of communion; he watches as their resistance and fear fade away, overtaken by the same hope he first saw flicker in Dr. Sanchez. Royce feels a growing confidence in his capacity to reach every single person in the room.

As he speaks to the room and trains his inner humanity from one individual to the next, Royce marvels at how his brain can conduct all of this work at once: supervising the delivery of factual data and complex, rigorous scientific methodology at the same time his mind—or some other essential part of his being—transmits messages of kindness, love, and support. He's aware of controlling both processes as they occur; at the same time, he feels like an independent observer, watching it all unfold.

He eventually turns his eyes toward the hostile parties in the room, the elder statesmen of cardiology and orthopedics as well as several skeptical board members.

"How will we not look like fools when this gets out?" huffs the chief of dermatology.

"Wait a minute," interjects the head of psychiatry, who had responded to Royce's silent, soul-to-soul outreach with a gentle brim of tears in his eyes. "This is the vanguard of medical science, to say the least. But Dr. Royce has shown us a rigorous set of study objectives and methods that deserve our respect. *He* deserves our respect."

Royce turns his gaze to the dermatology chief. They lock eyes. The chief seems uncomfortable, afraid even. "We can't lead with fear. I believe that by not pursuing this inquiry, we're letting fear take the lead over reason and ethics." As Royce speaks, he's maintaining his unspoken connection with the doctor, who he sees as struggling to accept this line of inquiry into death. "It's not the job of the scientist to worry about how our results will be perceived. It's our job to pursue knowledge and apply it for the good of humanity." Holding his gaze, Royce feels himself diving into this man's innermost core. It's an almost dizzying sensation of connection. He watches as the doctor's resistance crumbles.

Royce pauses and takes his eyes off the physicians, turning his gaze to the money managers. "I understand that many of you in this room are tasked with managing the perception of this hospital and its finances. I'm not ignorant to the importance of that task." Along this side of the table, chins are up and arms are crossed, as if asking Royce to prove it. He takes a deep breath and begins working the line of bean counters, gaze by gaze.

"Someone is going to go here—some scientist at Harvard or Penn or UCSF—is going to run first into the breach and take this on. Why can't it be us?" Royce sees chins begin to drop in thoughtful anticipation of accolades.

He turns his eyes at last to Evelyn Price. He's kept her in the corner of his eye throughout his presentation. She's sat still and silent. He's not so much as seen her shoulders lift as she breathes.

He can feel it now, the room swaying to his side. But he knows it won't matter if he can't get her on board.

Her green eyes are electric with intelligence. It's as though they give off a physical spark that startles Royce. But he doesn't give up her gaze. Rather, he catches that electricity and turns it back around toward her. It's like a dance they're doing, the two of them, and he watches as the surprise behind her eyes turns to respect and then something more, something like ardor; not sexual, but passionate and intense. He's not sure how long they do this, eyes locked, passing understanding back and forth between them before he finds himself speaking.

"We can change the world. At least, we have to try."

Evelyn P. breaks their gaze and lifts her eyes skyward, closing them in a moment of exquisite reflection. She takes her time; she's on nobody's clock.

"You've given us a lot to consider, Dr. Royce," she says. Royce sits down. Heated conversation continues at the table, but he can barely hear it. This meeting is to all intents and purposes over. Royce will be dismissed soon as the board goes into executive session to vote. But the fate of his study has been decided already. He heard it in the voice and saw it in the eyes of the only person in the room who matters.

CHAPTER 7

Royce wraps his arms around Alesha's waist as they tumble out of the Uber that ferried them home from the final bar of the night. It's been a long, buzzy evening of celebration out with the research team as well as Manny and some friends from the hospital. Gary Sanchez even stopped by for a drink early in the night and took Royce aside.

"You just had to go out on a limb all by yourself on this one, huh," his boss said, sounding equally pissed and proud.

The call came from Evelyn Price herself as Royce sat in his car in the hospital parking lot, watching sheets of rain batter the windshield. He felt utterly spent, mentally and physically drained. He wasn't sure if it was the gravity of the stakes at hand or the intensity of the way he'd communicated with each person in the room. He suspected the latter. He'd locked eyes with every board member and compelled them to his side, communicating at a level beyond words. Had he manipulated them? Maybe, but he wasn't sorry about it. What he knew was that in that board room, he'd tapped deeply into a power that he'd previously only flirted with, in all his compassionate conversations with patients, in all his romantic and sexual dalliances with women.

Most people assume that when a person's eyes express sadness, happiness, or anger, it's the muscles and skin around the eyes that do the work of revealing emotion. When someone smiles, the cheeks tend to elevate, making the eyes appear more almond-shaped. Similarly, anger and sadness change the shape of the eyes through the action of the facial muscles. Royce knew all this, but he had never been more certain that something lives behind the eyes that also broadcasts information.

"You've got your funding, doctor," Evelyn Price said, followed by a long pause that carried the full weight of her power. "Don't make me regret it." Hearing her voice, he's momentarily transported back to their passionate, wordless dance, her unwavering eyes flashing in recognition and admiration as he spoke to her without speaking.

"You won't be sorry, Mrs. Price."

She laughs, sounding almost girlish, before her voice drops to its typical low register. "Yours was quite a performance today. Call me Evelyn."

The next few hours are a blur. Royce can't remember where he's gone next, or who he's shared the news with first. The next thing he knows, he's doing a tequila shot with his research team in a crowded bar downtown, as friends from the hospital arrive in a stream to congratulate him and take advantage of his credit card holding an open tab. In between rounds and the toasts that grow increasingly juvenile—"To Mike Royce, a superhero who's going to kick the grim reaper's ass"—Royce notices that a few of his ER colleagues, including Adele Washington, haven't joined them. News travels like brushfire in the hospital; he expected there were some colleagues who are uneasy about his study.

. . .

Alesha leads him into her house by the hand, then turns around and wraps her arms around his neck. Flushed from a night of camaraderie and Aperol spritzes, she leans up and kisses him on his chin, pressing her body against his. "Are you staying?"

Royce holds her bright pink cheeks in his hands. "Do you want me to stay?"

She rolls her eyes. "Mike Royce, you're the bravest man I know . . . except when you aren't."

He doesn't know what to say. She's right, of course; he's been cagey and indecisive with her about their romantic status for years, freezing up whenever they get too close. Before he can fumble out a weak response, she takes his hand again and leads him upstairs, kicking off her shoes as she goes.

Royce follows, struck by his attraction to her, which is equally physical and emotional. It's almost too intimate, too close. Maybe that's why he shifts into neutral so often with her.

At the top of the stairs, Alesha lets go of his hand to shake a dress strap loose from her shoulders. Her back still to him, she shakes off the other strap, letting the light, loose fabric fall to her feet. She's not wearing underwear. *Classic Alesha*, he thinks. Royce feels his body respond as he drinks in her strong, slim shoulders, the dip in her lower back, her small bottom, her taut and powerful legs. Her body, which has been through so much, radiates with life and strength. As he follows her to the bedroom, he pulls off his already loosened tie and unbuttons his shirt.

Alesha turns to him with a smile, sweet and hopeful. "It's been a while for us. I feel kind of giddy, like it's our first time all over again."

Royce is momentarily shaken by her vulnerability. With

Alesha, he never needs to search for her deepest, truest self. She offers hers to him freely and easily, without restraint or condition. Her generous spirit fills him with awe, even as it leaves him grappling to respond in kind.

He kisses her deeply, at a loss for words and wanting to be the man who can reciprocate her emotional honesty. He feels her body shudder with pleasure.

She breaks away to run her hands over his chest and down his back, grazing his buttocks. Her mouth is dropping light kisses across his sternum.

Royce gently grasps her shoulders and pushes her body away from his. "Let me look at you for a moment."

Alesha looks surprised. Royce is a skilled and tender lover, but he typically approaches sex with an amorous version of his hallmark brisk efficiency.

Royce looks into Alesha's eyes, daring himself to seek her out there, in this wordless space that he's discovered. Her brown eyes brim with sweetness and humor and a love that he's never known elsewhere. It's like he's falling fast down a deep, dark chute. He's not in control of their connection; it's too vast and powerful for him to manage as he has with other people.

He pulls his eyes away from hers. "I'm sorry," he says as he sits up and swings his feet to the floor. "I can't tonight."

He turns to Alesha, who looks hurt and confused. He brushes the side of her face with his hand.

"I'm a crazy man not to ravish you right now." He tucks a strand of golden hair behind her ear. "Absolutely insane. You're beyond beautiful."

Alesha blushes as her eyes search out his. "What's the matter, Mike?"

Where to begin? He avoids her gaze as he speaks. "Something's been happening with me, lately . . . I don't know. I'm really turned around about some stuff and—"

Alesha takes his hand and clasps it against her bare chest. "You can talk to me."

Royce flops back across the bed. "It's just been a really long day."

Alesha gets up and pads to the bathroom naked, returning wearing an oversized T-shirt that Royce recognizes as one he left here months ago. She pulls down the bedcovers, slides into bed, and pats the space next to hers, inviting him to join her. He strips to his boxers and curls up next to her. Resting his head on a pillow, he feels like he's falling into a dream. Alesha leans on her elbow as she strokes his hair lightly at his forehead.

"Tell me about the meeting. You haven't said much about it."

Royce tries to explain what happened in the board room, but he struggles to find the words. He can't seem to remember the details of what he said to others and who said what to him. He's unable to reach back in his memory even just a few hours. *The tequila didn't help*, he thinks, shocked at how exhausted he is.

"I'll tell you tomorrow, I promise."

"Okay," Alesha says, as she wraps herself under his arm and curls her body next to his.

Royce doesn't hear her. He's already asleep.

The night passes restlessly for Royce. He alternates between a deep sleep that feels like being enveloped in a heavy, dark cloak, and dreams that take him veering into the last moments of his patients' lives. Their eyes, sometimes peaceful, are other times desperate and afraid. No matter what, they're always searching his own eyes for answers. He sees Harry Samuelson's eyes, full of life and then vacant. He wakes in the gray of dawn, a fresh idea fully formed in his mind.

"Good morning."

Royce rolls over to see Alesha smiling sleepily at him. He gathers her in his arms for a long, quiet embrace.

"You smell like tequila and lime," she says with a laugh.

"I'm going to shower, and then you and I are going to have an adventure."

Alesha breaks into a big grin. *It's been too long since we spent a day together*, Royce thinks.

"What do you have in mind?"

"Okay, this might sound weird, but hang in there with me." He goes on to explain his idea: to photograph people's faces in different emotional states and then strip away their facial expressions to see what their eyes communicate, completely on their own. "You know the vacancy of the eyes at death."

Alesha nods her head slightly, looking solemn.

"All the spark that lives in the eyes before that moment—that's what I can't stop thinking about. We don't pay it much attention—it's just there—but what is it, really? What do our eyes really convey on their own without help from our facial expressions? What lives there in the eyes, that we take for granted?"

Royce is suddenly self-conscious. "Am I being too impulsive? Does this make any

sense?"

"Call it spontaneous. The new Royce," Alesha says. "It's a great idea."

Alesha suggests they take a walk around downtown to capture candid photos of people going about their lives.

"I want to photoshop the images to eliminate the anatomy surrounding the orbit of the eye, and—"

Alesha jumps in to finish his thought, saying, "—see if we can determine what they're feeling, which eyes are smiling and frowning." She's smiling. Royce squeezes her shoulders and jumps up from the bed, excited to get their experiment underway. He takes a quick shower and cooks them breakfast while Alesha gets ready. Over egg-white omelets, toast, and coffee, they hash out their plan.

They'll both take photographs. Alesha will look for people who are smiling and upbeat. Royce will keep an eye out for people who are frowning or who appear angry or otherwise troubled.

"Once we get the pictures, we need to make a second set where we delete all the tissue and everything that surrounds the eye, erasing all the markers of emotional states that come from facial expressions. I want us to be able to look at just the globe of the eye itself."

"Right," Alesha says. "Then, we'll see if we can accurately discern what's happening with their mood, without the extra information."

"Exactly." If Royce's hunch is correct, the life behind the eyes will reveal itself, both with and without their surrounding tissue.

"But who's going to photoshop the images?" Alesha asks.

"I've got that covered, I think." Royce picks up his phone and shoots off a text to Rudy, one of the computer engineers.

Hey, remember all those drinks I bought you last night?

A minute later, Royce's phone pings.

I'm sweating Patron. It's going to be a lying down day for me.

Royce grins and types his response.

I've got a favor to ask. You won't have to get off the couch.

Royce and Alesha spend the morning crisscrossing the streets of downtown Albuquerque, snapping portraits with their phones. It's a glorious New Mexico spring morning; sunny, hot, and dry, with a strong breeze. *Thank god for the technology of camera phones with good zoom,* Royce thinks, as he sets up a shot of a teenage boy sulking and grimacing while walking behind his parents. They're able to capture a series of high-quality close-ups without having to get in people's faces. Only once, Royce gets too close: a middle-aged woman whose arms are loaded with shopping bags is arguing with a traffic cop over a parking ticket.

"Creeper," she mutters while darting into her car.

When they hit one hundred portraits between them, Royce and Alesha decide to call it quits. They send their photos to Rudy, who needs a couple of hours to alter the images.

Royce suggests lunch, and they find a French café with a lush garden patio in the rear, shaded by desert willow trees that make it possible to sit outdoors. Still, they're the only ones there in the midday heat. Royce and Alesha order wine with their crepes and salads, laughing about their morning escapade.

Royce feels light and euphoric; everything is clicking into place. The study he thought was impossible is proceeding, and he's getting some relief from the grind of the ER. Working together on the research project is good for him and Alesha. He feels closer to her than ever. Sitting across from her now, watching her hands fly around in front of her as she recounts a story, he wonders if they might be able to make things work as a couple. She is the epitome of a woman and a partner to him. And he likes who he is when he's with her. Why has he been so reluctant to really try with her? *So many impossible things seem possible these days.*

While Alesha is deeply immersed in the dessert menu, Royce excuses himself to use the restroom. Washing his hands, he catches a glimpse of himself in the mirror. He notes the faint lines around his eyes. He also notes that he looks happy and relaxed. It's been a long time since he saw that face in a mirror.

He strolls back to the patio, calling out to Alesha as he ducks beneath a low awning. "Hey, let's split the bête noire—"

The patio tables, empty when he left a few moments ago, are filled with lunchtime diners. But his table is empty; Alesha is nowhere to be seen. She must be in the bathroom. Settling back into his chair, he feels a hint of irritation when he sees their plates and wine glasses have been cleared. He opens his phone and scrolls the news, looking up every now and in hopes of catching the waiter's eye for the check.

Ten minutes pass, and Royce begins to wonder what's keeping Alesha. A flare of worry surges inside him, but he tamps it down. His concern for Alesha's health and safety rumbles like a quiet engine that's always running in the back of his mind. Before she was his colleague, friend, and lover, she was his patient, critically ill. He carries a strain of worry for her that never ceases.

Five minutes later, he can't sit any longer. He threads through the crowded patio and slips back into the restroom hallway. He knocks gently on the women's bathroom door.

Over the din of chatting diners and the clanging bustle of the kitchen, he hears, "Out in a minute."

Royce leans back against the wall and slides his hands in his pocket, preparing to tease Alesha for her slowness as soon as she comes out.

The door opens.

"What, did you fall asleep in there or—"

The twentysomething woman exiting the bathroom gives him a strange look as she scoots down the hallway.

What the hell? He walks back to the small, intimate indoor dining room, where a dozen tables sit cozily close to one another.

He scans the room once, then again. No Alesha. He stalks back to the patio, stopping briefly to pop his head down the narrow hall that leads to the kitchen. He scans the tables, and sees their own table now taken by another pair of diners. He approaches the couple.

"Excuse me. Have you seen a woman, mid-thirties, long blonde hair? We were just sitting here together a few minutes ago."

The man and woman give him an odd look as they tell him no. He's in such a rush to get to the front of the restaurant again that he barely takes the time to thank them and hardly notices how deep they are into eating their meals.

Royce races to the front door and steps outside. He looks up and down the street in both directions. She could have stepped into any of these stores. Except that's not something Alesha would ever do, just leave without letting him know. He turns back and heads toward the bar, looking for the maître d, who is chatting with a table of diners. As soon as the maître d leaves the table, Royce pounces toward her.

"Excuse me, I'm looking for my . . . friend . . . We were having lunch together on the patio and she's just . . . disappeared. Do you remember her? She's tall, with long blonde hair, wearing a yellow sundress—did you see her leave?"

The maître d looks concerned. "I haven't, sir. Where did you say you were sitting?"

Royce waves an impatient hand in the direction of the garden. "Back there. You sat us about an hour ago."

"Sir, I'm confused, I don't recall—"

"Have you seen my friend?" Royce struggles to keep from screaming.

"I have not. Have you tried calling her?"

"My god, I haven't." Royce whips his phone from his pocket and fumbles to find Alesha's contact information. As he dials, the maître d takes a few steps to the bar. Royce watches her lean in and whisper to the bartender.

His call goes straight to voicemail. He listens as Alesha's cheerful voice greets him.

"It's me. Where are you? I'm at the restaurant, still. You're not here, still. Will you call me please and tell me what the fuck is going on?"

He hangs up and immediately texts her.

"Sir, can I get you some water? Would you like to sit down for a moment?" the maître d asks.

"I don't want any fucking water," he snarls. "My god. I'm so sorry; that was awful." Royce feels panic beginning to bloom.

Then his phone pings.

CHAPTER 8

ell Alesha she left her phone at my house. Rudy's text flashes on his screen.

She's at Rudy's? Or was? His fingers fly over the keys. *Alesha was at your house???*

He watches the three dots flash.

She just left with the flash drive of photos.

Royce lets out a deep sigh. Alesha went to pick up their pictures. But why would she go without telling him? Royce calls up an Uber and rides to Alesha's house in a daze. He knocks on her door but doesn't wait for an answer before entering. He calls out to her from the entryway.

"In here," she calls from the living room. Her voice sounds bright and relaxed.

He turns the corner and finds her setting out paper and pens on the coffee table. She's barefoot, and wearing a loose, pale-blue mini dress.

"What happened? Why did you leave?" Royce is torn between anger and a powerful urge to wrap her in his arms.

"What are you talking about?" Alesha gives him a quizzical look.

"You left in the middle of lunch without saying anything." Royce rubs his forehead with his finger and thumb. "I was fucking worried about you."

Alesha laughs. "Mike, what are you talking about?"

"I went to the bathroom and when I came back, you were gone."

Alesha's laughter ends abruptly. "Mike, are you being serious right now? We agreed I'd go and get the files from Rudy while you went back to your place to grab some clothes and get your car."

"I don't—" He's about to tell her that he has no recollection of that conversation. He's stopped by a surging sense that whatever the hell is going on with him, he needs to keep it to himself, at least for now.

"Sorry. I misunderstood the plan." Royce does his best to smile and shrug it off for her. "Lack of sleep these past few days must be catching up to me."

Alesha grabs her laptop and sets it on the coffee table before saying, "I thought we could look at both sets of photographs together, but we'll make our answers separately and then compare them." She looks excited. Royce has almost forgotten the second part of today's experiment: to gauge their ability to correctly read the emotions in the eyes of the people they photographed.

He sighs. "Sure, that sounds good. I'm just going to splash a little water on my face." He ducks into the bathroom to pull himself together. He has no idea what's happening with him, but something isn't right with his mind.

When he comes out, Alesha is sitting to one side of the couch, her long legs curled underneath her. "Rudy made us an answer key, so we can easily identify the original photographs with the sets that he's altered."

Royce puts on a smile as he sits next to her.

"Ready?" Alesha asks, handing him pen and paper.

"Let's do it."

Alesha clicks open the first of Rudy's files. This set of photos are cropped to show all one hundred individuals' eyes with their surrounding upper and lower lids. Working in silence, Royce and Alesha independently make note of the photos as either smiling or non-smiling. When they've scrolled through them all, Alesha grabs the answer key so they can score their guesses. Neither of them is surprised when they discover they've both guessed correctly one hundred percent of the time.

"The lower lids always bulge as the face draws up with a smile," Alesha says.

Now fully re-invested in their experiment, Royce clicks open the second file. He is eager to get to the next set of photos, which show the eyes without the upper or lower lids and absolutely no surrounding tissue. This time, they're only looking at the globe of the eye itself.

They'd worked through the first set of photos in a matter of minutes. The second set, they discover, requires intense concentration. They move through the photos slowly, sometimes taking five minutes with an image before logging their guesses. After two hours of deep attention, they make it to the end of the series.

"Do you want me to tally up our scores?" Alesha asks. Royce nods and she eagerly grabs the answer key. He watches as she works through both of their sheets. He feels a rush of affection for her. Who else would ever do this weird experiment with him and be as excited about it as he is?

Alesha finishes and looks up at him. "You guessed correctly eighty times, so eighty percent. I scored eighty-two."

"Wow, that's high," Royce says. It's a testament to the power of the eyes themselves as communicators. "Let's look for patterns in our guesses."

Sitting shoulder to shoulder, they weed through their answers and analyze them against the original photographs.

"This is interesting," Royce says. "We almost never mis-labeled a smiling eye. Almost all our mistakes came when we thought a non-smiling eye was a smiling one."

"What do you think that's about?" Alesha asks.

"I'm not sure. But it's pretty clear from these results that there's something about the globe of the eye itself that communicates and reveals our emotions."

He looks at Alesha and sees wonder growing wide in *her* eyes.

"And maybe more than emotion," Alesha says. "Maybe intention, too."

Royce thinks about his experience in the board meeting. "Go on. What do you mean?"

"Well, what about the uncanny sensation that someone behind you has their eyes on you? What's that about?"

"Maybe paranoia," Royce retorts.

Alesha pushes back. "But how can eyes be threatening? Hands can cause physical harm, but we don't have an uncanny sensation of hands behind us."

"True enough. And that sense of fear, or threat, can feel as clear as if it was spoken aloud."

Royce thinks about Harry Samuelsson's eyes in the moments leading up to his death. He'd seen something shift in the man's eyes well before he expired. It was as though the determination, joy, warmth, and rebellion that was so clear in his eyes had receded prior to his death, even as he remained lucid, alert, and talking. Royce recounts this experience to Alesha, who agrees: she has also seen a change in patients' eyes that takes place before they die, different from the change that occurs at the moment of their death.

"There's a profound energy enlivening the body," Alesha says. "Maybe there's a concentration of that energy that is somehow connected to the eye, and what we're seeing is the beginning of the dispersing of that energy out of the body."

Royce mulls this over. "When you talk about profound energy enlivening the body, it makes me think of the vibration that initiates electricity and magnetism in 'dead' mass."

"Okay, so it's a primal pulse," Alesha says. She sits up on her heels and leans in close to Royce. "But what primes the pump?"

Royce's breath catches in his throat. "Are you talking about God?"

Alesha puts a hand on his arm and gently strokes it. "Don't worry, I'm not going to make you have a conversation about God," she says.

"What if I want to?" Royce's voice is barely above a whisper.

Alesha's eyes widen in disbelief. "Okay, then. I don't know who God is—or even that God is a 'who'—but I do think there is godliness in all things. You know that I believe there is an order and a cycle to life and death, to the energy in all living beings, that extends beyond what we've been able to see and measure and comprehend with science. At least so far."

"And the soul?" Royce can scarcely get the words out. He didn't know until this moment how much he wanted—needed—to have this conversation with Alesha.

"Do I believe in the soul?" Alesha asks. "I do."

Alesha looks calm and certain, her tone matter-of-fact. It's clear there's no doubt in her mind. Alesha speaks about the soul as if there were no controversy regarding its existence. *Why is this so easy for her, and so fraught for me?* Royce wonders.

"Have you always?"

"I'm not sure." Alesha pauses in thought. "I can't recall a time when I didn't. But there was—" Alesha cuts herself off midsentence, her face tightening in pain.

"What?" Royce reaches out and takes her hand in his. "What were you going to say?"

Alesha exhales a long breath. "When I was sick—the aneurysm—it all became really clear. Not intellectually—I mean, I felt it. I knew there was an essential part of me that existed inside me that was distinct from my physical body."

"How did you know?"

Alesha is silent for what feels to Royce like an eternity.

"Because I felt it preparing to leave."

Royce is taken aback; he has known Alesha for many years, but he's never heard this story before.

"It's hard to describe," Alesha says. "You of all people know how sick I was. How close I got to dying."

Royce's eyes fill with tears as he recalls Alesha in the trauma room with a brain bleed.

"I was so scared and in so much pain. My head felt like it had been cut in two. I was having a hard time seeing; everything was getting really blurry."

"That was likely the aneurysm," says Royce. He pauses, considering how to say what he wants to say next. "There is speculation that near death, eyesight goes first, before hearing."

"Well, I felt something shift inside—I don't know how to explain it. But I knew it wasn't related to my condition, my illness."

Alesha closes her eyes in recollection. "It was like something became unmoored inside me."

Royce shudders at the thought of Alesha's soul preparing to leave her body. "I wonder what happened."

She smiles at him. "You did."

Royce is confused. "I didn't treat you, not enough to save your life."

"No—I don't think it was that. I mean, the surgery saved my life, of course. But you stabilized my soul, for the time it took to get the operation."

Royce can't believe what he's hearing. "What do you mean?"

"Don't you remember?" Alesha's eyes well with tears. "We had a moment I'll never forget. You took my hand as I was being wheeled out of the trauma room. You looked right at me, square in the eyes. You saw me, and I saw you. Not the doctor you, *you*. You spoke to my soul with your own, Mike. I literally felt the unsettled part of me settle."

Royce can't believe she's talking about soul-to-soul communication. He's maybe just discovering this, wondering if it's real or if he's a delusional megalomaniac. And she's saying she's known about it all along.

"You think it's possible to communicate with another person's soul?" Royce holds his breath.

"Yes," says Alesha. "I think it's more than possible. I think some people are better at it than others." She grasps his fingers tightly with her own. "You are very good at it, whether you know it or not."

Royce lets out a short, sharp cry, a sob that's a mixture of grief and relief. He pulls Alesha into a tight embrace and feels her heart beating next to his as they sit in silence.

He's not sure how long they've been wrapped in each other's arms when Alesha says, "Mike?"

"Yes," he says softly.

"I'm starving. Could we get some food?"

Royce laughs and releases her from his arms. "Yeah, let's do that."

"I'm just going to change quickly. I'll be right back," she says.

While he waits for Alesha, Royce leans back on the couch and closes his eyes. He feels a sense of peace and confidence wash over him. He's not crazy or delusional. There's a power and an energy that he can use to communicate with others, and if Alesha is right, that power and energy are the soul at work. If Alesha's own experience is any indication, there's some kind of transition that takes place with that energy when death is close by. What can they learn about this in their research? Just thinking about the possibilities makes him euphoric.

Eyes closed, he hears Alesha's light footsteps coming down the stairs. *Such a comforting sound*, he thinks. Maybe it's time to start thinking about not living alone.

"You ready to go?"

Royce opens his eyes to Alesha standing in front of him. She's wearing her yellow sundress.

"I heard about this sweet little French place with a terrace dining room," she says. "Want to try it?"

CHAPTER 9

The boy's eyes were blocked by the dark, oversized hoodie that hung over his face. But in the seconds— Was it seconds? They were giant-sized, impossibly stretched—that the boy stepped toward him, Royce met his gaze. There was anger first, a sharp and brittle menace, and then Royce saw the rest: the fear, the pain, the desperation to be noticed, the thrashing for power in a world that told him again and again he was nothing. And then his chest exploded like a too-hot potato and Royce saw only his own blood spilling down his blue scrubs.

Something heavy falling from his hand startled him awake, and his feet fall off his desk. Royce bolts upright in his office chair, instantly aware of a stinging sensation across his chest. He grabbed at his shirt, pulling it up to inspect his torso. No bullet wounds. Hot coffee. Royce gets up to change into clean scrubs and gather the mug now spilling coffee across the floor.

The dream. How many times had he had it? Three, maybe four? It was hard to recall. And something about the dream was always playing in the back of his mind. The last couple of times, he'd felt as though he could exert some control over the dream, directing his attention to explore certain details, zooming in to see particular elements. This time, he chose the troubled, pained eyes of the young man who shot him. Taking a bit of control within the dream makes it no less frightening. But it gives his curiosity and confusion an outlet at least within his dreamscape. Awake, his confusion runs wild, barely controlled.

Royce doesn't understand what is happening in his mind. The recurring dreams of an ER shooting that never actually happened alternated with dreams from his past that feel viscerally real. When he is awake, he is uncharacteristically forgetful. And he's experiencing strange gaps in time that he can't account for or make sense of. The mystifying lunch with Alesha. Finding himself in the grocery store, no idea how he'd gotten there. Leaving the gym and being suddenly back at work, without a memory of the hours he'd spent off shift. He'd given himself a full blood workup and was regularly checking his vitals. The results are the same every time. Completely normal, nothing looks off. But something feels off. Something feels very wrong. He's thought about talking to Allan Schmidt, the head of neurology, to get an imaging study of his brain. But it's too risky. His study is up and running. Four weeks in, the team has collected reams of data and is beginning some preliminary analysis. He can't risk telling anyone—not even Alesha, much less the neurology chief who sits on the hospital board—how disoriented he feels at times. He'd most certainly get pulled from his ER shifts, and his research project would be suspended. He could probably live with the former. But the latter would be unbearable, his life's work screeching to a halt before it even has a chance to get going. He'll have to find another way to get a look inside his own brain.

Today's ER shift has been unusually slow. No trauma, no

strokes, no heart attacks, no overdoses. A rare morning during which Royce could sit down, sip a cup of coffee, and relax. He'd fallen asleep in his chair almost immediately, judging by the amount of coffee he's dumped across the room.

Grabbing a towel to wipe up the spill, Royce tries to focus on his research. It's a big day. The first batch of analyzed data is ready for him to review. But right now, he can't seem to train his mind on the details of what he'll be looking at or the finer points of what he'll be looking for in the results. This, despite designing the study protocols himself and working closely with the engineers on designing the computer program. It's another disturbing pattern he's noticed in himself lately; when he's not physically in the research laboratory, he finds it hard to concentrate on the details of the project. In the lab, though, he's sharp as a tack. He's been spending four to six solid hours there on an almost daily basis, his mind riveted on his work.

His pager beeps and Royce pulls it from his waist. Halfway through his shift, it looks like a genuinely ill patient has arrived.

Royce strides down the hall and into trauma room two, where a middle-aged man is sitting on a gurney, his wife and two young daughters huddled together at his side.

The nurse hands him a chart that he scans quickly, keeping one eye on his patient, who is pale and struggling to sit up.

"Mr. Grimes?" The man nods as Royce helps him to lean back on the gurney. "What's going on today, sir?"

"My chest hurts. A lot." He sits up slightly. "I feel the pain all the way around here," he says as his hand moves from the front of his chest to the middle of his back. He winces, and one of his daughters starts to cry.

Royce immediately thinks thoracic aortic dissection, a probable cause when a patient complains of tearing chest pain that radiates to the back. In layman's terms, this means the main artery in his chest that feeds blood throughout the body is tearing. Instead of blood flowing through the lumen of the vessel, it's carving away part of the lining of the vessel and flowing into the vessel wall. If Royce's suspicion is correct, Mr. Grimes could blow out his aorta at any moment.

"We're going to get you right in for a CT scan to get an idea of what's going on."

Royce turns to the nurse. "Let's get Mr. Grimes on his way up and give radiology a head's up that he's coming." Royce and the nurse together wheel Mr. Grimes on the gurney out of the trauma room, flagging down a pair of attendants to ferry the man to imaging.

"Fast as you can," he murmurs to the attendants, as the nurse grabs a phone to alert radiology. Royce turns to the man's wife. "He won't be gone long, and we'll start to get some answers. I'll show you where you can wait until he gets back."

"What will the scan tell you? Is he going to need surgery?"

"We'll know more soon." He puts a hand on the woman's trembling shoulder. "I know how scary this is. We're going to take good care of him."

Royce kneels and meets the eyes of two frightened girls, both with their arms wrapped tightly around their mother's legs.

"The hospital is a scary place, huh."

The older girl dips her head in an almost imperceptible nod, as her younger sister buries her face at her mother's side.

Royce smiles gently at them. "I promise; you're safe here. And I promise to take the very best care of your dad, okay?"

. . .

Royce has just enough time to suture a wound in trauma room three before he's notified that Mr. Grimes's CT images are ready. He steps up to the computer next to the radiologist. Royce's prediction is correct: dissection of the thoracic aorta. Royce's own heart feels heavy as he scans the images. Mr. Grimes's aorta is torn from the very top, where it arises from the heart, all the way down to the lower abdomen. A thoracic aortic dissection is always a life-threatening event, but this man's tear is so severe that his prognosis is even worse than most dissections. He puts a call through to the vascular surgeon on call.

After hearing Royce's rundown of Mr. Grimes's condition, the vascular surgeon says, "I can get him into surgery in ten minutes, but I'm not the best option, Dr. Royce. There are only a couple of surgeons in the country with this experience." The good news is one of these surgeons is based in Las Vegas, making it possible to get the patient there by plane in about ninety minutes; the unfortunate reality is Mr. Grimes needs surgery immediately, and this relatively short delay could be fatal.

Royce's legs feel heavy as he walks back to the trauma room two to deliver the difficult news to the patient and his family. The elevator opens as he passes by, and Mr. Grimes is wheeled out. The man manages to put on a tired smile as his wife and daughters rush out of the family waiting room to meet him at his side.

Royce approaches the gurney. "Let's get you all back inside so we can talk—"

Royce sees confusion spread across the man's face as his eyelids flutter and then close. His body trembles and twitches. "He's seizing," Royce calls, pushing the gurney toward the nearest open trauma room. Two nurses jump to help.

By the time Royce makes it to the head of the bed, Mr. Grimes has regained consciousness, his eyes wild with fear.

"I'm right here. Focus on my face and take an easy, slow breath." Mr. Grimes meets Royce's eyes with his own. Royce sees the fear beginning to recede slightly, replaced by a sadness that clenches his heart.

"Good, good," Royce says quietly. "Now take another." Behind him, one of the nurses is murmuring quietly to the man's wife and daughters. Royce glances up at the monitor. Mr. Grimes's blood pressure is 70/40, dangerously low. Dr. Royce orders the nurse to begin IV fluids to increase the man's blood pressure, just enough to maintain consciousness. He's walking a medical tightrope right now; increasing the pressure could cause the partially torn aorta to completely blow out. Royce beckons Mrs. Grimes to join him at her husband's bedside. Quietly, in simple terms, he explains the severity of the vascular damage. Mrs. Grimes places her cheek against her husband's, and her tears roll down both of their faces.

Royce prepares them for the choice they must make. Option one is to undergo surgery by the on-call surgeon, who doesn't have sufficient expertise but does have the ability to get Mr. Grimes on the table in a matter of minutes. Option two is to undergo surgery by one of the two most capable surgeons in the country. The risk of choosing option two, he explains, is that Mr. Grimes's aorta might blow out well before the plane lands.

"Sweetie, what do you think?" Mr. Grimes asks his wife.

"I don't know how to make this choice," she says, her voice strained with desperation.

"Doctor, what do you think is best?" Mr. Grimes's eyes fix on Royce's, allowing Royce to see below the fear, below the sadness, the man's steely, desperate hope to stay alive.

The emotional weight of the moment hits Royce like a bullet. It doesn't matter how many times he's been in this position before. If anything, it feels harder now than it ever has, to hold his patient's life-and-death decision in his hands. The words come out slowly, with effort, like cold molasses from a bottle. "Get to the best surgeon you can."

The couple looks at each other, silently coming to an agreement. Royce steps away immediately to arrange an air transport team. When he returns to the room, Mr. Grimes is holding his daughters' hands in his own.

"Dad's going to have an operation, so you won't see me for a little while—" he stumbles over the words "—but I'm going to get all fixed up, and then we'll go for a bike ride, okay?"

"It's time to go," Royce says quietly. He walks alongside the gurney with Mrs. Grimes and the girls as Mr. Grimes is wheeled to the ambulance bay. His family crowds around him as he's about to be lifted into the ambulance.

"Love you, Daddy!"

"Daddy, we love you so much."

"I love you, I love you so much," says Mr. Grimes, "Be good for Mom." He looks at his wife. "Sweetie, I—"

"We'll see you soon," she says, her voice staying firm and clear through her tears. "We'll be at the hospital when you wake up."

As the ambulance rolls away, Mrs. Grimes heaves with sobs that shake her shoulders. Royce puts a strong arm around her shoulders and walks her and her children to the elevator to the parking lot.

"Thank you, Dr. Royce."

"Your husband has a lot to live for," he says, "and he's going to be in the best hands."

He's just got to make it to the surgical table, Royce thinks.

. . .

The ER is quiet again after Mr. Grimes's departure, and the rest of his shift is uneventful, leaving Royce plenty of time to worry about how the transport is going, and whether Mr. Grimes made it into surgery. Royce discharges his last patient at 7:30. Still no word on Grimes. Wound up with anxious energy, Royce drops his bag immediately after arriving home and goes straight to his weight bench. Working through his weight circuit, he pushes through to yet another set of personal bests; his mind may be fraying, but physically he continues to be stronger than he's ever been, and his strength continues to grow almost by the day. Tonight, he bench-presses 250 pounds for ten repetitions, a feat that not long ago was unfathomable to him. As he finishes his final set, his phone rings. He returns the weight to the safety arms with ease and grabs his phone.

"Hello?"

"Dr. Royce, this is Emily Foster, I was with Mr. Grimes on the flight." Royce thinks he remembers the paramedic from earlier, but he can't quite conjure her face in his mind.

"What's his status?"

"We were diverted west en route to Vegas. Thunderstorms," she says. "It took us four hours to land."

"How is he?"

The paramedic sighs, and Royce feels an instant knot in his throat.

"He died five minutes before we landed."

Dr. Royce hangs up the phone, walks into the bathroom, and stares in the mirror. He inspects all the little flaws in his face that seem magnified. The dark shadows under his eyes seem darker. The creases in his forehead look deeper. The lines running down each side of his mouth that make his expression look even more dour and defeated than he feels. It's as though he's aged a year since yesterday. It feels like each one of these gut-wrenching events sucks away at his lifespan. Only the jet-black stubble on his face reminds him he is still young.

"Please, God. Help me make a difference."

The words fall from his mouth before he realizes what he's saying, and they shock him. Where did that come from? Not his own, hyper-rational, agnostic, God-indifferent mind. They couldn't have. For a single, bizarre instant, he wonders if it was actually his own thought that provoked the remark. Before he can do any further contemplation, he's overtaken by a powerful surge of exhaustion. Feeling like he's been drugged, he drags his feet along the floor to his bed, where he falls into a deep sleep.

In his dream, he's a crying, tiny child wailing with such ferocity that he hurts his own ears. His limbs feel jerky and wild, as though he's being controlled by a set of strings. He wants to stretch his arms and legs, but he can't. Something is holding him back. The sounds he longs for come closer, voices rumbling near him now, low and soothing. He's swept up by a pair of hands and smells the familiar scent that he knows as home. The hands deposit him into the crook of an arm and his wails begin again, for a moment, before he finds the delicious, warm comfort of the body he's nestled against. His mouth finds a nipple, colder than he expects, but the warm milk is there. He's in his father's arms.

CHAPTER 10

"Fifty-eight."

The woman in front of him looks at him expectantly.

"Excuse me?"

"That'll be fifty-eight dollars."

Royce sees the cash register that separates them. He turns around to see a line of people behind him, many in scrubs, holding trays and to-go cups. He looks down at his hands, holding a tray piled with sandwiches, doughnuts, and cups of fruit. An ice cream bar balances on a lidded cup of what he guesses is soup. It's enough food for three hungry people, and most of it is stuff Royce would never allow himself to eat.

It's happening, again. How did he get here? The last thing he remembers, he was showering at the gym. Now he's buying lunch fit for a carbo-loading teenage football player. Or two.

"You okay?" The cashier's tone straddles patience and irritation. "Doctor?"

"Yeah, sorry. Here you go." He fumbles for his wallet. "Wait, could you add a large coffee, please?"

The cashier moves firmly into irritation mode, rolling her eyes at him as she re-tallies his bill. Royce scans his credit card. A fifty-eight-dollar lunch he won't eat feels like a small price to pay to get out of this line as quickly as possible, find a place to sit down alone, and get his bearings back. He hoists his tray and makes a beeline for a small table in the corner of the hospital cafeteria. He sits and takes a long sip of hot coffee, hoping it will clear his head.

Where is his mind going, that's what he wants to know. His last firm, clear memory was of standing under a searing hot stream of water, washing the sweat of his long, high-intensity workout from his body. It's maddening. His brain is malfunctioning somehow. He's deep inside a hospital with all the tools to find out why, and he can't get answers without putting his career—and the fate of his research —in jeopardy. Is he so consumed by everything that's on his plate— he casts a wry glance at his actual plate—that he's moving through chunks of his day in some kind of trance? Is it something more serious? He's about to head down a wormhole of thought about dissociative episodes and fugue states when he sees Dr. Adele Washington heading toward the elevators. *Please, don't let her see me.* Royce doesn't want to make small talk, or any other kind of talk right now.

Too late.

"Hey, Mike. How are you feeling?" Dr. Washington says as she approaches his table. She scans his free-for-all lunch tray with a look of amusement but keeps her comments to herself.

"Hi, Adele, good thanks." Royce is hoping to keep this short.

"How's PT going?"

"What?" Royce is momentarily confused.

"Mike. Tell me you went to see PT." The way she raises her

eyebrows at him tells him she's prepared to be disappointed with his response.

It takes Royce a few seconds to figure out what she's talking about. His rib injury. The truth is, he didn't go to PT because he didn't need to; his rib healed remarkably fast. But Adele won't believe him. And she shouldn't. The speed with which he healed makes no medical sense.

"I know, I know," he says, putting on his best guilty-as-charged demeanor.

"Ugh, so typical," she says. "It never fails with doctors. Y'all are my worst patients."

"I've just been flat out with shifts and the study going now." He watches a dark cloud pass across her face at the mention of his study.

"How's the research going, then?" she asks.

Royce opens his mouth to reply and realizes he doesn't know what to say. He can't organize his thoughts to make a coherent reply. He can't recollect precisely how much work they've done, or what trends are beginning to emerge from the data. His mind is swathed in a thick fog that he can't cut through.

"You know how it goes," he says, fumbling for an anodyne response. "Early days, still."

Dr. Washington now looks as uncomfortable as he feels. "Well, good luck...I guess." She nods a goodbye, and Royce senses they're both equally relieved this conversation is now at an end.

He looks at his watch. Three o'clock. A wave of relief moves through him. It's time to head to the research lab. His concentration gets a boost at about three every day. The fog clears, and he can focus. He's fallen into the habit of giving his best hours of the day to his laboratory work. For four to six hours thereafter, he is consumed with his research, his mental energy soaring, his mind razor-sharp.

He takes a final slug of coffee. Standing, he spots the ice-cream sandwich still propped on the paper canteen of soup. *Fuck it.* He tears the thin white paper and pops half the sandwich in his mouth.

Alesha is waiting for him as the elevator doors open. "I thought we'd walk together," she says.

He immediately remembers; they're going to do an initial and preliminary review of the data that's been analyzed by the computer program the study's engineers have designed. His mind starts clicking, anticipating what they might discover in this first batch of data.

Alesha looks up at him and smiles, and Royce notices she looks tired, her face thinner than usual. Working together on the study means they've seen a lot of each other this past month. But coolness has settled in between them. Outside of the lab, Royce has been distant, deliberately so. She knows him so well, he was sure she'd see right through the façade he's putting up these days. He's masking his mental confusion well enough with everyone else—at least he thinks he is—but it won't fly with Alesha.

Then there are his mood swings. He's either elated or rageful, blissed-out or despondent; there's little in between. One minute, he's thinking about proposing to Alesha. The next, he's feeling chained down by a commitment that doesn't even exist between them, a commitment that Alesha has never pressed him to make. He knows she's confused by his distance; he can see it in her eyes. So far, she's been too patient and too proud to call him on it. It's not exactly the first time he's pulled away from her after they've gotten close. His remoteness, her quiet patience; it's a cycle they repeat. And they always somehow manage to find their way back to the intimacy that thrills and terrifies him.

"How's it going?" He drops his bag next to his desk. Alesha is already settling in at a computer terminal.

She shifts in her seat, pulling her shoulders away from him slightly. "Yeah, good. I'm just pulling up the data sets now."

"No, I mean—how's it going. Like, how are *you*?"

"Oh." She lets out a tense little laugh. "Fine, thanks. You?"

"Great. Good. Yeah." *Am I only capable of having awkward conversations now?* "Ready to take a look?"

He pulls up a chair and sits down next to her, and they begin to slowly review the first batch of analyzed data on the two hundred patients enrolled in the study. After an hour, Royce pushes back his chair and groans. The results are fairly unimpressive. So far, there seems to be no correlation between any of the historical or laboratory data and the number of days patients have left to live. Amazingly, there were two people with the same type and staging of cancer and nearly identical historical and laboratory results. One of them died thirty days after entering the study, and the other has been in the study for ninety days and is still doing well.

"We've got to increase the number of patients," Royce says. "It's the only way to get a broad enough swath of data to be meaningful."

"We could bring in other hospitals, go nationwide?"

Royce shakes his head in irritation. "That's going to take a lot of time. Too much time." He's trying to stay measured and optimistic, but it's a struggle. The truth is, he's agitated and desperate for a path to a breakthrough. Why does it matter how much time it takes to build a study population large enough to see correlations that they're not seeing now? The simple answer is that patients are dying every day, and the faster they can generate results, the sooner he may have the answers that can prolong their lives. The not-so-simple answer is a ticking clock within him that he doesn't quite understand. This work on this project has overtaken his life. It's become his obsession, his compulsion. Everything else in his life has become a fuzzy, unpleasant, and unwelcome interruption from his mission in the lab.

The door opens, and the team begins to file in. Royce wastes no time getting their weekly meeting started.

"Welcome, folks. And welcome, Dr. Rangupta." From her seat across the table, she lifts her hand in a quick wave to the group. After Margo walked out, Royce needed another physician consulting on the study. He was surprised at how long it took him to find someone willing to step in. "Dr. Rangupta is joining us starting this week. We're really fortunate to have her expertise." The group murmurs their hellos before Royce cuts them off. "Let's get down to business."

Royce walks them through the same preliminary data analysis that he and Alesha reviewed. The issue at hand is clear to everyone: they've got to find a way to increase the volume of patients. Lucy, a research assistant, suggests extending the study to include patients and hospitals countrywide.

"We've already nixed that idea. Unfortunately, it will chew up time we just don't have," says Royce.

"Not to mention the bureaucracy of having so many hospitals involved would totally sink us," Dr. Rangupta says.

Royce nods in heated agreement. He's encouraged by her no-nonsense attitude.

"I'll open it up to you all. Anyone else have thoughts on how we might proceed?"

There's a long silence in the room. Some lower their heads in thought. Others fidget with pens. Royce lets the silence linger. It makes its own point: there are no easy answers. He has a thought that's been brewing for a while, well before he saw today's disappointing analysis. But he wants them to stew in the difficulty of their current predicament before he floats it.

When the silence becomes unbearable, Royce clears his throat. "I have an idea for how to increase the volume of patients and narrow the focus of our inquiry to improve its accuracy."

All eyes are on him now. He's got one chance to deliver this idea successfully. Before he speaks, he makes sure to meet the gaze of every one of his colleagues, a brief but potent moment of connection that he hopes will prime them to agree with what he's about to propose.

"We could recruit terminal patients who are seeking physician-assisted suicide," Royce says. "And then we perform controlled evaluations before and directly after death."

There's a collective gasp around the table. He sees Alesha's jaw drop and her tired eyes widen.

"This would require some serious lobbying," says Dr. Rangupta. "Do you think we could get permission to perform assisted suicide within the context of our study?"

Royce is thrilled to hear this question. If Meera Rangupta is already thinking about practical considerations, it means she's not hung up on ethical ones. He's less sure about the rest of the group, who look in varying degrees of shock and discomfort. Alesha is the first to speak.

"We'd be intervening to end their lives? So that we can study them?" Alesha sounds incredulous. There's an angry edge in her tone that sets him off.

"Well, we're not going to be bribing anyone, Alesha," Royce says with a hint of contempt for her question that he chooses not to control. "We'll be recruiting patients who have gone through the legal preparations and psychological vetting to end their lives voluntarily."

"But who decides when it happens? When we terminate their lives?" Alesha presses him.

Royce feels himself getting angry at her challenge. "They will. Of course." His voice drops a full register as he tries to restrain himself.

"And you think they won't feel any pressure or undue influence coming from us, and our stated agenda?"

"I do not."

"I can't imagine how they won't, Mike. I think this is a dangerous idea. We're talking about hastening someone's death in order to—"

"Dr. Royce."

"Excuse me?" Alesha's jaw drops. The rest of the team cast low glances at each other.

"You can call me Dr. Royce," he repeats with a calm he does not feel.

"Well, Dr. Royce," she says, her wounded anger crystal clear. "I think you're kidding yourself if you think this isn't going to affect the trajectory of their lives and the time they have left. You're talking about vulnerable people making profound decisions with the precious time they have left to live, and you want to interfere—"

"Whoa, whoa." Dr. Rick Davies rises halfway out of his chair, hands outstretched. "Let's slow this down—"

"Yes, I want to interfere." Royce thunders his response. "That's the fucking point, Alesha. I'm not going to push a patient to end their lives until they are fully ready. I don't know how you could even think something like that. But we are trying to disrupt death."

"You're delusional." Alesha's words fall out in a barely audible whisper.

"And you're naïve," Royce spits back.

The rest of the team is frozen in their seats. Dr. Rangupta looks like she's wondering what the hell sort of melee she signed on for.

Alesha picks up her notebook and tosses her messenger bag over one shoulder. "Nurse Simmons."

Royce is momentarily speechless, stunned at the disintegration of their debate and that she is walking out. "Excuse me?"

"You can call me Nurse Simmons," she says as she pulls the door closed behind her.

Royce sits in the lab alone, his body shaking. The team left moments ago. They'd reached a fragile consensus that his suggestion is indeed the best way to amplify the power and accuracy of the study. A few seemed eager. Others clearly seemed to be searching for a reason to veto the idea. In the end, they came to an agreement to proceed, if only because there seemed no viable alternative.

He'd apologized to them for his outburst with Alesha. "That was wholly unprofessional. I'll make no excuses for it. But I promise, it won't happen again."

Sitting here now, he's shaking with anger and something else —what is it? Fear. He'd been unfair to Alesha and cruel to her. She'd voiced a reasonable concern, and he made things personal to spite her for it. When she hit back, she'd landed a bullseye, gotten deep under his skin. Was he delusional? Was she, or others, noticing the oddities plaguing his mind that he'd been working so hard to hide? He's got to find out what's happening inside his brain. He thinks about Rick Davies, the radiologist. They don't know each other well, but Royce admires the physician's acumen, and his cool headedness. He could ask Davies to perform a CAT scan, but could he trust the man to keep confidentiality, no matter the results?

And as angry as he'd been and still was, Royce is terrified at the thought of continuing the study without Alesha. He's got to make things right. He's got to get her back.

But first he needs to reckon with another powerful, perceptive woman in his life.

Royce picks up the phone and calls Evelyn Price's office to request a meeting.

"Hello?"

He's surprised to hear her deep, patrician voice answering her own phone.

"Mrs. Pri—er, Evelyn. It's Michael Royce."

"Dr. Royce. What a surprise." He's pleased to hear a lilt in her voice. "How goes the research?"

"That's what I'd like to talk with you about. We've seen some early results and I think we need to make some adjustments, that are . . . well . . ." Royce searches for the right words. "It's a big ask."

Evelyn's response comes without a hiccup of hesitation. "Come by my office at six."

"Tonight?"

"Is there a reason to delay?"

Royce laughs to himself at her impatience and feels once again that flash of recognition, of alignment between them. "I'll see you then."

Her office is nothing like he expected. He imagined lots of mahogany and modern art, furnishings that cost more than his yearly salary. Instead, the light-filled walls were lined with family photographs and cheerful plein air landscapes. Evelyn stands from behind a simple wooden desk to greet him. She invites him to sit on an attractive but surprisingly well-worn leather sofa.

"Not like visiting the queen after all, huh."

He laughs. She doesn't miss a thing.

"Drink?" She holds up an outstanding bottle of bourbon and he gratefully accepts. She settles herself slowly into a wingback chair opposite him. It's the first time he's seen a sign of frailty and age in her.

"So, tell me," she says. "What's the 'big ask' that's brought you here tonight, doctor?"

By the time he finishes explaining his idea, she's drained her drink.

She holds out the empty cocktail glass. "Would you mind?"

"Not at all." He leaps up to retrieve her glass and pours them each of them another finger of bourbon, neat.

"I'll take two," she calls from her chair. He splashes her glass, and then his own.

"Thank you, Dr. Royce. Once I'm sitting—especially by this time of day—it's often easier to stay put, sadly." Her hand shakes slightly as she accepts her drink. She watches him watch her tremble.

"Parkinson's," she says flatly. "It's early, but it won't be long before people know. And then the vultures will start to surface."

"Evelyn, I'm sorry."

"Don't be." Her spine already perfectly straight, she sits up a little taller in her seat.

"You must know, the board will never go for this change of course in your research," she says. "Even I can't get them to fund work that involves assisted suicide."

Royce feels like a balloon has been deflated in his chest. He nods silently, trying to accept the unacceptable.

Evelyn sips at her drink. "Here's what I suggest. We migrate your study's financial backing to my family foundation. The application process will be faster than dealing with the hospital bureaucracy. My program officers can help you network with hospitals around the country to recruit patients. And there's more money to be had—if your funding request is approved." She delivers the last line with an almost mischievous grin.

"Evelyn, I don't know what to say." Royce can't believe what she's offering.

"Say you'll go back to your office and get started on the application."

Royce wonders to himself whether this is a conflict of interest considering her role as hospital board chair and president of her private foundation.

She seems to read him like he's used to reading others. "The hospital will be glad to get your work off their balance sheet. If you get a breakthrough, they can take credit, and if you screw up, they can show their hands were off this thing, financially. It's perfect for them—private funding will give them the distance they need should you fail to return results." Evelyn pauses with her drink at her lips. Her eyes are boring into his over the horizon of her glass. "But you're not going to fail to return results, are you, Dr. Royce?"

"No." Royce looks back at her, meeting the intensity of her gaze. Once again, it's like dancing with a phenomenal partner.

Without breaking eye contact, he asks, "Why? Why are you putting yourself out there for me like this?"

Evelyn laughs mirthlessly. "Men. You all think it's all about you." She tips her drink back and closes her eyes as the bourbon hits her throat, then returns her eyes to his. "I need you to be successful. I don't believe in God. There is no afterlife waiting for us. This is everything we get. And I don't want it to end."

* * *

"To Dr. Mike Royce, who never fails to find a way to keep this incredible project alive."

It's an uncharacteristically heartfelt toast from Rudy, the study's chief engineer. "Thank you for pursuing this mission, Dr. Royce. It's an honor to play a part in it," Rudy says as he hoists his glass.

Royce's crowded loft erupts in cheers. He stops for a moment, opening his hands in front of his chest in a gesture of thanks to Rudy and the friends and colleagues who've gathered to celebrate the next stage of his study.

Manny claps him on the back. "Congrats, buddy. I wouldn't want to be in your shoes, but I'm proud of you." Manny's eyes drift over Royce's shoulder. "By the way, who's the beautiful brunette who's very enthusiastic about your champagne?"

Royce looks over his shoulder and laughs. "She's my downstairs neighbor. Single. I'll introduce you." He hands Manny a beer and moves on through the crowd. Royce has been manic at the party, filling drinks before they're empty, turning up the music, trying to dance with everyone. He can't keep still. Elation and anticipation course through his bloodstream, on the precipice of this giant next step. He's convinced that working with terminally ill patients and having the opportunity to observe them closely, will unlock the scientific secrets that have eluded him—and the whole of the scientific community—until now.

He hears the doorbell chime and sprints to answer it. His ER boss, Greg Sanchez, has just arrived. Royce starts to close the door as Evelyn Price walks in. With a ripple across the room, the energy of the party shifts at her presence. True to her word, she'd made things work with the hospital board, shifting funding of his project to her private family foundation and allowing the work itself to continue within the hospital. Through months of paperwork and meetings with program officers at the Price Family Foundation and with hospital administrators and attorneys, she'd been a steely champion for his cause, all while somehow maintaining a flawless, irreproachable veneer of impartiality and professionalism.

Evelyn had made only a single demand of him that surprised him: that he agrees to reside within the hospital when the study resumes and physician-assisted suicides began. He had been taken aback by the request, but she made it clear that his constant presence was a dealbreaker for funding, given the complexity and sensitivity of the project. Dr. Royce saw this as a small price to pay, and unequivocally agreed. In a matter of weeks, he'd leave the comforts of his loft and move temporarily into a suite in the hospital.

Royce grabs a chair from the dining table and pulls it to the center of the room. He stands on the chair, and the rumble of conversations ceases. Someone turns down the music.

"I want to thank everyone for coming tonight and drinking all my liquor."

The crowd laughs.

"Seriously, though. Thank you, one and all, for your support.

We're about to embark on an incredible journey, and it wouldn't have been possible without each and every one of you."

He scans the room, taking in the gazes of these friends, colleagues, and research partners. Except for his mother, who couldn't make it to the party, everyone who matters to him and his project is here in this room. Except for Alesha. Her absence is like a giant tear in a sailcloth; the boat is still moving, but without crisp clarity of direction. Outside the essential communication in the ER, they've not spoken in two months.

Determined to shake off the cloud of Alesha's absence, Royce forces his glass into the air again. "You all must realize that the work our team is doing may alter the life span of at least one of the people in this room in the very near future."

A chilling silence spreads through the crowd.

Royce stands above the crowd, feeling the scrutiny of every person in the room. It's like being battered by a hundred sets of existential fears. He could drown in the turbulence of the emotion that's silently erupting.

Then, a laugh. It's Rudy, from the back of the room. The laughter spreads slowly then quickly, as a hundred relieved souls —yes, that word—find an escape hatch from their momentary existential crises.

Well, not quite a hundred. Royce, chuckling to himself, spots her dead center of the crowd. A stony look of challenge on Evelyn Price's face, she raises her champagne flute in his direction. Her eyes tell him one thing: *your best better be good enough.*

CHAPTER 11

"**G**ood morning, Dr. Royce," the nurse says, her eyes flashing warmth as she passes him in the hallway.

Royce returns her smile with a friendly nod, mimicking the familiarity in her gaze. He can't remember her name. Have they worked together in the ER? His stomach drops a notch when he realizes he's not sure. She could be new this week, or they could have been in the emergency room trenches together for a decade. He keeps moving in the direction of his hospital room, shaking off the fright that rises every time his mind stumbles or fails him. He's getting better at brushing past the confusion and memory gaps, the disorienting twists in time. At least he thinks he is. Reality feels fragile and temporary, like a calm pond just before a rock lands and the water ripples.

He drops his bag on his perfectly made bed and pulls out his lucky shirt. As he changes into T-shirt and scrubs, he thinks about the meetings he has lined up back-to-back in the lab, starting tomorrow. With funding from the Price Foundation and approval from the hospital to proceed, his research is at last about to resume, after a painful, monthslong hiatus. It's time to scale up the team and get back to work. Royce's calendar for the next several weeks is packed with interviews: physicians, nurses, social workers, psychologists. He'll work with his core team to collect data on patients before and after they die, supporting and counseling patients through the process, and, when the time comes, to administer lethal drugs. Even at his best, the details of Royce's schedule—names, dates, places, CVs—would be hard to keep straight. And Royce is not at his best.

Or rather, his best comes and goes in unpredictable ways. He continues to be physically stronger than he's ever been, and yet exhaustion overtakes him out of nowhere. His mind is often a leaky sieve, playing tricks on him everywhere but the lab. So far, he's managed to avoid any adverse events in clinical shifts. But it's only a matter of time, he worries, before he makes a lethal mistake.

He's got to get some answers. A CT scan won't rule out many types of pathology, including insidious dementias, but it at least would rule out a brain mass. His pulse racing and throat dry, Royce picks up the phone and dials Rick Davies's extension.

"Rick," he says, hoping to sound casual, "I took a nasty fall the other afternoon, went headfirst over the handlebars on my bike. Had my helmet on, of course, but I really hammered my head. Lost consciousness for—I don't know—a few seconds." Royce takes a breath and closes his eyes. "Wondering, could you get me in for a quick head CT?"

"Sorry to hear it, buddy. I crashed out a couple of years ago and completely fucked up my knee." Davies sounds sympathetic, but Royce anticipates what comes next.

"What are your symptoms, Mike? Are you disoriented?"

Is Royce paranoid, or did Davies's voice drop a register with that last question?

"No, no, none of that. I just want to be sure I'm all good."

Davies lets out a soft sigh of irritation. "Do you really think you need a head CT for a brief loss of consciousness?" he asks. "I'm not trying to tell you your business, Mike. You know trauma medicine at least as well as I do. But seriously, a head CT for this? Come on, Mike . . . You think maybe you're overreacting just a little?"

Royce puts on a laugh. "Yeah, maybe . . ." he says. "But I'd feel better if we could play this one safe. Can you squeeze me in?"

Royce hangs on the silence that follows, until he hears Davies sigh again, this time in surrender.

"Sure, Mike. We can do a scan. Come up to the lab in fifteen."

Davies voice crackles over the intercom. "Okay, Mike, you're all set."

The low whir of the CT scanner halts, and the table Royce is lying on exits the scanner. He ignores the technician who's waiting to help him off the table. Royce leaps up and walks to the observation window, where Davies sits on the other side.

Royce says loudly, "Let me see the pictures."

Davies lets out a startled laugh. "Jesus. Slow your roll, will you?"

Royce grabs his scrubs from a chair and starts dressing underneath his hospital gown. "No, actually. I won't. I want to see the pictures."

"Look, I did you a favor getting you in here right away. But I'm backed up now, in the middle of a few things. I'll call you within the hour, okay?"

It's not okay, Royce thinks as he slips on his scrubs. He's been tormented for months about the condition of his brain; waiting another hour feels unbearable. "Fine," he says, "I'll be in the lab."

True to his word, Davies calls him sixty minutes later. "Good news. Your scan is clean, as we expected. No bleed; no mass. Normal study."

Royce doesn't know whether to feel relieved or disappointed. "Okay, okay, great. But I'd still like to see the images, Rick."

The pause on the other end of the line lasts a beat too long, just enough time for Royce to wonder whether Rick Davies is stonewalling him.

"Yeah—ugh—you know what? Let me get back to you," Davies says. "Our system just went down. I'll call you when it's back up."

Royce throws his phone in frustration.

A research assistant drops a large shipping box on the table next to Royce and begins tearing it open with his hands.

"Find another place to be," Royce thunders to the assistant. "And find yourself some scissors. You're ripping into that box like a child."

His watch beeps, timer set to remind him that his shift is starting, a new habit he's using throughout the day to help keep himself on track. Grabbing his pager and ID, Royce heads to the ER floor. He picks up a chart from the admit desk and walks to trauma room three.

The patient—female, middle-aged, overweight, slightly

disheveled in a rumpled sweatsuit and unwashed hair—sits upright on the gurney with her face pointed toward the floor.

"Good morning, Ms. Folgerty. How can I help you today?"

No reply.

"Ma'am, how are you feeling?"

Her lips remain squeezed shut, her eyes fixed firmly on the alternating squares of the worn linoleum floor.

Royce scans her chart. Delilah Folgerty has no prior medical problems. Except one. She suffers from dissociative identity disorder.

"She was bleeding when she pooped this morning."

The voice makes him jump. He hadn't noticed the man sitting in a corner chair, wearing a sweatsuit that matches Ms. Folgerty's, equally rumpled.

"Are you her husband?"

"I am." The man stands but keeps his distance from his wife. "George Folgerty."

Rectal bleeding is generally not a significant problem for an emergency physician to manage. A rectal exam will generally reveal either bright red or maroon blood, suggesting the patient has a lower GI bleed, or a black and tarry stool, indicating an upper GI bleed.

"Ms. Folgerty, can you hear me?" Royce turns to her husband. "Do you know why she won't talk to me?"

"Oh, 'Ms. Folgerty' isn't here now. This is Juju."

"Another personality?"

"Yup." George Folgerty is matter-of-fact. "She's been in charge for the past few days, and she's bent on hurting my sweet Delilah."

"Will Juju talk to me, do you think?"

"Hard to say," says Mr. Folgerty. "Juju is a stone-cold bitch. I don't mess with her, myself."

Royce struggles to keep a straight face as he kneels next to his patient, trying to make eye contact.

"Juju, I'm Dr. Royce." He leans in a little closer. "Have you done something to make Delilah bleed from her rectum?"

No response.

"Juju, did you hurt Delilah in the bottom?"

Juju lets out a low *humph*.

He turns back to George. "I need to do a rectal exam. That means I need to get her pants down. What do you think is the easiest way to do that?"

"Oh, I wouldn't look up there." George shakes his head rather violently. "You don't know what she might've put up there. You could get hurt."

"Okay," says Royce. "Thanks for the heads up."

"No problem," George responds. "Fucking Juju," he whispers under his breath as he drops back into his chair.

"I'm going to order an X-ray, and we'll take it from there," Royce says to the couple, glancing between George and Juju. Turning to George, he continues, "And I'm going to bring another doctor in to make sure Delilah—er, Juju—understands what's happening."

"You mean a psychiatrist, right?"

"Yes."

"Juju hates headshrinkers," George says flatly.

Royce puts an order in for X-rays of Mrs. Folgerty's abdomen and pelvis. He also calls for a psych consult. Hanging up the phone, he spots Alesha at the admit desk, chatting with a couple of other nurses. He feels a pang of longing. He wants nothing more than to slide up next to her and tell her about the crazy case in trauma three. He wants to talk to her about staffing the new positions on his—on their—research project. He wants to talk to her about everything. He's about to turn away when Alesha looks up and sees him looking at her. He expects her to freeze him out, to dodge his gaze. Instead, she breaks into a warm, beaming smile that makes her eyes shine. Royce looks behind him to make certain the smile is for him. Across the floor, Alesha laughs as though he's playing around. He returns her laugh with a puzzled smile and a weak-handed wave.

An hour later, Royce is staring at an X-ray screen, mouth agape. Mrs. Folgerty's rectum is crowded like a junk drawer. He's looking at a pen—"Yeah, that's probably her favorite one," Mr. Folgerty will tell him.—a golf ball, and a razor blade, with the sharp end pointed at her anus. Had Royce performed a rectal examination, the blade likely would have cut him. Dr. Royce breathes a sigh of relief as he picks up the phone to call the surgeon who takes Ms. Folgerty—Juju—to the OR to remove her rectal contents.

Royce looks up just as Alesha is walking down the main hallway toward the locker room. Her shift is ending. If he's going to capitalize on the sudden goodwill between them, now is the time. Summoning a courage he doesn't quite feel, he steps into the hall and calls to her. She stops and turns around, breaking into another mystifyingly cheerful smile.

"Hey, Mike," she says, rerouting her path toward him.

Royce manages to muster a hello as he watches her come closer. "Can we talk?"

"Sure," she says. "What's up?"

What's up? How about the fact that we've avoided each other and barely spoken in the past two months?

"Come in here, will you?" Royce gestures to an empty office where they won't be disturbed. Alesha follows him into the room, humming a tune under her breath. She's awfully happy, even for

Alesha. Close to her now, he notices she's dropped some weight from her already slim frame. It seems as though these past couple of months have taken a toll on her, too.

He closes the door, and she gives him a quizzical look.

"Okay, I'm not great at this stuff—and you of all people know that—" Royce stammers before blurting out the only thing he's sure of. "—I was being such an ass in that meeting, Alesha, and I've been such a coward since then." He runs his hands through his hair. "I really fucked up and I just want to get back to—"

"Mike . . ." Alesha holds up a hand to stop his blabbering. "You don't need to keep doing this."

"What do you mean?"

"I mean, I'm happy to move on. I *want* to move on."

"You do?" Royce would be thrilled if he weren't totally mystified.

"We both made mistakes that day," Alesha says. "My concerns about the suicides were important to me—and totally valid. But I shouldn't have walked out. I should have stayed to hash things out, to work through the process. Though, let's be clear—you *were* a giant ass that day." She grins. "Despite my better judgment, I've missed you . . . Somehow."

Royce's knees buckle as a ribbon of joy runs through him. He's not sure how it's happened, but she's forgiven him. How is that possible?

"I can't tell you how happy this makes me." Royce wants to reach out to her, to take her into his arms. "But I need you to hear me out. I need to apologize for my terrible behavior—and I want to explain what's been happening with me, not as an excuse but—"

"Mike, seriously, you don't have to do this again." Alesha puts a soft hand on his bare forearm.

Again?

"Your apology the other night was enough. I really think it's best for us to try to move on, for our sake and for the project."

Royce is stunned. The other night? What is she talking about? His mind starts racing back in time to recall the events of the past few days when it's hijacked by another thought. "Wait, you're going to come back to the research?"

Alesha squints at him, looking confused. "I told you the other night at my place. I hold by what I said. I think there's a vulnerability to this arrangement with these patients, and I think we need to be exceptionally careful in how we proceed." She looks into his eyes and he sees her wisdom and compassion, both boundless, shining back at him. "But this is important work, and I want to be a part of it. I want us to do this together."

Royce whistles a sigh. "I do, too. I really do." He pulls out his phone. "I've got meetings scheduled tomorrow to start interviewing some new people," he says, pulling up his calendar. "Could you sit in with me?"

"It's already on my calendar."

* * *

The rest of his shift is a blur. Royce moves from patient to patient, going through the motions, relying on muscle memory and years of expertise to function while his mind is consumed by his conversation with Alesha. Not the conversation he'd just had with her— the conversation he can't remember having with her. At some point in the past few days, he'd apparently gone to her place, delivered an apology for his reprehensible behavior, and persuaded her to return to the study. If he didn't know Alesha, maybe he'd wonder if she was yanking his chain. Or even, if she were sound of mind herself. But he knows Alesha wouldn't fuck around with him that way. And he knows that it's his mind, not hers, that's full of black holes and dead ends and wrong turns. He just doesn't know what to do about it.

Still wrapped in the fog of his muddled, runaway mind, Royce heads to trauma room one to see his final patient of the day. A look at the chart tells him that Jarvey Woods is here, and he's complaining of back pain. He notes that Woods is schizophrenic, newly diagnosed by the hospital's psychiatric team a month ago.

Royce pushes open the trauma room door. "Good afternoon, Jarvey, I'm Dr. Royce—"

He stops cold, his feet locked in place. Jarvey Woods is standing in front of the gurney, feet angled at forty-five degrees like a soldier at attention. His hands are in his pockets. His eyes are lit with mania.

"Jarvey, I hear you're having some back pain."

"Worse than that, doctor," he says.

"Tell me what's happening, Jarvey," Royce keeps his voice measured and calm. "I'm here to help you."

"I know you are. You and everyone else."

"That's right, Jarvey. Everyone here is here to help you."

Jarvey shifts his weight from one leg to the other and back again. Royce begins to relax a little and takes a step toward his patient.

"I need everyone's help," Jarvey says.

"We're all here for you," says Royce.

Jarvey's left hand slides out of his pocket. Royce catches a glimpse of something shiny and then he's looking at a silver handgun in Jarvey's outstretched hand, pointed directly at his chest. "I need to kill each one of you. It's the only way for me to stay alive."

Before he knows what his body is doing, Royce lunges forward and tackles Jarvey to the floor. The force of Royce's body against Jarvey's slight frame knocks him over, and he drops the handgun to the floor. Jarvey goes limp as Royce lies on top of him, screaming for help. Within seconds, the entire ER security staff swarms the room and immobilizes Jarvey Woods.

Royce steps back to give the security team room and slips out the door. Keeping his head down amid the chaos and alarm in the hall, he walks quickly back to his office, where he strips off his scrubs and lucky T-shirt, which lived up to its reputation once again. People will have questions for him about the incident; he'll need to fill out paperwork and be debriefed by administration and the head of security. They'll have to wait until tomorrow.

He changes into a set of running clothes. Royce takes a stairwell to another wing of the hospital, where he can get outside without being pulled back into the administrative nightmare that happens after a near-shooting in the building. He launches into a trot that quickly becomes a sprint and completes the fastest three-mile run that he's done in two years. He hasn't been that fast since he ran track competitively in college. *Maybe I should visit a psych ward before every run*, he thinks. He tries not to think about whether he ought to check himself in.

CHAPTER 12

R oyce rolls over in bed and opens his eyes. He's looking out a window at a view he doesn't recognize. The tree-tops swishing in the breeze are unfamiliar. So is the ugly, squat building that hulks beyond them. A parking garage, he registers. Where is he? Where has his mind taken him this time?

He rolls over on his back and squeezes his eyes shut, preparing for the cognitive dissonance, the fear, the mental gymnastics that are part and parcel of living with his rogue brain these days. Reluctantly, he opens his eyes. The industrial squares of the ceiling above bring it all back in a flash. Wary of his own mind, he looks down at his feet to confirm. Yep, he's in a hospital bed. He's flooded with relief and excitement. He's not on a psychotic mind trip—at least not yet.

He's just spent his first night in his new, temporary residence within the hospital. He's been given a suite in an old wing that's scheduled to undergo renovations. Looking around the sparse room, with depressing fluorescent lighting, decrepit floors, and nothing more than a lumpy loveseat and a bed, he wishes for a moment that he'd gotten in here after the room was refurbished. It'll do. It puts him closer to the only thing he cares about, the work that begins as soon as the first cohort of patients arrive. He'd grabbed some essentials and moved in yesterday. He's waiting on a call from the doctor who's leading the prospective squad—hospital physicians, nurses, and social workers who are interviewing and selecting suitable candidates for physician-assisted suicide in his research—to let him know when the first dozen patients from around the country will arrive on-site.

He grabs his Dopp kit and fishes out his toothbrush. He can't deny it feels intensely strange to be leading a euthanasia team, to be assisting in death after spending his career battling against it. He keeps telling himself that his way is a different—and better—way to fight the fight. Physicians back to the ancients and right up to today have been showing up with a knife to a gunfight when trying to defeat death. He's going to change everything by making death irrelevant. He stares at himself while brushing his teeth. He almost doesn't recognize his own eyes; they're filled with a gritty energy he's never seen there before.

In addition to Group I, the Prospective Squad, Royce will be overseeing Group II, the Investigative Squad, made up of the technicians who will collect data on patients before and after they die. Then there is Group III, the Implementation Squad. This subgroup will counsel each patient before euthanasia and, when the time comes, administer the drugs. The Implementation Squad is made up of Royce and Alesha. Royce can't bring himself to hand off this work to anyone else. And while both he and Alesha will be involved in counseling patients ahead of their euthanasia, it will be Alesha who delivers the lethal cocktail of drugs.

"I said you would be my conscience, and I was right," Royce said to Alesha late one night in the lab after a full day of interviewing prospective team members. Alesha's face clouded with concern. "I don't know, Mike, I'm not sure I can do that once, much less again and again."

"I'll be right there with you."

"Why me? Why not another experienced nurse or doctor?"

"I don't trust anyone else to do it. Including myself." Royce slides his chair over to hers and pulls her around so that they are knee-to-knee and face-to-face. Her eyes are pools of compassion.

"If you aren't sure that they're prepared and ready to move forward, without pressure or interference at the most subliminal level, then we don't proceed."

With a solemn, almost sacred, understanding passing between them, Alesha agreed to take on this responsibility.

Royce walks into the lab with Lucy, one of his research assistants, in tow. They've taken over a larger space to accommodate the expanded team. He feels a runaway thrill at the sight of his colleagues, new and old. He has a sudden, irrational urge to leap onto a desk and scream with joy. He restrains himself but feels like he's floating on air as he walks toward his desk at the back of the room. He listens and watches as techs from Group II—the Investigative Squad—work with the engineers to make sure intake forms that guide data collection are coded correctly in the computer program. He sees Alesha through the window of a conference room, meeting with Dr. Anil Radapathya, a consulting psychologist who will advise them on enacting implementation protocols as they work with patients in the upcoming weeks and days, hours and minutes, eventually leading to euthanasia. It's really happening.

"Dr. Royce. Call for you." Peter, another research assistant, holds up a landline phone.

"It's Dr. Bowers," Peter says, as Royce pulls the phone to his ear. Royce feels his heart quicken; Dr. Peter Bowers heads up Group I, the Prospective Squad.

"Pete, what's the word?" Royce can barely catch his breath.

"We're good to go, Mike. The first twelve patients will be at the hospital in three days. Hope you guys are ready."

Royce slams the phone down with excitement, catching the attention of his colleagues. He can no longer hold back on his impulses. With two deft steps, he climbs to stand on the top of his immaculate desk.

"Our patients are on their way!" he shouts, his arms high above his head, both fists reaching for the ceiling. He feels like he's flying. Everyone turns to stare at him. Some of his colleagues cheer; others look at him strangely. He doesn't care. He's no longer at odds with himself at the thought of inducing death. He's ready to be a new age explorer.

Royce's watch beeps, telling him it's three o'clock. It's the only alarm he doesn't need. His body and his brain inevitably let him know when three p.m. laboratory time is near. His mental and physical energy surge. He steps out of the maddening brain fog that dogs him throughout the rest of the day and into a clarity that shines like a cut jewel. And today, of all days, he needs no reminder. He's about to meet the first cohort of patients entering his study. Twelve of them, most of them late-stage cancer patients, and a few with progressive, degenerative diseases. All have elected to die by lethal injection. And each one of these pioneers has volunteered the final weeks of their lives—and their deaths—in the service of science. His eyes fill with tears thinking of their bravery and generosity.

He and Rudy walk together into the conference room, which is already full of clinical research staff and the new patients. Everyone is standing around the perimeter of a large conference table. Alesha and a few other clinicians are talking with patients. But the two groups are mostly segregated on either side of the table. To his left are a group of white-coat scientists conferring. To his right are the group of patients—most of them rail thin, many bald, several in wheelchairs. Everyone, on both sides, looks hesitant and nervous.

"Good morning." Royce's voice thunders over the quiet chatter. Everyone turns to look at him.

"Guys, help me get these chairs out here." He motions to the wide empty space beyond the conference table. Two investigative techs jump to their feet and together they pull two dozen chairs into a large, loose semi-circle.

Royce looks around the room with a gentle grin. "Now, let's do this summer camp style. Sit next to someone you don't know."

Nervous laughter rumbles across the room as the clusters break up and people take their places in the circle. He waits until everyone has settled.

"Welcome, everyone. Welcome Mary, Oscar, Juan, Susan, Tiffany, Jake, George, Odette, Preethi, Tim, Charlotte, and Martin." No name tags are needed at this moment. Royce ticks off each patient's name from memory and matches names to faces flawlessly, taking his time, looking each one in the eyes, establishing the connection that will bond them through the challenging days ahead. Every patient is different, a universe unto themselves. Still, in each pair of eyes, he sees similar combinations of anxiety and curiosity. These people are pioneers, and there's a spirit of adventure he sees in each of them. He watches them respond to his attention and the wordless empathy in his gaze. In every face he sees a flash of recognition and a burst of confidence and comfort.

Royce introduces the individual members of the clinical and technical staff. "We are known—around the hospital and among ourselves—as the Euthanasia Team."

"Do you have T-shirts?" asks Martin, a seventy-six-year-old with colon cancer.

"What? I—"

"If you're a team, you oughta have a T-shirt." The room erupts in laughter.

"You're quite right," says Royce. "We'll get that done."

"I'm going to talk us all through the protocols in a moment. But first, I want to say this." Royce begins to choke up with emotion. He glances at Alesha. Her steady gaze steadies him. "No one has ever done what we're about to do. We are honored you have chosen us to help you live out this most profound choice. And we're grateful you are willing to help us learn what we can about the transition from life to death. Every step of the way, we are right by your side."

Several of the patients have tears in their eyes. A number of them are holding hands with the clinicians sitting next to them. It hits Royce fully at this moment, how emotional this work will be, that the emotional roller coaster has launched.

Royce reviews the process each patient will undergo. Upon entering the study, all patients will have vital signs measured, including body weight and laboratory testing of blood. A brain PET scan will be performed on each patient.

"PET scans are different than other imaging," he says. "CT and

MRI scanners reveal the anatomic structure of the object of study, but PET scanners display the metabolic activity."

All tests, including the brain PET scan, he explains, will be repeated one hour prior to injection of the lethal cocktail. The blood tests will be repeated five minutes post-mortem.

"What is the PET scan looking for?" asks Preethi, a sixty-year-old woman with liver cancer.

Royce works methodically through an explanation. A radioactive tracer is injected into the patient's vein, where it enters the bloodstream and is circulated all over the body. Organs, such as the brain, that are very metabolically active, will pick up more radioactive tracer than other organs. The scanner will then take photos, and the computer will assign different colors to the object, depending on the amount of tracer that is concentrated in the area.

"For example, if we ask a person to solve a puzzle and we image his brain while he performs the task, we will see regions of the brain that are labeled with various colors. Regions that are very metabolically active during this thought process will receive a large blood flow and will show up red on the scanner, while other regions of the brain that are not required for this process will show up blue or black. In layman's terms, if it's a hot spot of activity, we'll see red. If nothing's happening, we'll see black."

George, another cancer patient, shoots up his hand then pulls it back down, laughing to himself.

"What is it?" Royce asks. "Did you have a question?"

"I did, but it's stupid," says George, still chuckling. "I was about to ask if any of this stuff is potentially harmful. Then I remembered, it doesn't matter!" The patients among the group burst into waves of boisterous laughter. The clinicians follow their lead and begin to laugh out loud.

Laughing himself, Royce wonders what it is like to feel so free. It's an unnerving thought; imminent death as freedom. That's what he's fighting to eliminate. He stuffs that thought in the way back of his mind.

Odette, a forty-five-year-old with ALS, uses her augmentative communication device to ask, "Will any of this testing be painful?"

"Beyond the pinprick of the blood draw, no, it will not."

"Will we be seeing the same nurses and techs every day? There's always so much turnover in the hospital."

As Royce fields their questions, he's reminded how much he loves working with patients. His ER grind—day after day, year over year, of churning through trauma—has nearly ground that love out of him. He feels it resurrecting today. By the time he's answered the last question, his patients seem satisfied, relaxed, and even happy to comply with the protocols.

"Now it's time to hear from you." Royce touches his gaze lightly down on each of his patients, offering silent encouragement.

Royce and the Euthanasia Team listen as each patient tells a story. Some talk mostly about their lives before their illness and all that has changed and been lost to them. Others recount years of treatment, the ups and downs, the dashed hopes, the isolation, the dual pain of disease and of treatment. All eventually come to express why they have decided to end their lives.

"I lost my autonomy a long time ago," says Mary Gordon, a thirty-five-year-old with stage four cervical cancer. "My body has been taken over—by cancer, by radiation and chemo, by a million different people poking and prodding me day and night. It took me a long time to get here. I wanted to fight, fight, keep fighting.

Now, I'm ready. And I get to decide. I get my autonomy and my dignity back."

Royce wipes his eyes and watches his colleagues struggle to compose themselves. Whatever they discover in their research, it feels good to give these brave souls—yes, he said it, souls—agency over their lives and deaths.

When the final patient has finished talking, Royce can feel the exhaustion in the room. He thanks everyone for coming and closes the meeting. The doctors and nurses from the Investigative Team help the patients back to their rooms.

Royce feels a heady mix of solemnity and excitement. This first meeting went better than he dared expect. He pulls his notebook into his bag. He's going to spend another four hours or so working in the lab before he calls it a night. He catches sight of Rick Davies leaving the conference room and sprints to his side.

"Thanks for being here today, Rick," says Royce.

"You bet. Quite a remarkable group of—"

"I'd like to see those CT scans, Rick." Royce has tried to pin the radiologist down a few times since the initial scan, but Davies always has a reason he can't show Royce his own brain CT.

Davies doesn't bother to hide his irritation. "Mike, you're good. No abnormalities. Aren't we both a little busy for this?"

Royce is not going to take no for an answer this time. "Agreed. We can stop wasting each other's time when you show me my—"

"Dr. Royce?" a kind voice calls behind him. He turns to see Dr. Radapathya. Behind him, Rick Davies takes advantage of the interruption to slip out the door. Seething inside, Royce turns to shake the psychologist's hand.

"That was a triumphant beginning," Dr. Radapathya says.

"Thank you."

"I wanted to extend my condolences. I heard about your mother's death."

Royce is dumbfounded. He spoke to his mother just yesterday. Or the day before. The days and nights bleed together now that he's spending all his time in the hospital.

Before he can form a reply, Alesha breaks in. "You're thinking about Dr. Rice, Anil. He lost his mother last week. She apparently had severe coronary artery disease."

Dr. Radapathya looks pale, mortified. "Dear god, I'm so sorry."

Royce puts a hand on the man's shoulder. "Not to worry, Anil."

He's not due to call his mom for another few days. But Royce makes a note to himself to call her tonight. His mental reminder vanishes the moment he leaves the lab.

CHAPTER 13

"The beach at Plum Cove."

"What?"

"It's the beach at Plum Cove. Late afternoon, must have been the middle of summer because it was still hot—I can feel the warmth on my shoulders—even though the sun was starting to drop."

Mary Watson leans back on her pillow. Her face is pale and sunken, a bright green wool cap covers her bald head. She opens her eyes. Her voice is cracked with exhaustion and emotion.

"I've been trying to go all the way back, to figure out my very first memory. I think I've got it. My dad was there—I'm sure my mom was, too, but I remember my dad, lifting me up by my shoulders as the waves rolled in. I can feel the cool salt water on the bottoms of my feet, the sand sticking to the backs of my wet calves. God, I can smell the salt water in the breeze. I really can. My dad smelled like sunshine and Ivory soap and sweat—the most comforting smell, you know? I was three, almost four, I think." She sighs. "It was a good day, I think. A really good day."

Alesha takes Mary's hand. A look of deep understanding passes between them, these two women who were strangers to each other a month ago. Alesha leans in closer, her eyes speaking for her, saying, *Tell me more.*

Royce sits in a chair on the other side of Mary's hospital bed. He shifts in his seat to get a careful, covert glance at his watch. Five-fifteen. In exactly forty-five minutes, Mary Watson will receive a lethal injection. At five o'clock precisely, Mary was weighed, had her blood drawn, and underwent a PET scan of her brain. Now Mary lies on what will shortly be her deathbed, wandering through the memories of her thirty-five years like a child rambling through a field of flowers, stopping to pick one, then another, and another, looking at them with fresh eyes, untainted by disappointment or expectation.

In the past month, patients from all over the country have entered the study by the droves. Thirty patients have already undergone their preliminary laboratory testing, and forty-five more are expected within the next few days. The original dozen patients enrolled are about to undertake their physician-assisted suicides. Mary is the first.

Royce sits silently at Mary's bedside, listening to the two women talk. His demeanor is calm and collected; Royce knows how to present a tranquil, steady, and compassionate façade in a patient's last hours. Inside, he's roiling with emotion. He has sat with hundreds of patients at their deaths, held their hands, whispered words of comfort, listened to their last words, taken final messages to ferry back to their loved ones, even cried with them. Today, for the first time, he will take a life.

". . . You know, I was a week away from leaving for Paris."

"I didn't know that," Alesha says. "Paris, my goodness. What were you going there for?"

Mary lets out a dry, ragged cough and Alesha lifts a cup with a straw to her mouth. Mary takes a small sip, then pushes the cup away.

"Thank you," she says. She clears her throat. "Cooking school. I'd been accepted at Le Cordon Bleu. I quit my tech job and moved in with my parents for the summer to save some cash. Had my flight booked. I was ready to go. Then the biopsy results came back."

"You must have been heartbroken." Alesha's hand flutters to her chest.

"It was worse for my parents. I was so young, I thought, 'Okay, this sucks, but I'll get it taken care of and get back to my life.'" She sighs. "It didn't exactly go that way."

Mary's family visits with her for the last time this morning. Her parents and her boyfriend linger in her room, their arms wrapped around her shrunken shoulders, laughing and crying and holding each other close until the last possible moment. In keeping with study protocols, Mary's family can't be present at the time of her death. It's one of the great sacrifices his patients have made in joining his study. Royce is flabbergasted by their bravery and self-lessness.

Royce stands and clears his throat. "Mary, it's getting close to six," he says. "I'm going to start preparing the injection, okay?"

Mary takes a long look out the window, watching the shaggy tops of cottonwood trees along the riverbank dip and roll in the wind. She drinks it in, the swaying of the branches, as though it's the most beautiful, miraculous sight she's ever seen. When she's at last able to tear her eyes away, she looks squarely at Royce standing at the cart that holds the syringe with a lethal cocktail of diazepam, digoxin, morphine sulfate, and amitriptyline. He gasps inwardly at the faraway look in her eyes. She's looking at him and looking right through him, as though she's still gazing at a horizon he can't see. "Okay."

Alesha squeezes Mary's hand. She casts her eyes at Royce, and he sees the wild, flickering emotion in them. Like fighting a tarp in a windstorm, she's battling to hold down her fright and her pain.

"Did I ever tell you I almost died once, already?"

Alesha swivels her attention back to Mary. "No. What happened?"

Royce is startled; he can't remember any mention of another serious illness in Mary's medical history.

"It was so dumb, really. I almost choked to death. On a first date, if you can imagine."

Alesha grabs Mary's frail arm playfully, taking care not to grip her too tight.

"A first date! You've got to tell us what happened."

"Honestly, it was as embarrassing as it was scary. I hadn't been on a date in eons. For months, my whole life had been treatments. Then I was in remission, and I thought, 'Okay, give this a try, right? My hair is growing back, my body has scars, but so what—if you can't handle cancer, you're not the one for me, you know?' So, what the hell, I got on an app, matched with a really cute guy. Oh my god, I was so nervous, I'm sure that's why it happened. It was one of those jumbo shrimps, those gigantic, oversized things. The guy was really cute, really funny and sweet, and I just—" Mary flutters her skeletal fingers in the air. "—I don't know, I forgot to chew, or something.

"I remember that I started to black out. Things got really fuzzy around the edges of my vision, and what I could see all seemed really far away all of the sudden." Mary's voice drops. "For just a second—maybe a little part of a second, it was over so quick—I think I got a glimpse of what comes next."

Royce hangs onto her next words.

"What did you see?" Alesha's voice is a notch above a whisper.

Mary sighs. "I'm not sure. It was more feeling than seeing. Definitely not a bright light or anything like that. It felt cloudy in there, foggy—but like no fog you've ever seen."

Mary's faraway eyes are fixed on the wall opposite her bed, as if in a trance, as she works through the memory.

"It felt like . . . Well, like a road. Not a tunnel—there was space all around, endless space, but I couldn't see any of it clearly. I just knew it was there, all around me, all this space. And in front of me, some kind of path. It wasn't marked in any way, or even visible, I just knew it was there."

"How did it feel to be there, on the edge of something . . . somewhere . . . beyond this life?" Alesha's voice is quiet and calm, but its tenor rings clear; she's comfortable in this terrain that Mary is traveling. Royce feels no such confidence. His fascination is overmatched by a roaring discomfort. His blood feels hot inside his veins. His heart is racing. He wants to jump out of his own skin. There's a powerfully bitter taste on his tongue. His entire body is reacting with revulsion to Mary's story. Is this a panic attack? He tries to claim control of himself. Just when he thinks that he can't take it anymore, that he's going to have to get up and run out of the room, Mary falls silent.

"So, can I ask, what happened with the guy?"

Mary's laugh rings like a tiny, delighted bell. "Well, he saved my life. Pulled me out of my chair and popped that stupid shrimp right out of my throat." She smiles. "You met him this morning." A cloud thick with sadness sweeps over her face. "I can't believe I'll never see him again." Another wordless gaze of understanding passes between the two women. "I mean, who knows, maybe I will. Maybe I'll sit on his shoulder at his wedding to someone else. Maybe I'll get to be with him when it's his time. Maybe I'll get to be the first soul who greets him on the other side, or whatever it is."

Royce lingers behind the medicine cart, the injection ready. He's not sure he could move if he tried. Inside, he's torn between awe for his patient's courage and a sort of physical revulsion he can't explain. He feels nauseated and his skin is crawling.

"You know something that most of us have to rely on faith for," Alesha says. She and Mary lock eyes. "Death isn't final. It only marks the end of this lifetime."

"Maybe it'll look familiar." Mary shrugs. She pulls the blanket up to her chest and grasps it with both hands.

Royce returns to stand next to Alesha at Mary's bedside, holding the syringe in his hands.

"You and I haven't known each other long." Alesha reaches out and takes Mary's hands in her own. Royce can see the blue veins running the length of her pale hands beneath her fragile, translucent skin. "I want you to know that you've changed my life." Alesha swallows a sob.

"I can honestly say, there's nobody I'd rather die with than you two," Mary says, with a sad grin and mischief in her eyes. Alesha laughs and catches a trickle of tears with her forearm.

Royce steps in and kisses Mary on the cheek. She looks up at him. Gazing into her eyes feels like traveling a great distance. "It's time. Do you want me to walk you through what's about to happen one more time?"

Mary shakes her head. Royce takes her hand. Alesha asks

Mary if she's ready.

Mary nods. "If it's okay, I'm not going to watch." She closes her eyes and begins to hum a song to herself.

Royce hands Alesha the syringe. Her fingers quiver as she picks up the IV tube. She fumbles a little as she finds the injection port.

Royce reaches over to steady her hand.

"God be with you, my friend," she says as she injects the solution into Mary's IV.

At 6:01 p.m., Royce and Alesha stand side by side at Mary's body. They stare into her eyes, watching as her vitality seeps away. Her face takes on a pale, blue-ish hue. Neither of them seems willing or able to break the strange, silent space they now occupy like a cocoon. Royce is still holding Mary's hand.

Royce moves first, sliding his fingers to Mary's wrist to feel for a pulse, then pulling the stethoscope from around his neck to listen to her heart. He looks at Alesha and nods.

"Mike . . ." Alesha can't find the words.

"I know." Royce opens his arms and she steps into them. Her face against his chest, her body heaves against his. He wraps his arms around her body, rocking her as his own tears fall on her silken blonde hair.

"It's the hardest one because it's the first one," he says. "Remember, she wanted this. We helped her today."

He feels Alesha nod against his chest. They continue to rock slowly together, a strange, sad dance of mourning, before Royce squeezes her tight, bringing them to a stop.

"They're going to be here any minute," Royce whispers.

Alesha reluctantly pulls away from him and takes a few deep

breaths to collect herself.

At 6:05, right on schedule, the technicians arrive to begin the final phase of data collection. They will draw blood, weigh Mary's body, inject the tracer for the last PET scan of her brain. The techs enter the room silently, eyes going first to Royce and to Alesha, who have stepped back from Mary's body to make space for their work. The techs work through their appointed tasks methodically and in silence; their every move and gesture reflect a care and solemnity meeting the gravity of the moment. Watching them, Royce feels another swell of emotion; this time, gratitude for the people working with him on this most difficult stage of his research.

As they prepare to take Mary's body to the imaging room, Royce steps forward. He feels compelled to say something, but the words rattling around his brain feel empty, inadequate.

"Thank you, all of you," he says. "You're doing a hard thing today, and you're doing it flawlessly. This is the first time, but it's not the last. As we prepare to do this this again and again in the coming days and weeks, I want you all to take care of yourselves."

Mary's room empties out, leaving Royce and Alesha alone.

"What are you going to do now?" asks Alesha.

"Maybe go for a run. You?"

"Honestly, I don't know. Home, I guess. I feel shaky—shaken. I'm having a hard time putting one foot in front of the other."

"Come with me," Royce says, taking her hand.

They walk in sorrowful silence down the long hall. Alesha keeps up with his long strides at first. When she falls back, he turns and sees her hands clutching her cheeks, and panic rising in her eyes.

"What are we doing, Mike?"

"I thought maybe we'd go back to my room and just—"

"No, I mean, what are we doing? What have we done?" Alesha's eyes reflect a dawning horror. He remembers that he doesn't really know what it's like to be the hand of death for a patient. Alesha pushed the injection in.

He walks back to her and wraps an arm around her waist. He's startled at how thin she is. She buckles against him, now sobbing. He doesn't speak. What is there to say? They are in uncharted land, and it's just the two of them. They stand together for an uncountable number of minutes—Royce has become untrusting of time since it's played tricks on him so often—before he leans down and whispers in her ear.

"Wanna see my dorm room?"

Her body still plastered against his, he feels her laugh through her tears. Relief washes over him. If Alesha is laughing, everything is okay. He starts to laugh, and they giggle like teenagers the rest of the way to his hospital suite, a grief-stricken silliness overcoming them.

"Wow, not bad." Alesha whistles as she walks into the spacious private suite. "Evelyn Price really set you up."

Royce kicks off his shoes and pads to the small refrigerator located in the pass through to the en suite bathroom. "You want a beer?"

"Sure," she says, not bothering to turn around. She's looking at the small bookshelf, filled with mostly medical texts that Royce keeps here, rather than in his office. Her eyes shift upward to a row of framed photographs. He hasn't brought much with him to his hospital room, but in a stray moment of sentimentality back at his loft, he gathered a few pictures into his bag. Alesha scans the line of photographs of Royce with his mother as a teenager, and at his med school graduation, glowing with the pride she's showered on him since he can remember.

"Hey, you feeling okay?" Royce asks. "I mean I know today is tough, but I'm wondering if maybe you're pushing yourself too hard."

"That's rich, coming from you," Alesha says, without turning around.

"Seriously, Alesha. You're practically disappearing. I'd like to run some bloodwork."

He watches her shoulders tighten, her back still to him.

"It's hard to eat sometimes," she says. "It's hard to sleep. It's hard to do a lot of normal stuff when I'm with these people I know I'm going to have to kill."

"You're talking like a murderer, Alesha," Royce says hotly. "This is their choice—"

"I know, Mike. I know. It's still hard to make peace with what I have to do." She finally turns toward him. "Could we not talk about it right now?"

He hands Alesha a beer and drops down on his hospital bed. As his body hits the mattress, he's overcome with a deep, pervasive exhaustion. It's as if he's taken a powerful sedative; his limbs feel heavy, his mind suddenly awash in fog. Struggling to keep his eyes open, he sees Alesha's face light up when she spots a photograph of the two of them, from a hiking trip to Big Bend a couple of years ago.

"When was the last time you spent a day outdoors?" he hears Alesha ask. "Maybe we could sneak off for a couple of days for your birthday."

Royce can't make his mouth open to reply. He's tumbling fast into a deep sleep.

In his dream, he's riding his brand-new bike along the wide, familiar streets of his childhood neighborhood. It's dusk, and the wind is making the trees whistle, a sound full of portent, both ominous and comforting to his ears. As he's sweeping his bike in big, wavy lines back and forth across the road, he comes upon a group of neighborhood kids, a little younger than his twelve, huddled in a circle, squealing and pushing each other.

He slows down to hop off his bike before it comes to a stop, eager to see what the center of their circle holds. He looks over a boy's shoulder and sees a red squirrel, half-mangled, likely from a car's glancing blow. The squirrel pants, its tiny torso heaving with staccato breaths, back legs flattened useless, tiny front arms clawing at the pavement to move its immovable body, trying to escape its fate. Two of the boys are poking at the squirrel with sticks, sending the others into fits of shrieking laughter.

Mike Royce knows this is wrong, and cruel. He feels the wrongness in his bones. At the same instant that he feels a sharp stab of sorrow for the pitiful animal, he also feels a twisted sort of awe at the boys' ruthlessness and savagery. He shouts at them, grabs a stick from one of the boys and swings it overhead to scare them away. He scrambles back on his bike, cycles around the corner to home, races into his mother's garden shed and comes out with a short, heavy, flat-bottomed spade. He pedals back to the squirrel, spade tucked in the back of his jeans. It's no longer clawing; the body is still.

Probably dead, Royce thinks, but he can't be sure. He stands for a long moment over the tiny body, spade held in two hands above his head. He wants one blow to do it, quick and merciful. He takes a deep breath as he drops the flat weight square on the squirrel's head, but only after glancing over his shoulders and making sure he's alone. He scoops the body onto the spade and gently releases it into the bushes. Riding slowly home, the sun nearly setting, he knows he'll be up tonight wondering: was he a killer or a savior?

CHAPTER 14

Royce has always preferred to work on his birthday; it keeps him from dwelling uncomfortably on the passage of time. This year is no exception. Today, he couldn't have paused to reflect if he'd wanted to. A steady stream of patients and a doctor out sick last minute has made for a hectic shift. He's got to remember to call his mother. She doesn't like to call him when he's working. But Royce knows she'll be heartbroken not to talk to him on his birthday.

As the end of his shift nears, Royce decides to sneak off to his office and zip through some paperwork so he can meet up with a few of his buddies for drinks. He knows that Manny, and probably the others, will be looking to meet women while they're out, the same old routine they've been at for years now. They'll be expecting him to want to do the same. To his surprise, he's not feeling up to it. Sure, he's tired, but that's never stopped him before. It's the whole dance of casual, no-strings romance: the flirtation, the looks, the charming, the dancing, the first touches, the moment you decide to go back to her place, the knowledge that it's all fleeting, that they will drink each other in for a few hours and then move on. It's always energized him, been the perfect antidote to the emotional weight of his work.

Since the study resumed, something has shifted. The thought of a mindless, soulless hookup leaves him cold. These days, when he thinks about making love with a woman, it's only Alesha who comes to mind. His mind is a tortured, jumbled mess, but she's a constant presence in his thoughts and his fantasies. Her physical body, yes, but also her faith—in the work they're doing, her faithful devotion to their patients, her faith in some kind of God, and her faith in him, Mike Royce. He never imagined that faithfulness would be a heat score for him, but lately, he's obsessed with hers. And the work they're doing on the induction team has cracked open a new level of intimacy between them.

Could they be together, making it work as a couple? For days, he's been working up the courage to talk to her about their future, about a future together. Maybe tonight is the night. After a beer or two tonight with the guys. If anything, watching his friends do their usual routine with a room full of single women might help him gear up to broach the subject with Alesha. Royce is rounding the corner to his office when a nurse calls to him from the charge desk.

"Dr. Royce, a patient for you." He turns to see her waggling a chart in his direction. He sighs and shuffles in her direction. Hopefully it's nothing complicated. He can taste that cold beer. He flips open the chart. Female, twenty-six, pelvic pain.

"Suzanne, can you take this one with Dr. Royce?"

Great, he thinks. Suzanne Santiago is one of his favorite nurses to work with. She knows her stuff and they have a great rapport. They ought to be able to wrap this one up quickly.

"My pleasure," says Suzanne. Royce catches her casting a

weird, furtive sort of glance at the charge nurse. *What's that about,* he wonders. Are people talking about him? He's hyper-vigilant about keeping his mental chaos under wraps. Now, his thoughts begin to race as he wonders, is it working? Can his co-workers tell he's not himself?

Suzanne holds up a fist as she meets him outside the GYN room. He bumps it. "Let's do this," she says.

Inside the room, the first thing he notices is a police officer uniform draped over a chair. He shifts his gaze to the patient. To his surprise, she's already on her back with her legs spread in the lithotomy position, feet in stirrups, her bottom hanging just past the edge of the exam table. *Well, that's some initiative*, he thinks.

"Ms. Carson, I'm Dr. Royce."

"Hello, doctor. Please, call me Anna." Her voice is a kind of purr that tickles his ears.

"You're a police officer?"

"I am. A very dedicated one." Her feet still in stirrups, she twists one set of toes in his direction.

"Good for you. Nurse Santiago and I will be examining you today." He looks up at her and smiles. "I see you've gotten yourself all set up here for a pelvic exam."

"Yes, I'm looking forward to it."

Royce chuckles. "Well, that makes you a very unusual patient. Now, before we go ahead with the physical exam, can you please describe to us your pelvic—"

It happens in a flash. Anna Carson grabs his hand. Before he can pull away, she's ducked her other hand under her hospital gown, pulled out a pair of handcuffs, and handcuffed his wrist to hers.

"What the fuck!" Royce thrashes his arm and spins around in a panic.

The door bursts open and the entire ER staff—technicians, nurses, secretaries, and doctors—spill into the tiny room, grinning like naughty children.

Still confused, Royce turns back to his patient, who is clicking open the lock on the cuffs that bind them. "I'm ready for my exam, Dr. Royce," she says in a cheeky drawl. His heart is still beating out of his chest with adrenaline as she takes him firmly by the shoulders and pushes him down onto a stool, shrugs off her hospital gown, revealing her lithe, naked body. Somebody has turned on some music. She swings and rocks her bare pelvis around his face. She hops back up on the exam table and proceeds to probe her vagina repetitively with the vaginal speculum.

The staff is wild with laughter, and Royce's shrieks of embarrassment only make them laugh harder.

Sliding back to the floor, she finishes her dance by turning her back to him, dropping her head and shoulders forward, and flashing her anus and vagina in his face. The crowd bursts into applause and cheers. Royce is red-faced and laughing.

He turns to Anna Carson and tosses her a playful salute. "Thank you for your service, officer."

"Anytime, doc." She winks at him.

"Let's get you out the door, honey," Suzanne quickly ferries Ms. Carson out of the room, no doubt to escort her from the hospital before anyone in administration catches wind of these birthday antics. The charge nurse links arms with Dr. Royce and pats him on the forearm.

"To the breakroom, kiddo," she says, escorting him from the room with the rest of the staff in tow. In the staff lounge, Suzanne is lighting the final candles on a giant birthday cake with a chocolate statue of a nude dancer sitting on top.

"You're all demented," he says, smiling ear to ear.

"Takes one to know one," someone shouts from the back of the room.

An innocent barb, but it stings, and Royce's anxiety spikes again. *What do they see,* he wonders. "No other bunch of deviants I'd rather spend my birthday with." Someone hands him a paper cup, and he lifts it. "Thank you."

"Will you blow out the damn candles and cut the cake? I skipped lunch for this," says the charge nurse.

Royce obliges, and as he hands out slices of birthday cake, Manny steps up behind him.

"Let's get out of here. McHale's, thirty minutes?"

"God, yes," Royce hisses under his breath. "See you there."

His phone pings as he walks into the bar, a local hangout for hospital staff and professionals in downtown Albuquerque. An emoji-filled text from Alesha, wishing him happy birthday.

Got plans?

His thumb hovers over the screen, then he shoves his phone into his pocket. A quick beer and he'll text her back, maybe see about meeting up. Manny, Greg Sanchez, and a few other guys from the hospital are at a table in the middle of the packed room. He waves to them, but they don't see him. He heads directly to the bar for a beer.

Royce hadn't realized it until this moment; he can't remember the last time he was outside the hospital walls. He shakes his head as if to clear the fog of memory, to shake off the gravity of the past month of immersion in death.

The music blares, a folksy song about doomed lovers that reminds Royce of the tune that Mary Watson hummed as she died. He feels a set of eyes on him. He looks up and sees Anna

Carson sitting at the bar. She dips her chin down toward her impossibly sculpted shoulder, a nod hello. He laughs and gives her a playful salute. She smiles and holds his gaze, long enough to make her interest clear. He hesitates for a moment. And then the old Royce comes roaring back to life. As he walks over to join her at the bar, he slides his hand into his pocket and silences his phone. His birthday night is going in a different direction than he planned, and right now, that feels just fine with him.

His watch alarm, now his constant guide, wakes him. Royce rubs his eyes. Three o'clock. He's continually surprised at how comfortable he finds his hospital bed. Once, he'd have been full of self-recrimination for sleeping until mid-afternoon. Now it barely registers as he races through a shower and a shave and throws on a fresh set of scrubs. He casts a wistful glance at the weights. He needs to get to the gym tomorrow, no excuses. He runs his hands across his torso. He feels toned, lean, and ripped. It's remarkable what he's been able to do in the past few months to increase his muscle mass and further purge his body of fat. He can't let up. He's thirty-nine now.

Royce tries to remember details of the night before. There was that business with the dancer in the ER, and then, did he see her again? His memory comes in zig-zag flashes, dodging him from seeing anything straight on. And how did he get back to his hospital suite? He can't dredge up a single detail. He checks his phone for Uber activity. None. He'd have needed to swipe his badge to get into the wing where he's staying. He makes a mental note to ask the security staff to confirm for him what time he came back to the hospital.

He bumps into Rudy outside his door, and they walk together toward the elevator. "I'm taking the stairs, man. You want to join?"

Rudy rolls his eyes and follows Royce to the stairwell. His steps are light and eager as he jogs his way up the final flight of stairs. Not the gym, but not nothing, either. He's got a meeting with the technicians and the radiologist to review data results for Mary Watson.

When he arrives, the team is waiting for him at the conference table.

"Good morning, folks—I mean, good afternoon. Have we got data?"

"We do," says the senior tech. She pushes a laptop across the table. Royce opens it to a tabbed spreadsheet that compares Mary Watson's data collected before her death, to the post-mortem data.

The group waits in silence until he's had a chance to review the results.

"I see no significant differences here," Royce says.

The lead tech concurs. "The patient's weight was unchanged. And review of the blood chemistries showed only changes that one would ordinarily see directly after death."

Royce stares at the screen as if willing the numbers to show something they don't, something that shows they're on the right track. He pulls up Mary's PET scans and scrolls through them slowly, catching his breath as he gets near the end of the series. "Whoa. On the final PET scan before euthanasia, there's some interesting stuff here. Do you see that?"

Rick Davies nods. "There were hot spots behind both eyes, as well as in a brain region called the temporo-parieto-occipital junction, which is believed to be involved in consciousness and is activated during dreaming, seizures, and out-of-body hallucinations. It caught me by surprise."

"But it's not really all that surprising, if you think about it. Of all the senses that one would expect to be on double secret alert, with one hour left to live, it's the visual sense."

Royce shoves the laptop across the table. Rick Davies looks startled, and the senior tech recoils. He gets up and starts to pace the room.

Davies and the techs trade glances. "One patient can't tell us much," the radiologist says. "Anything, really."

Royce spins around. "Don't you think I know that?" he demands. "I'm not a first-year med student, Rick. And I don't need to be appeased."

"Of course not, Mike." Davies gives him a look of sympathy mixed with the kind of strained patience one shows a toddler. Royce reckons he's earned that with his outburst, but he's too embarrassed and tangled-up inside to apologize.

"When is the next euthanasia?" Davies asks.

Royce feels his body begin to calm. Another one today, and starting tomorrow, they have three physician-assisted-suicides scheduled per day for the next twelve days. It's a crushing schedule, but it means they'll have the beginnings of an actual data set soon.

"Let's look through this stuff again," Royce says, pulling his chair back to the table and motioning for the laptop. With some hesitation, the senior tech slides it toward him, and they spend another hour reviewing Mary Watson's data. It's all thoroughly unenlightening, and it makes Royce want to scream, but he manages to keep his impatient frustration under wraps.

His watch beeps, telling him it's time to head to the induction room. Royce stands and looks around the table. "I'm sorry I got a little hot there, guys. No excuse for that." As he walks toward the door, he pauses next to Davies and extends his hand.

"Sorry, Rick. I shouldn't have spoken to you that way."

"Don't sweat it, Mike," says Davies. "We're all on edge these days."

Royce raises a hand to wave goodbye to the team. At the same time, he leans in close to Rick Davies's ear. "I want to see my fucking scans."

Royce's white-hot irritation dissolves as he enters the induction room and sees Paul McNee. "Hey, doc."

Paul's automated voice sounds cheery, generated by the speech device he directs with his eyes. Four years ago, not long after his ALS diagnosis, Paul recorded his own voice, anticipating a time when he'd need to rely on augmented communication. "I didn't want to sound like a robot around my kids," Paul told him when they met a month ago.

Royce takes one of Paul's hands in his own and puts another hand on the man's shoulder, giving it a warm squeeze. He's struck, again, by the faraway look in Paul's eyes, the same look he saw in Mary's gaze as she readied herself for her death.

Alesha greets him wordlessly from her seat next to Paul. Royce flinches with guilt—is it guilt?—an unfamiliar feeling for him in relationships, one he's worked diligently to avoid. He wonders, *is this about last night*? He never responded to her text and spent the night with Anna Carson. But had they spent the night together? Royce still can only reclaim snippets of memory of the woman's exquisite body, which he'd seen plenty of at the hospital.

"Dr. Royce." Alesha's voice brings him back.

Royce sits next to Paul and listens as his computer-generated voice talks about his teenage children and his abiding love for his ex-wife. "I fucked things up with her before I got sick, and she still took care of me. I got luckier than I ever deserved. If you don't count this blasted disease."

At the appointed time, Royce stands to prepare the injection. The second time around feels different, he's less frightened, more assured. He's repeating steps now, not fumbling for his way, right up to kissing Paul on the cheek before Alesha administers the injection through the IV. Mary's song floats through his mind.

As Royce hands Alesha the syringe, he sees her fingers trembling. For Alesha, it will take many more deaths before this procedure becomes less heart wrenching, if it ever does. As they stand together over Paul's body, watching the life drift from the man's eyes, Royce once again takes her in his arms and rocks her. This time, though, it's for her sake; he needs no such comfort. As Alesha cries into his scrubs, he sheds no tears.

CHAPTER 15

Royce hums to himself as he waits for the computer to boot up. It's the song Mary Watson sang quietly in the last moment of her life. It's been stuck in his head for weeks now. After Mary died, he sang to himself at Paul's bedside. Then again, and again. Thirty times in all, he's watched his patients die by lethal injection, holding their hands as the cocktail of drugs stops their hearts, silently humming this song in his head. Thirty times, he's sat with them in the hours leading up to their deaths, watching them say their goodbyes to their families, listening to them tell stories for the last time, bearing witness to their relief—sometimes even a strange sort of joy—as their suffering came to an end. Thirty times, he's felt the strange mix of wonder and revulsion at their welcoming acceptance of death. And thirty times, as the designated time of death drew closer, he's seen appear the same faraway look in their eyes. He is convinced, beyond a shadow of a scientist's rigorous doubt, that he's observing a pattern. What he doesn't know is whether the data they've collected will prove him right and tell him anything about what it means.

Trust your gut. Evelyn's words echo in his mind, the aftertaste of her unfailingly excellent bourbon lingering in his throat.

"Look at us, a couple of shut-ins." Her laugh earlier was tinged with bitterness, but her green eyes twinkled with the sharp humor Royce has come to appreciate in her. With his living quarters now in the hospital, he's taken to visiting with her in her office on the occasional evening. More than occasional. They'd struck up a regular routine of bourbon and conversation several times a week. She's become, if not a friend, a confidante. Not a cheerleader; that's not her style, he's learned. But she is a welcome sounding board. And she has a way of seeing beyond his veneer of confidence to prod him when he's losing hope. He leaves their chats feeling determined, the steel returned to his spine.

"How are you feeling?" In the soft evening light, he casts a subtle gaze over the deep purple bruises on her face. She took a fall last week, and she's kept herself largely out of sight. He feels an almost childish pride that she's continued to grant him access for their nightcap chats. Tonight, her assistant waved him through without a word.

She looked peeved at the question, and waved a wobbling, lacquered hand in his direction, as if swatting away a bothersome fly. "I'm ugly as a puckerfish, but otherwise fine. Today was number thirty, correct?"

"It was."

"So, you'll be taking stock, now, yes?"

"I have a meeting with the techs and radiologist on Friday—tomorrow."

After his meltdown in the lab when reviewing Mary's death,

he'd sworn off on looking at the data. Until now. He promised himself—and Alesha insisted—he'd give the scientific process time to work. They agreed he'd wait until they'd collected data on thirty acts of euthanasia before he reviewed any more numbers. Had it not been for the bourbon, he felt he might fly out of his own body with impatience.

"Whatever's there, you'll find it."

"I'm glad you're so sure."

"You're not?" She raised an eyebrow.

"It's like looking for sunken treasure at the bottom of the sea. We've marked our search field and cast our nets into the darkness —but are we even looking in the right place?"

Evelyn leaned forward in her chair, her ring-clad fingers grasping the knob of her cane. "You're sure as hell not smarter than I am, young man. But you are smarter than the rest of them." Again, a trembling hand moves as if to dismiss the entire hospital that sits beneath them, maybe the entire medical profession at large. "I bet a lot of money on your gut. You'd damn well better trust it yourself."

Royce laughed. "Point taken, ma'am."

"And don't tell me you're going to wait until tomorrow's meeting to see what's in those results."

She was right, of course. He escorted her to the private entrance where her driver met her. Now he's in the lab. He has nowhere else to be. And there's nowhere else he wants to be.

On the computer screen in front of him are the blood work, vitals, and PET scan results obtained when each of the thirty patients entered the study, results taken one hour before their lethal injection and five minutes post-mortem.

Royce first analyzes the blood chemistry data for each patient.

Over and again, he scans the data tables, reading hard and slow. Just like he encountered nothing surprising in Mary's results, he sees nothing noteworthy.

The weight of his frustration sinking like a stone inside his chest, he moves on to the vitals. It's there, on his first, careful pass through the data, that he sees something unexpected. Three patients had a slight weight loss—0.1 kilograms—five minutes post-mortem, as compared to their weight taken one hour prior to injection. The weight loss itself is interesting. But what are the chances of the three of them losing precisely the same amount of weight?

Slow down, he reminds himself. He peruses the data more closely. This time, he sees something that stops him cold. In collecting vitals for each of these three patients, the study protocols were broken. Instead of being weighed sixty minutes prior to injection, the technician weighed them at fifty-five minutes. Royce ought to be furious. An error like this can render weeks and months of work useless. But as the weight-loss anomaly sinks in, Royce thinks he may just have to track this tech down and give him a giant hug.

What is happening in the body between fifty-five and fifty-nine minutes prior to death that can account for this weight loss? Were it not for the tech's mistake, he'd never have known to wonder.

With that question in mind, Royce turns his attention to the PET scan photos. He scrolls slowly through the thumbnails, enlarging each one at a time. Halfway through, his heart begins to pound. By the time he's finished the full set of thirty scans, the hair on the back of his neck is standing on end, and a chill is rising through his body.

Twenty-seven of the thirty PET scans taken an hour before death look similar. They all have the hot spot behind the eyes and the temporo-parieto-occipital junction, indicating increased blood flow. Three of the thirty scans, however, look different. In these three scans, the hot spot is nowhere to be seen.

All attempts to take things slowly now cast aside, Royce scrolls frantically through the data associated with each scan.

What he finds makes him shriek like a wild animal. The same timing error that occurred with the final weigh-ins for three patients persisted with their final PET scans. Instead of having their final PET scans sixty minutes prior to injection, these same three patients had PET scans fifty-five minutes before their lethal shots. He can barely catch his breath as he grabs his phone and calls Rick Davies.

"Rick, have you left for the night?"

"Dr. Royce?" Davies sounds confused.

"Are you in the hospital?"

Royce picks up the irritation in the silent pause that follows. Through the phone, he hears piano music tinkling in the background.

"Mike, it's Saturday night. I'm having a late dinner with my wife."

It hits him again. The now familiar spin of disorientation. A couple hours ago, he was having drinks with Evelyn Price in her office. He heard her assistant confirm tomorrow's date. Friday, October 15. Now, Rick Davies is telling him it's Saturday evening. He feels his mind spinning, making him dizzy, and he pushes down the rising nausea. He's got no time for it. He forces himself back into the moment.

"I'm sorry; I lost track of time. Look," he says, pulling out his most collegial, reasonable sounding tone. "I need you to come into the lab. Tonight."

"Christ, Mike, are you serious? What's this about?"

"I need you to look at some scans with me."

"Why can't this wait until Monday? I can meet you early, before the team meeting if you want—"

"It can't wait." Royce unleashes the desperation in his voice.

Davies reluctantly agrees, and Royce spends the next thirty minutes in a manic cycle, looking at the three anomalous scans and jumping up to pace the room like a caged animal.

At last, Davies arrives and Royce practically shoves him into a chair in front of the computer terminal.

It takes the radiologist almost no time to concur. "No hot spots. Back to baseline blood flow for each of them." Davies takes off his glasses and rubs his eyes. "This is really striking."

"We've got something here! We do." Royce wants to leap on the table and howl, as adrenaline surges through his veins. He holds himself back and claps the radiologist hard on the back.

"Still, this could have waited until Monday." Davies pushes his chair away from the computer, putting space between himself and Royce. "You're too close, too wrapped up, Mike. You gotta take a breath and slow down—"

Royce isn't listening. He's texting the research team, calling an emergency meeting for the next day. Sunday or not, he wants to schedule it for first thing in the morning. Fingers flying across the keys, he reconsiders, and tells everyone to meet in the lab at three. That's when he can count on being awake and alert.

* * *

At three on the dot, Royce is stalking down the long, empty hallway to the laboratory. One of his lab techs trails behind him, headed for the emergency meeting in the lab, but Royce hardly notices his colleague; he's so wrapped up in thought. The lack of hot spots in the PET scans, the slight weight loss . . . Something is happening to their patients in the first five minutes of the final hour before their death. They need to immediately revise their protocols before the next euthanasia.

He hears a ring and instinctively reaches for his watch to silence the three o'clock alarm. It's not his watch. It's his phone, pinging with a call from Lucy.

"Hey, Lucy, I'm on my way—"

"Dr. Royce, you've got to get down to the ER."

"I'm not on shift today. I need you to get up here to the lab. We're meeting—"

"No, Dr. Royce."

Then he hears it. The dread in her voice.

"It's Alesha."

It's the strangest feeling. His body feels as though it might fly upward, tethered only by feet that suddenly feel like they're encased in cement.

"What happened?" Moments later, he's towering over Lucy. She takes a cowering step back, fear lighting up in her eyes. "Sorry," he says, lowering his shoulders and putting out his hands in a peaceful gesture. "Please, just tell me what's going on. Is it her heart?"

Lucy shakes her head. Alesha had been talking with a group of their terminal patients, wrapping up a daily group support session, when she'd suddenly dropped to her knees, holding her hands to her head. "Her arms seemed to go totally limp, and her legs just crumpled." Lucy's lip trembles as she fights off tears. One of the social workers called for a nurse, and as Lucy helped get Alesha onto a gurney, Alesha told them she had a terrible headache and numbness all over her body.

"Do you have her chart?"

"No, I—"

"Why the hell not?" Royce thunders.

"Dr. Royce, I'm not ER staff—they wouldn't let me if I asked."

"God, of course. I'm so sorry. Where is Alesha now?"

"Imaging. They took her up about ten minutes ago."

When the elevator opens, returning Alesha to the ER, Royce is waiting at the doors. She's asleep on the gurney. The nurse whispers, "She's so exhausted that she fell asleep on the way down."

Royce instructs the nurse to get Alesha settled in an empty trauma room and calls the elevator back to take him to radiology on the third floor.

"Can I see Alesha Simmons's pictures, please?"

The tech pulls them up without a word, and steps back so Royce can get a close look.

The PET scan shows Alesha's body rife with small tumors.

Typical for a Sunday afternoon, the ER is humming. It's the story of most weekends, when all the doctors' offices are closed and the ER, on top of dealing with trauma, also functions as a primary care facility. Royce stands in the middle of the thrumming activity, doctors and nurses and orderlies zipping past him, children crying in the waiting room, having no idea how he got here. The last thing he remembers is staring at Alesha's ghostly, ghastly scan. Somehow, he made his way back down to the ER floor.

Royce ducks his head into the trauma room where Alesha rests, just long enough to see she's still sleeping. He wants to crawl in bed next to her, gather her in his arms, and shield her from everything that's coming. Instead, he wanders out onto the frenetic

ER floor. She's going to be moved to a room upstairs shortly. That's when she'll learn the results of her scans, and the miserable flood of consultations and testing will begin. Royce will be at her side for all of that; until then, he'll let her rest.

The radio at the central ER desk crackles.

"En route with three-year-old male, drowning. CPR in progress. Five minutes out."

Royce feels a familiar churn in his stomach. When an adult dies, it's a shame, but when a child dies, it's heartbreaking. Royce has known no greater sorrow than after failing to resuscitate a child.

"I'll take this one."

The admin nurse looks up at him. "You're on today?"

"I'm here. You want someone else?"

Four minutes later, EMS rushes the gurney through the ambulance bay doors. One paramedic is performing chest compressions while the other ventilates the child. A nurse sweeps the child's frantic parents into a private waiting room.

Royce steps in beside them as they head for a trauma room. He looks at the monitor and sees a flat line. The paramedics quickly present the history: the child was seen swimming five minutes before he was found face down in the pool. EMS worked on the child for approximately twenty minutes in the field. During this time, they proceeded through Pediatric Advanced Life Support protocols while intubating the patient: placing a tube into the trachea, which is then attached to a bag that feeds oxygen directly into the lungs.

Dr. Royce glances at the child's pupils. Fixed and dilated—a bad sign. He proceeds directly to the child's airway to check the placement of the endotracheal tube. He's hit with sudden, overwhelming grief that falls upon him like a boulder. The endotracheal tube has been inserted into the child's esophagus, not his trachea. This child will die, or worse, remain alive with no brain function. In one long, swift series of motions, Royce removes the misplaced tube, throws it on the floor, and inserts a new tube in the trachea.

He barks his orders to the respiratory therapist. "Bag this kid."

He shuts his eyes tightly, waiting. His heart bottoms out in his chest when he hears the blips from the monitor. This child's heart now has a rhythm. Unfortunately, for the boy and his parents, this child will live. His heart is strong, as is the rest of his body. It is his brain that has been wasted into ruin by a twenty-minute lack of oxygen. Opening his eyes, Royce turns to see paramedics silently watching the scene unfold at the edge of the room.

Anger and grief rendering him senseless, he calmly asks them to step out into the hallway. He does not yell or scream. Royce lowers his head and without looking at them, he informs them that they have killed this poor child. Leaving them stunned and speechless, he turns and walks back into the room to complete the resuscitation. When the child is stable, Royce makes the long walk to inform the parents of their child's prognosis. He hugs them and cries with them, so familiar with the machinations of his role in sudden, horrific tragedy that he can do it without thinking, without even feeling. He does not tell them about the errant intubation.

When he is finally able to leave the parents to begin their new, ruined lives, he walks directly to his office and closes the door. Only then do his senses return, in a rush that lights his body on fire with rage.

"How dare you! Who do you think you are? You abominable bastard." The anger in his shouts comes from the deepest well within him, so black and tarry he can taste the spitefulness on his tongue. It takes him a moment to realize who he's talking to. When he does, he laughs, a bitter laugh like Evelyn's, but devoid of her spirit. It seems grotesquely fitting that his first real conversation with God is an angry one.

"You can't have them all. You can't have *her*."

CHAPTER 16

"It is what it is, Mike."

Royce feels fear circling him like a stiff, icy wind. His body tingles with dread. He reaches out a hand and brushes a strand of Alesha's hair from her face. Just for an instant, she leans her cheek into his hand and closes her eyes, taking comfort in his touch. Before he can reply, she sits herself upright and squares her shoulders. This, he thinks, is what they mean when they talk about an indominable spirit. She's never looked more beautiful.

"Remember, we've been here before," she says. "I wasn't supposed to make it five years ago." She sweeps her arms out to the side. "And look at me now," she laughs, wiggling her shoulders under her hospital gown in a girlish twist, as though she's anywhere but trapped in a hospital bed about to undertake a fight for her life. She wipes the smile from her face and looks at him with steely eyes. "I'm here."

The bloodwork and biopsy results have confirmed what Royce

already knew. Her cancer has returned with a vengeance, metastasized to her brain.

He takes both her hands in his. "I'm going to fix this, my darling. I'm going to fix this for you."

Alesha hoots with laughter. "Wow—'my darling'—you must really be scared shitless right now."

Royce forces himself to grin. "Lucky for you, fear makes me sharp."

The day Alesha collapsed, everything changed, and Royce saw his research with entirely fresh eyes. Gone was any pretense of objective non-involvement. Everything he does, from this point forward, will be in the service of her recovery. If this had happened before he embarked on his study, he'd be furiously researching upcoming trials and the latest drug regimens, frantically putting together a diet and sleep and mental health regimen to optimize Alesha's energy, immune strength, and emotional resilience while her body was battered by treatment.

Now, he'll do none of that. Everything he has—every ounce of energy, every waking breath—will go into remaking his study to move faster and do more. He can't believe he hadn't seen it sooner, that he required a personal crisis to realize what he needs to do. In the days since her illness became apparent, two things have become clear. They need to speed up the rate of suicides. They must have more data, and they need it fast. Dying patients around the country are clamoring to get into his study, looking for a way to end their suffering on their own terms as they take part in something extraordinary for humankind. Speeding up the euthanasia will be the easy part. The hard part will be the second thing he knows he must do. An observational study won't do a damn thing to help Alesha. He doesn't know how, not yet. The data has only begun to reveal its secrets. But he will find the answers.

He will build a clinical trial.

And Alesha will be a participant.

Royce feels like a guy short of cash who buys a lottery ticket, giddy with hope, manic with desperation, knowing the odds are a million to one. But he's out of options. And the anomalies in his data mean something. He knows they do.

Royce's watch beeps. He checks the small screen and grimaces. "My shift starts in ten minutes. I'm going to call out."

"No, you're not." Alesha unwraps his hands from hers. "Go to work. I'll be fine."

"I don't want to leave you."

"What are you going to do? Sit here and watch me take a nap?" She pats his hand. "I'm okay. I really do need to get some sleep. These damn nurses had me up all night checking on me." She shoots him a wry smile. "I love that you want to stay, but, well, I think I could use some time to myself. I need to sit with this new reality for a while."

"We're going to change the future—you and me." Royce kisses the top of her hand. "We're going to change your future, and a whole lot of others' futures. And then we're going to run off to Bali and celebrate, drink rum, run around on the beach, for like, a month—a year, if we want—okay?"

She stayed silent for a few moments. "We're both going to do what needs to be done, Mike."

Stepping out of the elevator at the ER, Royce rubs his temple and tries to focus. Morning shifts used to be a breeze for him; lately they feel brutal and painfully difficult, as though he's wading through chest deep water to stay awake and focused. And today, he feels resentful for having to be here at all, begrudging of the time away from Alesha and even more so the loss of time in the lab. He's never experienced this before, a kind of preemptive anger at the people who will need his help today, contempt for the carelessness and ignorance and arrogance and plain old bad luck that today will drive them into his ER in droves. *No physician should think this way*, he chastises himself. He's always prided himself on not being one of those physicians who has disdain for their patients.

Ahead of him in the hallway, Royce sees a slight, bespectacled young man shuffling outside his office door. He's wearing an oxford shirt and a tie that has been knotted crookedly. His memory flashes back to the days when tying a necktie was a challenge. The young man sees Royce, and his hand flies up in a nervous, slightly manic wave. Royce squints as he walks closer, trying to figure out who this kid is, and why he's so happy to see him.

"Dr. Royce! Hello!"

Royce waves a bewildered hand in response. *I am definitely supposed to know who this is*, he thinks.

The young man extends a hand and shakes his vigorously. "Excited to get started."

"Excuse me, I don't mean to be rude, but . . . started with what?"

The kid freezes. "My ER rotation starts tomorrow. I'm the new intern. I'm shadowing you today, remember?"

Royce does not remember. *Why isn't this kid with the chief resident*, he wonders.

The young man seems to recognize Royce's confusion. "We met at the welcome reception a couple of weeks ago? You invited me to come and work a shift with you." He extends his hand once again and Royce grasps it. "Charlie Hsu."

"Charlie, of course. I'm sorry, it's . . . it's been a morning. Why don't you come into my office?" Royce unlocks the door, hoping young Dr. Hsu doesn't see his hand shaking. If he attended an intern reception a couple of weeks ago—and apparently, he did—he has no memory of it. Ditto for inviting this eager, earnest fellow to tag along on a shift with him. A year ago, he was voted teacher of the year. How things have changed. He's about to pry Charlie loose from his day when he reconsiders. Having a student to lecture throughout the day could be just the distraction he needs to get him through this shift.

Royce pastes on a smile. "Charlie, I'm glad you're here." Royce grabs his white coat and stethoscope. "Let's go grab a chart."

"Right on, doc," says Charlie, practically skipping at Royce's heels.

As they head to the GYN room to see a patient complaining of pelvic pain, Dr. Royce shifts into teaching mode. "What are the three most common gynecological emergencies?"

Charlie straightens his already rail-straight spine and leaps into his answer. "Ruptured ectopic pregnancy, acute pelvic inflammatory disease, hemorrhagic miscar—"

Royce pushes open the door. In front of them on the gurney is a full-term mother bearing down as her baby's head pops out of her vagina. Royce grabs at a pair of gloves. "Get us some help in here, now."

Charlie stands frozen, eyes wide.

"Now, Charlie!"

Royce suctions the baby's nostrils. "Hang in there, mom; your baby's almost out." As a nurse strides into the room, a sweating Charlie Hsu trailing closely behind her, Royce delivers a baby girl and places her on her mother's chest. The nurse moves to the young mother's side, and Royce sits and waits for the placenta to exit the uterus.

Charlie paces in tight circles behind him. "I'm not sure I need this kind of excitement in my life, Dr. Royce," he says breathlessly. "I need time to think. Maybe internal medicine is more my speed. You know, a gentleman's specialty. Isn't that what they say?"

Royce laughs. "How you doing up there, mom?" His eighteen-year-old patient smiles the smile he's seen on a thousand new mothers, one of elation, relief, pain, and awe.

After several minutes, Royce turns to Charlie. "I'm going to need to sweep the uterus to aid the descent of the placenta."

Charlie nods gravely, as though it will be he him with half his forearm venturing into the patient's vagina. Royce explains to his patient what he's about to do before gently and firmly reaching inside her to help dislodge the placenta. After a moment, the patient starts to moan.

"I'm sorry this is painful, ma'am," Royce calls to her. "It's essential that the placenta come out."

"No, please, don't stop."

Royce and the nurse trade puzzled glances. Charlie's jaw drops open.

"I think—I think . . ." the patient is panting now, her moans escalating. ". . . I think I'm going to cum."

Royce and the assisting nurse do their best to stifle their chuckles. It's quite the first day for Charlie.

The placenta comes down on its own, and Royce gives his

patient a moment to regain her composure before wishing her the best and leaving her with the nurse, taking Charlie with him.

"So, I guess you give the best pelvic exams around here?" Charlie says with a smirk.

Royce roars and claps Charlie on the back. "I needed that laugh, Dr. Hsu. You'll never know how much. Let's go see what else is in store for us today."

At the end of his shift, Royce stops by Greg Sanchez's office. He requests a drastic reduction in his ER load, but it's a request in name only. He can't waste his time pulling shifts in the ER, not anymore. His boss is not surprised. Sanchez, like everyone else in the hospital, has heard about Alesha. Royce doesn't tell him what he plans to do with the time. It's true; Alesha's health is at the center of his every encounter and thought. And he intends to use every moment going forward to transform his research project into a clinical trial, all in time to save her life.

The next two weeks are a blur of activity as Royce pushes his team to expand their patient population and simultaneously implement multiple euthanasias per day. The clinical language of the process matches his increasingly remote stance with his patients. He's with every one of them in their final hours, holding their hands and kissing them on the cheek in the moment before they pass. He doesn't believe they'd ever know how automated the process has become for him; if not easy, then manageable and increasingly impersonal. He cares for his patients and admires them, even as they mystify him with their tranquility at death's door. But they are, irrevocably now, a means to an end for Royce.

Sitting together at the conference table, Royce, Alesha, Rick Davies and a handful of other staff members are silent with anticipation. Alesha has begun chemotherapy. But she's insisted on being present for every euthanasia and as many meetings as she can. Royce is watching her closely for overexertion. But knows better than to fight her when she's determined. And she wanted to be here today.

Thirty patients have been studied and euthanized under the new protocols. Patients are now being weighed every minute between sixty-five and fifty-five minutes prior to injection of the lethal cocktail. PET scans are now performed every minute on the minute, starting at sixty-five minutes prior to injection, images taken every minute, the last image shot at fifty-five minutes prior to injection. This schedule, they hope, will allow them to pinpoint the activity of the hot spots that appear—and then disappear—behind the eyes and temporo-parieto-occipital junction, perhaps revealing some more precise insights on the mysterious weight loss.

It's time again to look at data. Royce is almost manic as he thumbs through the sheets of information. As he absorbs the information on the pages in front of him, his chest begins to heave. It's here, the pattern that they found in those three anomalous euthanasias from the last round. In each one of the thirty patients, weight remained static until exactly fifty-five minutes prior to injection. At that point, each patient experienced exactly a 0.1 kilogram weight loss. Every single patient: the same amount of weight loss at the same exact time, relative to their lethal injections. Royce feels euphoria expanding like a balloon in his chest.

Rick Davies reviews the PET scans with the team. Between

sixty-five through sixty-one minutes prior to injection, every patient's PET scan appears normal, reflecting their individual existing conditions. But suddenly, at exactly sixty minutes prior to injection, their brains light up like light bulbs, and the hot spots behind the eyes and temporo-parieto-occipital junction.

It's too much for Royce, and he leaps from his chair and begins pacing the room like a wild cat. "What have we found—what have we found—"

Dr. Davies laughs uncomfortably. "Dr. Royce, how about you sit down so I can finish relaying the findings? Trust me, you're going to want to be sitting for this."

Davies continues. "At fifty-nine, fifty-eight, fifty-seven and fifty-six minutes prior to injection," he explains, "the separate hot spots behind the eyes and at the temporo-parieto-occipital junction appear to merge into one oblong-shaped hot spot, which then progresses toward the top of the head. Until, at exactly fifty-five minutes, it disappears." He turns the palms of his hands up as if to say, *who knows?*

No area of increased blood flow exists from fifty-five minutes on.

As Davies sits down, Royce's mind reels as he attempts to process the significance of their results.

Could it be that some energy exists in the body that works its way behind the eyes at approximately sixty minutes before death?

And, as this energy leaves the body within five minutes, upward through the top of the head, we can measure an actual weight loss?

Royce thinks about the faraway look in Mary Watson's eyes. And in Paul McNee's eyes. And in the eyes of every patient who has been euthanized in the past six weeks. He looks at Rick Davies, and at Alesha, seeing the same dawning questions reflected in their eyes. The next question, the one they're all thinking, he asks aloud.

"Is this proof of the existence of the soul? Are we charting the soul as it leaves the body?"

Royce, Alesha, and Davies stare at each other, stunned by the revelations in their data.

For once, even Royce himself is speechless.

CHAPTER 17

"I had to do something to move things along, you see." Royce's eyes dart around the room, avoiding Evelyn's steely gaze. He's torn between spilling all the details of his earth-shattering discovery and alienating the person who holds the purse strings and the power to propel his research forward or stop it cold.

His discovery of the migration of energy out of their patients' bodies between sixty and fifty-five minutes of death rocked him. But Royce's euphoria cooled quickly, replaced by a furious, all-consuming impatience to know more. The appearance and disappearance of the hot spots at the eyes and visual cortex. The small but precise corresponding weight loss. He's convinced he's pinpointed the exodus of the soul from the body and that this seminal event marks the moment that death becomes an iron-clad inevitability. What prompts the migration? Can they—how do they—stop it? And if they can corral this energy, stop it from disappearing, will that indeed forestall death itself?

Royce had known almost immediately what he needed to do

next. He also knew it to be a total rogue move that could put his entire research project in jeopardy. Still, once the idea came to him, he gave it very little thought before deciding to proceed. He had no choice, not with Alesha's life hanging in the balance. And if he was being honest, he relished the opportunity to test out the hypothesis that had been rattling around in his mind since watching those hot spots merge and then vanish on the PET scans.

"Well, did you get what you needed?" Her voice is halting as she speaks, a warbling, stilted version of her once smooth, assured contralto tone. But it is a classic Evelyn response. She's a principled woman who understands that the ends do often justify the means. Royce feels dizzy with relief: she's not about to rake him over the coals for taking a calculated risk, provided the results are worth it. He wasn't going to be able to make the leap to a clinical trial until he demonstrated that the migration of this energy—this soul—is the defining event in the march toward death, the tipping point that makes death an irreversible outcome. And he knew exactly what he needed to do to prove it so.

"Yes, ma'am. I did."

Once the idea came to him, he'd wasted no time in testing it out on the next scheduled euthanasia. The patient lies in bed in one of the induction rooms, counting down the minutes until their lethal injection. As Royce prepares the drug cocktail, Alesha sits by the patient's side, providing her unfailingly steady, quiet comfort. As he put his hands deliberately through the motions of mixing the drugs, Royce tries to remember whether this is euthanasia number eighty or ninety. He still knows their names and their histories, still feels the twin pangs of pity and admiration for their predicament and their service to his quest. But the connection he felt with his first euthanasia patients isn't there anymore. There are too many of them. After presiding over dozens of assisted suicides, Royce has achieved a peace about the process, his focus shifting to answers.

Alesha remains deeply emotionally invested with each of their patients, still coming undone at every death. It has become a point of contention between them. She says he's becoming remote with the patients. He's worried she's doing too much at the expense of her own health.

Royce hands Alesha the syringe and kisses the patient on the cheek, in keeping with all his customs. Only he knows that this euthanasia is different from the rest. Alesha pushes the cocktail and strokes the patient's face as she and Royce stand side by side to watch life slip away. Out of habit, they step aside in perfect sync, anticipating the tech team's arrival to ready the patient's body for the post-mortem blood draw, weighing, and PET scan.

As they watch the flatline on the monitor, Royce's heart pounds like a bass drum in his chest. It happened. Just like he believed it would. He leans close to Alesha's ear. They're still alone with the patient's body, but he feels compelled to whisper his confession.

"That cocktail I pushed? It was sterile water."

The ecstasy that Royce has been keeping just barely under wraps explodes, and he leaps around the room in giant strides of joy, throwing his hands over his head.

Alesha stares at him for a long, bewildered moment. "You did what?" Her voice is barely audible.

"Jake here—I mean Nate—whatever, this patient? They didn't get the drugs. They got water, Alesha, water. And they died anyway, right on schedule."

Alesha stares at him and at the patient, the significance of the moment dawning on her.

"What were you thinking? My god, Mike."

"What was I thinking? I was thinking we needed to know whether the disappearance of the hot spots—the goddamn soul leaving the body, Alesha—is the final, irreversible catalyst for death." Royce wants to shake her, just to wake her up to the staggering reality of what's just happened.

"I don't understand how this is possible." Alesha's already pale face has gone white with shock. "How is this man dead? Why?"

"I don't know. Not for sure, not yet. But I'm willing to bet my life it has everything to do with the movement of energy behind the eyes." Royce forces himself to slow down his manic pacing and reaches out a hand to Alesha. After a moment's hesitation, she extends her hand to his, and he squeezes it tight.

"They're going to be here any minute. We'll have PET scan pictures within the hour. I'm going to look at them right away. Will you come with me, please?"

It's all there on the screens before their stunned eyes.

"The hot spot recorded?" she asked him, though she could see it herself on the series of scans taken between sixty and fifty-five minutes before death. At sixty minutes, the hot spots appeared behind the eyes, merged into a single oblong configuration, and migrated toward the top of the head. At fifty-five minutes, there was no hot spot to be found. The patient's scans looked exactly like the dozens they'd seen after euthanizing patients with the lethal cocktail.

"Yes. Fifty-five minutes before like clockwork. And the 0.1 kilogram weight loss occurred at exactly fifty-five minutes, correlating perfectly with the loss of the hot spot."

This is what he'd hoped for, what he'd been counting on, what all his instincts told him would happen. And still, he is boggled by what he's looking at now.

"It's the hot spot that preordains death?" Alesha took a deep breath, her words catching the fire of urgent excitement that Royce had running through his own veins. "And what triggered the hot spot? Merely scheduling the shot? We thought certain death triggered it somehow."

Royce notes her brightening tone with hope. It doesn't sound like she's going to bail on him for his deception and his deviation from protocol. He can see her own potent curiosity taking over. What they've discovered is ground-shaking. It's making him lightheaded. The juxtaposition of events—no poison, only saline solution, yet death within minutes of the injection—is capsizing the last of Royce's own sense of traditional scientific boundaries.

Alesha's mind goes next to where any good scientist's mind would: to wonder whether this patient's death was caused by their underlying illness. "Could it have been a crazy coincidence that his death occurred at the time of the injection?" Alesha thinks aloud.

"It certainly could've," Royce says. "But that timing's too perfect not to consider a connection. Here's what I'm wondering. Could knowledge of impending death have pushed the psyche to unleash the hot spot, thereby killing the physical body?"

Alesha shivers. Royce thinks about Mary Watson's soulful eyes, growing remote they gazed at a horizon he couldn't see. Then he feels it, along the pathway of intimate, unspoken understanding that runs between them: the recognition that they had discovered the soul. And when the soul leaves, it doesn't matter what anybody does. Within fifty-five minutes, the individual will die.

Evelyn's green eyes are the size of saucers. She's stayed uncharacteristically silent, but it doesn't take her long to find her voice.

"Now what?" she breathes. Alesha is his partner in so many ways. But only with Evelyn does Royce's urgency meet its match. *She's got her own reasons for needing me to move quickly*, he thinks, watching her body jerk and writhe in constant revolt against her wishes. For a woman as supremely controlled as Evelyn Price, Parkinson's is an especially cruel disease.

"We're changing the protocols. Again."

The day after the non-lethal euthanasia—the saline suicide, as he's taken to calling it—Royce called a meeting with all supervisors involved in the project to discuss the results of the latest assisted-suicide and immediately implement new protocols, which he drafted himself. He outlines the broad basics for Evelyn:

Patients will be randomly assigned to Limb 1 or Limb 2.

Limb 1 will receive the lethal cocktail that is currently being used.

Limb 2 will receive a non-lethal mixture of Sodium Pentothal, Ativan, and morphine.

All patients still alive ten minutes after the cocktail has been pushed will be terminated with a solution of potassium chloride.

This will, of course, be a double-blind study, meaning neither the patients, nor those administering the drugs will know which mixture they are injecting.

PET scanning protocol will also change. As in the previous phase of study, scanning will be initiated at sixty-five minutes prior to injection. Going forward, scanning will continue until disappearance of the hot spot is observed. Weight will be obtained every minute on the minute starting at sixty minutes prior to injection, with the last weight measurement taken just after disappearance of the hot spot.

"The big issue right now is getting the patients on board," Royce says. There's no point in glossing things over with Evelyn. She's a master at seeing all the angles. "They're coming into the project expecting to die on their terms. It's going to take lot of reassuring that that's what they'll get, no matter which limb they get assigned to. But we're getting there." Whether patients fall into Limb 1 or Limb 2 will make no difference. The patients injected with the non-lethal cocktail will quickly lapse into unconsciousness and then, if necessary, receive the lethal injection.

"How does this get us to a trial, Dr. Royce?" Evelyn asks.

Royce leans forward. "If we can show that it's the exiting of the hot spots that triggers death, that's gives us the rationale to try to stop the hot spots from going away." He pauses, wanting his words to sink in. "No migration of hot spot out of the body, no death."

Evelyn's eyes glint like sharp stones. "What do you need from me?"

"We're going to need more money. Fast."

"Whatever you need, I'll make sure you get it."

* * *

The latest protocols usher in an exhilarating, exhausting stretch for Royce, Alesha, and their team. For this next round of thirty patients, who will randomly receive injections of either lethal or non-lethal solutions, Royce insists on stacking euthanasias at three per day, scheduled between the hours of three and nine p.m. That's when he's at his sharpest.

It's a grueling undertaking. With their patient population growing, Royce realizes they need to expand their staff, but they'll make do with the original team for this next, all-important round. Royce needs a new data set to formally analyze as soon as possible; it's the only way to know how best to build out the project going forward.

As part of their work implementing the injections, Royce and Alesha are now observing the cardiac monitors after patients' first injections. At ten minutes after the initial injection, they push the deadly cocktail on all those patients still alive. They stare at PET scan photos with mouths agape as they watch the soul escape the physical body, over and over again, in every one of their patients.

Royce almost makes it to thirty completed euthanasias before reviewing the PET scans against the remaining patient data. But after the penultimate night, he can't hold back any longer. He's already gone so far out on a limb to get where they are. Breaking the rules is getting easier and easier.

He convinces Alesha to accompany him back to the lab to review the data on their most recent twenty-seven patients and, as they correlate PET scan photos to the corresponding patients, the hermetically sealed secret to immortality begins to crack.

Every patient that was randomized to Limb 1, meaning they received the lethal injection, had hot spots appear at sixty minutes prior to injection. These hot spots always merged into one and disappeared at fifty-five minutes prior to injection. All patients randomized to Limb 2 had hot spots appear at fifty minutes prior to their non-lethal injection. Their hot spots merged and disappeared five minutes later.

As predicted, weight loss consistently correlated with disappearance of the hot spots in all patients in both Limb 1 and Limb 2.

His spirits soaring and his mind whirring, Royce begins to scribble down his thoughts in his journal. Alesha whips off the bright, linen scarf covering her now-bald head and jumps around the room like a child who just realized she's been locked in a candy store overnight. He looks up from his notes and they lock eyes, beaming at one another with a joy and awe that only they can share. A lot of people are about to share in the knowledge of these results. Right now, tonight, the discovery is theirs alone. For once, Royce doesn't want to race ahead. He wants to savor this moment.

Royce laughs at Alesha's shimmying around the room. "Okay, dancing queen. Let's walk through what we think this means."

Alesha plops onto a chair and rolls close to him, stopping when they're almost nose to nose.

Royce begins. "In both groups, the soul seems to leave fifty-five minutes before death occurs. In Limb 1 patients, the soul leaves fifty-five minutes before the lethal injection. In Limb 2 patients, the soul leaves forty-five minutes before the non-lethal injection—"

"But that's only because the lethal injection follows it ten minutes later," Alesha interjects.

Right," says Royce, still working to shake off his disbelief. "In all cases, death takes place fifty-five minutes after the soul leaves."

Royce knows it's time for yet another unorthodox leap of, if not faith, then calculated risk-taking. He's going to test his hypothesis further, without alerting the rest of the research team, by changing the protocol again in the next day's assisted suicides.

He selects the final euthanasia of the day for his latest rogue experiment. As Royce stands at the monitor, watching the patient's hot spot leave their body, he sneaks a peek in the protocol book and discovers that this patient is in Limb 2. They are scheduled to receive a non-lethal injection in forty-five minutes, followed by a lethal injection ten minutes later. While Alesha is consumed with comforting the patient, the techs are transfixed by the real-time PET scans. Royce quietly steps away from the patient's bedside and, with swift, clandestine fingers. switches syringes. This patient will receive the lethal cocktail first, and the non-lethal cocktail second.

For the next forty-three minutes, Royce stares at the cardiac monitor. When the patient's first injection fires, he holds his breath. He watches in wonder as the patient's cardiac rhythm remains normal. One, two, three, four, five minutes, and the patient's heart continues to beat. Royce is coming undone, his insides a wild ball of untamed adrenaline, but he manages to hold his composure as the time ticks toward the patient's second injection.

Ten minutes after the first, the patient receives a second injection. Only Royce knows this is the non-lethal saline injection and that this patient has remained alive for a full ten minutes, in the face of all conventional scientific explanation, after receiving a shot that ought to have killed him almost instantly. The cardiac monitor shows a flat line, and Alesha's thin, battered body crumples over the now deceased patient for a final, loving embrace.

There is no doubt now.

The patient will always die fifty-five minutes after the soul leaves.

He wants to tell Alesha, to relieve her of her grief by sharing the remarkable news. But he's hit with a wave of fatigue that takes his breath away. Wiping her eyes as she enters the observation room, Alesha takes one look at him and her face floods with alarm.

"Are you okay?"

Royce finds it difficult to speak through the exhaustion that drains him.

"Work catching up to me. I need some rest." He can barely stay awake. Alesha walks with him to his room. He's in REM sleep with dreams flurrying upon him even before he hits the bed.

CHAPTER 18

A steamy, humid Albuquerque night, and in the ER, the air is heavy and still. It's been one trauma after another: several gunshot wounds and a couple of stabbings, a kid with a gnarly hand and forearm injury from popping off fireworks, a parade of heat-related strokes and cardiac events. Royce hasn't had time to think. The hardships of his patients aside, he's welcomed the nonstop action. The past two months have been an unrelenting throb of planning and activity in the research lab. He and Greg Sanchez agreed that Royce would remain available for shifts just like these; all hands are needed on deck to roll with the relentless presentation of miseries. Royce feels surprisingly fresh; he's enjoying unpacking his ER skills for the night. Night shifts have always suited him, now more than ever. His months of residence in the hospital and his near-total immersion in the lab have made him strangely nocturnal, sleeping until mid-afternoon before putting in an intense stretch of work and falling almost immediately back asleep when he returns to his hospital suite.

He has time to take a quick swig from his water bottle before the next case is upon him, a

victim of an automobile accident. The charge nurse hands him the chart, and he strides into trauma one. Lying on the gurney, the fifty-two-year-old white male is struggling to breathe.

"Please," the man's voice croaks through his gasps, "don't let me die."

As Royce approaches the patient, the faint odor of alcohol hits his nose. "Try to relax. I'm going to take a look at you now."

The man has a football-sized bruise on the left side of his chest. Royce orders the nurse to call for an X-ray and bring a sedative. The patient is hyperventilating now, his panic escalating. Royce leans in and tries to comfort him.

"Easy, now." The pungent smell of alcohol makes his nose curl. "Gentle breath in, slow breath out." The man tries to stall his gasping breaths to little avail. His eyes bounce around in their sockets, his gaze wild with adrenaline and alcohol-fueled anxiety. A wet patch appears and broadens across his jeans.

The X-ray reveals a large amount of blood around the patient's lungs. Royce administers the sedative, and the man's breathing calms. His eyes come to rest on his own feet, sticking out at the end of the gurney in a pair of worn, scuffed sneakers. Quickly, Royce makes an incision in the patient's chest and inserts a large tube to drain the blood.

As the tube goes in, the patient screams in agony, his eyes once again lit with fear.

"I'm sorry, I know how much this hurts. We need to—"

"Don't bother treating this bag of trash like a human being." The state trooper strolls into the room like a tank. Royce gives the officer a glare as the man on the gurney writhes and moans.

"This wonderful specimen just killed two children." The

trooper looms over the patient on the gurney, taunting him with a bitter smile as he fills Royce in on the basic details of the accident. A family of four—two kids in the back, parents up front—were on their way to the airport.

"Headed to Disneyland or grandma's house, who knows," the trooper says, waving his hand with a savage mirth at the man. "Their luggage was coming loose from the rack on top of the car, so dad pulled over to the shoulder. It was dark, you know, so mom and dad got out but told the kids to stay in their seats. Good parents, looking out for their little ones." The trooper's face curls into a snarl. "This shitstain barrels into the back of the car at a speed of . . . Wait, let's make sure this is right." He makes a show of flipping open his notebook to check before saying, "Ninety miles per hour. Boom. The children were killed on impact."

Royce feels like he might vomit.

The trooper motions for Royce to step away from the gurney to talk. "Turns out, this asshole was just released from prison a week ago. Went up for eight years for killing a six-year-old boy while, you guessed it, driving shitfaced."

The voice from the gurney is slurred by intoxication and choked with the blood that Royce knows is still clogging the patient's lungs. "Go fuck yourself," the patient says.

The adrenaline rush of being back on the ER floor, the buoyant, upbeat feeling of being back to saving patients' lives, not taking them, it all rushes away. Royce is overcome by melancholy, dark rivers of anger and despondency suddenly course through his blood. He turns and walks slowly, one deliberate step after the next, until he's standing once more over the wounded man. He stares into the patient's eyes, long enough to see what he needs to see.

"Can you fix me, doc?"

Without a word, Royce turns and walks away, pushing the trauma room door open with both hands.

"Fuck you too!" the patient shouts.

Royce bolts upright in his bed. *Another dream*, he thinks. His next thought is, *Wait, was it?* Did I dream that, or is that what happened last night? He force-marches his mind back in time, but he cannot tell whether he's just awakened from a dream or awakened after a deep sleep that came on the heels of an ER shift where he abandoned a patient. Every day, it gets harder to distinguish between what's real and what isn't, when he's not in the lab. The hospital feels like a cage, and he's the wild, lonely animal trapped inside. He would fight to break free, but he has no desire to do anything except work on his research, and make sure Alesha is okay.

* * *

Royce's risky bank-shot, switching up the lethal and non-lethal injections for the final euthanasia of the set, horrifies many of his research colleagues. A few of the iconoclasts on the team defended his brazen move. In the end, after what feels like an endless debate, all but one of the physicians on the team—Rick Davies resigned in disgust—agreed that the finding must be explored, if only to explain it away properly as a bizarre anomaly. But Royce knows, in the deepest part of himself, it wasn't an anomaly. He knows that the exodus of the soul determines the time and the finality of death, overriding all other inputs, including lethal drugs. He doesn't know how it's so. And he doesn't know how to stop it. But he's on his way to finding out.

Royce races to overhaul the study protocols yet again, now to address the now looming question: how does foreknowledge in patients' minds at the time of their lethal injection affect the timing of the hot spots and the subsequent timing of death?

And Evelyn more than delivers on her promise: with a fresh influx of funding, Royce can scale up his experiment quickly and considerably. For the next round of assisted suicides using the latest protocols, they expand their patient population, yet again increasing the rate of euthanasias.

Patients, all terminally ill and seeking physician-assisted suicide, are divided into two groups. Patients in group one are notified twenty-four hours before their scheduled injection. Patients in group two consent to not know when they will receive their injection. For this second group, injection times are determined by a computer program that sets the time of each injection randomly. All participants receive injections automatically administered through their intravenous drips.

As in the previous protocol, patients in both groups are randomly and blindly assigned to receive either a lethal injection or a saline injection followed by a lethal shot. All participants are now equipped with headcaps and electrodes that track heat and electrical activity of the visual cortex, helping measure temperature and electrical changes sixty minutes before death. Participants' weights are measured by sensitive in-bed scales.

Once again, the results proved the doubters wrong, confirming Royce's hypothesis and the wisdom of his unorthodox interventions. In both groups, all patients died immediately after the lethal injections. The disappearance of the hot spot and corresponding 0.1 kilogram weight loss preceded death by precisely fifty-five minutes, in patients whose lethal injection was scheduled twenty-four hours beforehand and in patients whose lethal cocktail was randomly scheduled immediately before injection.

The most shocking finding, which floored even his most loyal and supportive colleagues, do not surprise Royce in the least.

He knew it was coming.

Among the patients in group two, whose time of death was randomly chosen immediately before lethal injection—and thereby unknowable both to patients themselves and to the research team—the hot spots behind the eyes and in the visual cortex appeared, merged, and migrated in time to disappear from the body at precisely fifty-five minutes prior to injection.

It's a maddening temporal paradox that thrills and delights Royce, even as it is unhinging like a crowbar his last bit of attachment to conventional wisdom about the human body, about the scientific method, about time itself. The exodus of the soul somehow precedes an unknowable time of death by fifty-five minutes.

"How can a future event, the actual injection, which is unknowable until immediately before death, cause an effect in its past—the appearance of the hot spot fifty-five minutes before?"

He's sitting at the bottom of Alesha's hospital bed. Exhaustion and depletion are written across her face; the dark circles under her eyes look like murky pools deep enough to swim in. She's been re-admitted to the hospital after developing chemotherapy-induced neutropenic fever. But her cheeks, which had a sallow pallor when his visit began, are now bright, flushed with excitement and enthusiasm over their latest round of discoveries.

Royce is trying to wrap his conventionally trained scientist's mind around the bend in linear time that their findings suggest. "This utterly violates the adage, 'That which precedes, causes.'"

Alesha nods furiously. Without his exclusive attachment to

conventional scientific principles at the expense of spiritual, extra-sensory and extra-temporal realms, she's three steps ahead of him in her questions. "So, which is the cause of death: soul migration or injection? How can death cause the soul's departure? Time-like-an-arrow, bending backward like a pretzel?"

"Like arriving at a location before departure." Royce dips his head into his hands. His body tingles with recognition, a sense memory, of all the lost time he's encountered since he began this study. All the missing pieces, the jumps, the confusion. Were these experiences, which terrified him as a sign of psychological break-down, in fact signs of the breakthroughs he had yet to make? Had this study itself dislodged his own mind from the illusion of linear time, opened up a portal to another, more flexible and knowing time dimension, before his scientific mind arrived at this incred-ible destination? For months, he's been carrying a secret shame, and a terrible fear, terrified of the decomposition of his mind. All this time, has the time-twisting chaos instead been a strange, remarkable badge of victory that he's only now able to understand?

Alesha, unaware of Royce's personal time-warp demons, continues to think out loud, saying, "The separation of past-present-future is, like, completely trashed, but strangely, the fifty-five minutes is replicated like clockwork. Crazy." Alesha takes a deep breath and her tired eyes sparkling with delight.

For Royce, it's a relief to see her totally engaged in their research questions, a temporary reprieve from thinking about her own condition. Her neutropenic sepsis was the latest in a series of distressing setbacks. The tumors in her brain, metastases of her breast cancer, did not shrink significantly from radiation. She's set to begin another round of chemotherapy as soon as her infection clears. Royce offers a silent *Thank you, Lord* to the universe. He may not ever be a religious man, but as the revelations from his research pile up and as time itself appears to bend back around itself like a serpent eating its tail, Royce himself is now bending toward a spiritual belief he'd never imagined possible.

"The good news is that anomalies open doors to new paradigms and out-of-the-box thoughts." Struck with a thunderbolt of elation and a desire to make her laugh, he leaps up and does a little tap dance, concluding with a hand flourishing in her direction. "Those are your bailiwick, m'dear. What's on your mind?"

Alesha does laugh, but her head remains stationary on the pillow. It's late afternoon, the time when Royce hits his stride. But Alesha is losing steam. He plunks back down on the bed and gently pulls her leg. "Maybe you hope this will finally bridge the gap between Western and Eastern medicine?"

"I'm picturing the quantum world, pure energy at play, where cause and effect can be simultaneous. Time and space conflate, things arriving as soon as they leave, simultaneity at a distance. Maybe we are—you and me and the team—going to open the portal that connects newest physics with traditional medicine."

Royce is pushing his own boundaries by the minute, crashing through walls that have housed his rigid, narrow thinking about the scientific process as well as the nature and purpose of the soul itself. Yet, he is not ready to stray into quantum mechanics. Nor is he willing to make room for a non-mass entity like the psyche as a link in the causal chain. "We've got 0.1 kilograms of mass and a spark of energy, in the form of the hot spots. Maybe there's a connection to mine between that and electromagnetic fields?"

"You're wondering if the 0.1 kilogram of energy can be held in the body by a magnet?" As only she can, Alesha completes his thoughts. It's as though her brain and his are connected, her intuition keen and supportive. Her body remains still, shackled by the invisible bonds of the cancer invading her body. And he remains concerned that her head stays on the pillow, even as her eyes move about. But her words leap into the space between them, blooming like roses crawling up and out of the rich, dark earth.

"Like we've talked about," he says, "all bodily cells contain charged ions that radiate electromagnetic waves."

"Hmmm," Alesha says. The excitement and engagement in her eyes flickers like a dying candle, replaced for a moment by a dull, dim gaze that sends a chill down Royce's spine. She can only muster a whisper, but her thoughts are quick.

"You're picturing a clinical trial and a treatment arm involving magnetism?"

"You know me too well," he says, thinking, *I'd do anything to help you recover.*

CHAPTER 19

Exiting sleep is like a journey from the underworld for Royce, a deep-sea voyage through tumultuous, pitch-black waters of his treacherous slumber, its powerful pressure holding him down as he fights to rise to the surface of consciousness. It takes concerted, almost painful strength to open his eyes. This morning, he pries them open to find a stunning pair of brown eyes looming over him. For an instant, he wonders if his mind has wandered off course into yet another dream.

"You were sewing lacerations in your sleep."

Alesha reaches out to take Royce's hands, which he realizes he's holding above his prone body. She lowers them to his sides. "Is this how you got so good at your job? Treating trauma in your sleep?" She smiles at him, a sweet grin tinged with sadness and concern. Looking up at her, he realizes her cheeks are less sunken than he's seen them in weeks. Her color is better too. Alesha has obviously recovered from her neutropenic sepsis. Chemo is scheduled to resume treatment next week. He shivers thinking about it.

"I think I was having a dream," Royce says, opting not to share with her the details of last night's gory, traumatic ER nightmare, currently flashing through his mind like the final lightning strikes at the end of a furious storm. His dreams are growing ever more vivid and bizarre, and he's still dreaming periodically about the terrifying infiltration of gang members that ends, inevitably, with him slumped on the floor, bleeding out from the chest.

Alesha laughs. "You think? You were talking to yourself—your lips were moving, but I couldn't make out what you were saying. And your eyes were flying around under their lids."

"Just how long were you standing here watching me, exactly?" Royce raises an eyebrow playfully.

"Long enough to see you're never really at rest, even in your sleep." Alesha looks almost mournful. "Are you, Mike?"

Her question stops him cold. He doesn't know what to say, how to explain to her the wild, often morbid ride he takes nightly. His getaway car is a pivot to charm. Even Alesha, who can practically read his mind and sees right through him into the deepest recesses of his own ragged soul, can't resist his charm.

"I'm not going to complain about what you're doing in my bedroom," he gestures with mock-grandeur at the hospital suite that's become home "but, um, what are you doing in my bedroom?"

She holds up his gray suit and navy silk tie.

"It's almost time."

* * *

Side by side, Royce and Alesha walk into the conference room. Her pace is slow; she's still a little weak on her feet. But Alesha was adamant about being here. Today, Royce will pitch his proposal for a clinical trial to the hospital board and executives at the Price Foundation. Walking into the conference room filled with people who among them hold more power and money than most sovereign nations in the world, Royce feels oddly calm. He's nothing like the ragged ball of nerves who presented his initial research proposal over a year ago.

Today, he comes with real data, findings that will rock the medical community and turn the scientific world upside down. These people used to intimidate him. He used to bend to their influence. Not anymore. The crowd gathered in this room is powerful in all the ways that the conventional, linear world defines power. Royce carries with him knowledge and a plan that will lay that conventional world to waste, replacing it with a new order. Stepping into the boardroom with Alesha at his side, he feels like a king among thieves.

Without rising from her seat—Royce knows she'll be damned before she lets this crowd see her bent, quavering body and her need for a cane—Evelyn Price calls the meeting to order at precisely three-thirty and invites Royce to speak.

He stands, his hands clasped in front of him, a small gesture of armoring himself. Otherwise, his body feels like an exquisite cocktail of electrified and calm. In the past, he thought he understood the notion of flow, of being utterly in the zone, riding the waves of skill and knowledge and insight and action with a focus both intense and effortless. Now, about to share his findings for the first time outside his research team, Royce realizes that what he thought he knew of flow, in all those ER shifts patching up patients and pulling them back off the ledge of death, was, as his mother would say, *Hogwash*. Or as Evelyn would say, *Bullshit dressed up for the prom.* Or as Alesha would say, *An illusion.* This, right here, right now, is flow; Royce feels grounded to the earth beneath him and light as a bird.

Remember to meet them in their eyes, a voice whispers. It's a voice so clarion clear, for a moment he thinks it's Alesha. Then he realizes it's coming from inside him. As he delivers his opening remarks, he casts his gaze slowly around the table, like a fly fisherman spooling out a long line, reeling them in, one big fish at a time.

"What would you do if you could live on indefinitely, without the stopwatch of disease and death clicking away at your side? It sounds like a purely, fantastically theoretical question. Today, I'm here to show you how it's possible."

Royce slowly, confidently, walks the group through his findings, beginning by explaining the discovery of the emergence, migration, and disappearance of the hot spots.

"This energy, which we have taken to referring to as the 'soul'—though that is not meant to connote any particular set of religious beliefs—obviously has some mass, since its disappearance consistently results in a 0.1 kilogram weight loss," he says.

He explains the persistence of the soul exiting the body fifty-five minutes before death. "It happens," he explains, "when the patient knows in advance when they are scheduled to die by lethal injection. It also happens when the timing of lethal injection is set randomly and follows immediately thereafter. It happens, too, that death occurs fifty-five minutes after the soul departs," Royce says, the tempo of his speech slowing, "even when the patient receives a lethal injection that ought to kill them immediately."

He watches their eyes go wide, every last pair in the room but for Evelyn's, whose eyes narrow with a greedy, desperate glee that radiates across the room and pierces Royce in his heart. Greg Sanchez puts his hand over his mouth in horrified disbelief. Melinda Dillion, chief of oncology, gasps. The chief of neurology lets out a hoot accompanied by a clownish clap of his hands. A few shouts of shocked protest are quickly shut down by Evelyn, who smacks her cane on the glossy mahogany table to bring to order, no longer seeming to care that her infirmity is on display.

"Enough," says Evelyn. "Dr. Royce, please proceed. Where do you propose we go from here?"

Royce gives her a short, grateful nod for the assist. "We strongly believe that our future work should revolve around attempting to forestall or even terminate the exodus of the soul. It is clear that death always occurs fifty-five minutes after the disappearance of the soul. Can we hold the soul within the brain? And if so, can we stop death from occurring?"

What he does not say, but what his premise implies, is that he's now watching the entire room wrap their brains around, is this: if the soul could be held, fixed, in the brain, will the individual become immortal?

The room remains deadly silent. Royce forges ahead, introducing them to the concept of the magnet as a soul stop. He's aware that many in the group haven't been educated as scientists; but then, what group is educated on the movement of the soul?

"All living cells maintain electrical charges," he explains, "usually negative on the inside and positive on the outside. Although we don't know what the soul is made of, it stands to reason that the soul maintains some type of electrical charge."

Dr. Royce then outlines the treatment protocol that has been his obsession since that day with Alesha in her hospital room. He proposes that they place a large magnet over the patient and attempt to affect the movement of the soul by manipulating the magnetic field.

He stops talking and looks around the room. They're all staring at him, hanging on his every word.

The head of pathology, Dr. Marian Hsu raises a hand. "How will you do that, Dr. Royce?"

Royce welcomes the question; he's more than ready to shift this conversation to an explanation of the clinical trial.

"The treatment arm of this study," he explains, "will consist of participants suffering late-stage cancer, for whom death is imminent. In the active treatment group, patients will be placed into one of two arms. Patients in both of these arms will undergo magnet exposure in hopes of stopping their souls' exodus from their bodies. In arm one, participants are those who choose to die naturally without treatment except comfort care and of course, magnet exposure. In arm two, participants choose to die by lethal injection while being exposed to the magnet. The control group will have no magnet exposure. The time of their injections will remain unknown to them and to the research team, and the time will be selected randomly by a computer that then immediately administers the lethal cocktail through IV drip.

"Small magnetic bars have been placed in heat-detection headcaps currently being used to measure the metabolic energy of the hot spots. The control group will wear heat-detection caps with bars that have no magnetic force. In the treatment groups, magnets among participants are kept in a 'turned off' position by shielding the bars in aluminum until the instant the headcap's heat sensor detects the spark of the hot spot. That rise in metabolism," Royce says, "will trigger the magnet to a 'turned on' position by releasing the bars from their aluminum shields.

"Each participant who survives the fifty-five-minute period—the time left of life after the soul has historically left the body—will have a magnet implanted beneath the skin near the visual cortex. So, we hypothesize, we can continue to hold the energy—the soul—in place over a longer term."

Royce concludes simply. "The endpoint of the trial is overall survival," he says. There's no need to gild the lily. He knows they know he's talking about life without a timestamp on clocking out, about eternal life. And he knows he's got them. Their faces—their eyes—tell him so. A few of them look green with fear, but nobody in this room is going to pull him back from the brink of the threshold he's on, which could change life and death as we know it, including for every single soul in this room. And for one soul in particular, sitting at his side, her chin held high, her clear brown eyes holding back tears.

"You did it, Mike." Alesha wraps her now frail arms around him, and he eases his muscled shoulders down close to her in an embrace. The vote was unanimous, each one cast silently by an individual swimming in a sea of their new existential reality. Their stunned, humbled silence swept them out of the room. Evelyn had been carefully shepherded out by her assistant. It's just the two of them left in the cavernous, dehumanized room where they got the green light to change human life forever.

"We did it." Royce holds Alesha closer, feeling her heart beating fast.

"Fair enough. You'd be nothing without me," she says, grinning up at him. "Where to now?"

"You're going home to rest. I'm going back to the lab."

* * *

Driven by Royce's relentless prodding and encouragement, his research team shifts quickly into the protocols for the now-approved clinical trial, and within two months, they have first stage results to analyze.

As anticipated, all the patients in the control arm who received no soul-stop magnetization died from their illness. Among the two groups being treated with magnets, no one dies. Not of their disease or from lethal injection.

But Royce and the research team are astounded by the differences in the trajectory of survival between the first and second groups. Among the participants in the first group, who chose natural death without lethal injection, a hot spot developed. The magnet triggered and held the hot spot, and death was delayed beyond expectation. Among participants of the second group, who received a lethal injection, no hot spot developed. The magnet never triggered, and the participants survived beyond expectation, despite the injection of lethal drugs that ought to have killed them almost instantly.

Royce and Alesha sit up late at night in the empty lab, sharing paper containers of Japanese takeout and trying to make sense of the thrilling, mystifying results.

Royce states, "The first group, the natural death group, establishes the hypotheticals—the *if clauses*—in the following: *If* the anticipation of death triggers the hot spot, *if* the hot spot triggers the magnet, *if* the magnet holds the 0.1 kilogram mass of the hot spot, and *if* holding the hot spot forestalls deaths. All the *ifs* occur."

"In the second group, the lethal injection group, it makes sense *—if you let go of the idea of a linear sequence of events*—that no death can be imminent. Why? Because no hot spot develops. Why? Because the magnet would trigger and hold the hot spot, which forestalls imminent death—and the emergence of the hot spot. The process is circular."

"I'm still not there, Mike." Alesha pauses to dig her chopsticks into her vegetable gyoza with enthusiasm. Royce's heart soars to see her with an appetite. "I understand the circular logic of what you're describing. It's wild, but I get it. But why the difference between the first and the second group?"

"Maybe the injection is the difference versus natural death. I don't understand it myself. "Not yet." Royce shakes his head. "The long-held certainties, of cause and effect, of linear time, unshaken since the likes of Aristotle proposed them, are crumbling before their eyes. "But death and the progression of symptoms is fore-stalled in all survivors."

Having seen these results, Royce wants to install a magnet immediately in Alesha. But the risks are daunting. Static magnetic fields become pulsating when the participants move through them quickly, and that's what's happening with the external magnet exerting such high force on the patients' heat caps. The voltage created by these pulsating fields causes heat, which can be lethal to the cells of the body. Until he finds a better way to deliver the magnetic force needed to hold the hot spots, he can't put Alesha into the trial.

"The magnet we're using is okay for temporary use. But long-term, it's probably not safe."

It's the primary roadblock right now in the trial. Traditional resistive magnets in the Tesla-range, like the one they're using, are too strong for constant, long-term use. The magnet holds the hot spots, which is remarkable. But his patients won't survive the effects of constant exposure over an extended time. The Earth's magnetic field pulls at one-half a gauss, or 1/20,000th of one Tesla. For comparison: a refrigerator magnet, is around fifty gausses. Magnets used therapeutically for pain-reduction exert a force of about 0.5 Tesla, and the most powerful human-made magnets put out somewhere between seventy-five to one hundred Tesla. The magnets in MRIs, strengthened by resonating radio frequency signals, make paperclips go ballistic at seven Tesla and re-align the nucleus of hydrogen atoms at 1.5 Tesla. Strong magnets can wreak havoc with patients' bodies. But a weaker magnet may not hold the 0.1 kilogram mass of the hot spots.

Crunching through a bowl of edamame, Alesha listens intently to Royce's description of magnetization. When he's finished, she chimes in with, "Are you familiar with what some Eastern religions believe happen as death approaches?"

Royce looks at her blankly and she laughs out loud. "Of course you're not. The body mass, which is yin, separates from its energy, which is yang. This causes energy to concentrate around the head," Alesha snaps her fingers, "which may be reflected in our visual-cortex hot spot.

"Historically," she explains, "this concentration causes the dying person great angst. For centuries, hands-on energy work has relieved patients' anxiety through resonance, which is achieved when a healer can match his vibes, or wave frequency, with the participant's."

Royce feels his mind thrumming with curiosity. Once again, it feels like Alesha is showing him the path. "Even insurance companies cover pain relief via hands-on resonance or acupuncture." Royce has long and quietly harbored an interest in the work of Dr. William Bengston, who focused his bodily energy to cure mice of cancer.

Her excitement growing, Alesha continues, marrying her

thoughts with Royce's own thinking. "This hot spot has a mass and emits electromagnetic waves, and we now know it responds to magnets. I wonder if resonant magnetic waves could hold the 0.1 kilo hot spot?"

"What's your idea?" Royce asks.

"Have you read anything about a resonance frequency device derived from Tesla's medicine, the Rife-Bare device? It generates a field several times stronger than earth's magnetic field, which might influence the 0.1 kilogram of mass?"

Royce winces to himself. He'd just spent ten minutes talking to Alesha about magnetism 101 as though she were an undergrad. "Tell me more."

Alesha explains that the device uses a plasma antenna that detects a target cell's frequency and replicates it, achieving resonance with it, which strengthens its field. "The field is made even stronger by the use of noble gases that may increase uniform polarity," she says. "That can look like billions of protons of the body's hydrogen atoms directing their magnetic fields in a uniform direction. The plasma-generated wave energy is absorbed by a cell, which stimulates, even resuscitates it. Or the cell can re-radiate the energy as heat and structural vibration."

Royce nods enthusiastically. "Re-radiation is the basis of magnetic resonance imaging—MRIs."

MRIs immerse the body in a magnetic field of 1.5 Tesla. The single proton of each hydrogen atom in the body acts like a bar magnet. But the protons' emissions are weak. To strengthen the signal, the MRI sends in a radio frequency that resonates with the protons' (at 1.5 Tesla, the protons' frequency is sixty-four megahertz) which generates a strong, measurable signal from the protons.

Then, the MRI turns the radio frequency signal on and off

repeatedly. When off, without resonation, the magnetic energy of the hydrogen protons in the body decays at different speeds for different bodily matter. The signals from the body's water and blood decay slower than fat, so the signals from water and blood remain more energized longer and show up brighter than fats, which themselves remain brighter than bone and lung tissue. Different types of cancer tissue are likewise distinguishable in the gray-tone images produced by MRIs. Royce shudders as he thinks of Alesha's initial scans, which showed her brain lit up with tumors.

"Yes, exactly," Alesha says, interrupting his dark thoughts and dragging him gratefully back to the present moment. "Like MRIs, the Rife-Bare device transfers energy to a cell by resonating with it. This has two purposes. The first one is interesting, but not useful to us. That being, if the resonant energy is greater than the cell can dissipate, the cell will fail structurally and die. That's great if we're killing cancer cells, but not right for the scope of our research. But the second purpose might apply to us. Moderate resonance is not only healing but also emanates a magnetic field."

"You're wondering if the magnetic aspect of that resonance can calm or hold the hot spot from burning out to avoid it chaotically exploding out of the top of the head?" Royce asks.

"I guess I am." Alesha grins and gives herself a pat on the back. "At the very least, we might reduce pain and anxiety. What do you think?"

Royce is hit with a tidal wave of feeling. He suddenly needs to hold back tears. He wishes, for one long, impossible moment, that he could stop time altogether, right here, right now, up late at night batting around big ideas with Alesha, who's eating and feisty and so alive. He clears his throat, hoping she doesn't notice the wet pools of his eyes.

"I think you're brilliant."

She reaches up to his face and wipes away a tear before it can fall to his cheek.

CHAPTER 20

Jennifer Wright is an almost impossibly beautiful twenty-seven-year-old woman with a heart-shaped face and eyes flecked with gold. To Royce, she looks like an angel in human form. And her demeanor is as sweetly soulful as her appearance. She radiates a pure, almost childlike cheerfulness and optimism despite the dire and cruel circumstances that have brought her into Royce's orbit.

Jennifer is dying from metastatic ovarian cancer. She was diagnosed her senior year of college when a young person of such promise—any young person—ought to be consumed by living fully in the moment and making plans that stretch inscrutably far into the future, as only the young can. Instead, she's been through several excruciating surgeries, chemotherapy, and radiation that have brutalized and weakened her body; remissions that gifted her with fleeting hope; and recurrences and metastases that would have crushed the spirit of someone less intrinsically hopeful.

She doesn't deserve to die, Royce thinks bitterly. None of his patients do. But Jennifer has gotten under his skin. Because she's young and beautiful and sweet, yes. And because he's coming off the agonizing, frustrating losses of several patients that his updated magnet has failed to save.

I'm going to keep Jennifer alive, he thinks, gazing at her through a large observation window. If he can keep Jennifer alive, he'll be one step closer to safeguarding Alesha's life.

Alesha is with Jennifer in the treatment room, where Jennifer lies serenely patient and smiling. Royce doesn't trust himself to venture in and talk to her again, moments before she undergoes this most experimental treatment. He's afraid he'll make promises he won't be able to keep.

In the wake of his provocative and enlightening conversation with Alesha about resonance, Royce practically drives his engineers into the ground to revamp the magnet, and the methodology for deploying it. He hopes to hold patients' hot spots in place without exposing them to potentially lethal side effects.

Their innovation, the hybrid magnet, sits in the room adjacent to the one where Royce now stands, preparing to observe Jennifer's PET scan. Their latest innovation employs traditional resistive magnets with superconducting magnets to lower the heat generation, utilizing the same resonating technology found in MRI scanners. The hybrid magnet's power can be increased simply by the push of a button, allowing an ever-increasing magnetic field. Royce's intent is for the resonating magnetic field to alter the course of the soul without harming the patient. But Royce's initial attempts to halt the flight of the soul from the body with the hybrid magnet have failed.

. . .

Jennifer is not the first patient to undergo exposure to the magnetic field. That tragic honor belonged to Jimmy Williams, a twenty-eight-year-old man with a baby face and metastatic testicular cancer. Royce stood beside the young man's bedside in the moments before, calling up all his experience as a compassionate healer to help ease Jimmy's anxiety, even as he felt a kindred storm of nerves raising havoc in his own mind.

"I'll be able to see the effects that the magnet has on your soul in real time, right here on this monitor." Royce gestured to the screen positioned near the bed where Jimmy lay. "That sedative we gave you should be kicking in any minute. You won't feel any discomfort. And it's going to help you relax."

Jimmy gave Royce a grateful nod, still too frightened to speak, as Alesha clasped his hand in her own. Nobody else can comfort these terminal patients like she can. Alesha doesn't simply bring to their bedsides compassion born of training and experience. She brings an authentic, boundless love and the understanding and solidarity that she shares with them as a fellow cancer patient.

Royce glanced at the clock on the wall. They were about to reach the sixty-minute-mark before Jimmy's scheduled lethal injection. It was almost time. As soon as the PET scan picked up the emergence of the hot spots behind the eyes, the magnetic field would turn on. And Royce would once again attempt to alter what God has so carefully contrived.

Jimmy lay motionless, less visibly anxious thanks to the sedative, but his eyes still flashing in frantic anticipation as the PET scanner revealed the hot spot behind his eyes. A technician flipped the switch, turning on the magnetic field. For five minutes that felt as though they stretched into years, Royce stared at the monitor. Standing next to him, Alesha had eyes only for Jimmy;

her gaze never wavered from his. Not once did she glance at the screen that held Royce's full attention.

At the fifty-five-minute mark, Royce watched as the soul, completely unaffected by the magnet, left Jimmy's body. He turned to look at Jimmy. No words passed between them. There was no need. Jimmy saw it in Royce's eyes. He knew his soul had escaped his body. Tears welled in Jimmy's eyes, and beneath the dampness Royce saw acceptance settling in, as Jimmy's gaze began to take on the faraway look Royce had seen so many times before. He was ready to die. Royce leaned in and hugged Jimmy gently and tightly before kissing him on the cheek. Alesha stepped in front of Royce to gather Jimmy in her arms, subtly blocking him out and releasing him from the need to be the primary comfort for their patient in his final minutes. He felt grateful.

Fifty-five minutes later, when the lethal cocktail was released and Jimmy peacefully passed, Royce wasn't discouraged. He'd instructed the technician to limit the magnet's power to only a 25-Tesla magnetic field. He planned to turn up the field to the magnet's maximal capability, if that's what it would take to stop the soul from departing.

After Jimmy's death, two more patients underwent exposure to the resonating magnetic field, one at 30 Tesla and the next at 35 Tesla. Both times, the soul marched on, leaving the body to die within the hour. After the third patient died—the dignified, stoic, grandfatherly Joe Pappas, who crumbled and wept like a child when he saw in Royce's eyes the news that the magnet had failed to trap his soul—Royce demanded that the PET scan monitor be moved to an observation room. He told himself it was for his patients' sake. The truth was, he couldn't bear to be the bearer of news of his own failure.

.   .   .

I will not fail with Jennifer. Royce stands in the observation room like a soldier readying for battle. The hot spots behind Jennifer's eyes appear, and the technician activates the magnetic field. Royce has started Jennifer's exposure at a whopping 40 Tesla. But he soon learns that matters not to a soul with a mission. Struggling to keep hold of his frustration, he watches for a full minute as the hot spots behind her eyes and in her visual cortex crawl toward one another. After another full minute, they are merged into a single hot spot.

Royce knows what is about to happen. This mass of energy that holds the crux of life will make its way upward and out of Jennifer's body. His mind is a simmering pot of impotent rage that is about to boil over.

Another thirty seconds, and Jennifer's soul is midway through its departure. Royce's desperation—to save Jennifer's life, to prevent his own failure—overflows.

"I will not let her die!" A guttural scream unleashes from his body at the same instant he lurches to his right and pushes the magnet to its maximum capacity, elevating the magnetic field to 45 Tesla. A couple of techs in the room react with alarm, and Royce shouts them down with a voice loud enough that Alesha, at Jennifer's bedside, turns toward the observation window. The technician operating the magnet shoots him a look of alarm, and Royce turns his back on her.

He looks back to the PET scan monitor. For the first time since they implemented the hybrid magnet, he sees a low-frequency, to-and-fro motion playing across the screen. It's as if there's a struggle between the powerful force of the magnet and the stubborn, determined intention of the soul.

And then it happens.

The soul stops moving.

Royce drops his hand from the keypad that controls the magnet strength. He stares at the screen in disbelief. For a moment, he wonders if he is dreaming or having another dissociative episode where time breaks open like a sinkhole. He wiggles his feet in his running shoes; he feels like he's in his own body, not traveling a dreamscape. But his dreams sometimes feel meant to deceive him.

He looks around the observation room and sees the technicians and radiologist staring at the PET scan, with looks of awe splashed across their faces.

This is real.

This is happening.

For what feels like an eternity, Royce and his staff watch the soul idle in neutral. Fifty-seven minutes pass after the magnet yanked the soul to a stop. Jennifer then receives her scheduled lethal injection.

Ten more minutes pass and the soul hasn't budged.

Royce enters the treatment room so elated he feels like he's hovering above the ground. Jennifer has fallen fully unconscious from the sedative effects of the cocktail. He approaches her slowly, noting again her angelic presence. The long-lidded lashes closed over gold-flecked eyes, post-chemo hair growing back in cherubic curls. The simple, noble joy that emanates from her being.

He can't bring himself to look at Alesha. Not yet.

He gently places his fingers on the inside of Jennifer's wrist. There it is. A strong heartbeat that makes it clear: for now, she has evaded death.

Royce removes his hand from Jennifer's radial pulse. A smile breaks across his face and his tears begin to flow. They flow as if he had saved a lifetime of tears for this one occasion.

He turns to Alesha. Looking in her eyes is like looking in a mirror. Tears stream down her face, and he sees his own amazement and elation reflected in her gaze. He opens his arms, and she steps into his embrace. Holding her body close to his, he can't tell whose pounding heart he feels knocking on his chest.

"You did it," she whispers.

"We did it."

Royce and Alesha sit together at Jennifer's side, their hands almost grazing, waiting for the effects of the sedative to wear off. As Jennifer begins to come around, Alesha leans in and whispers to her something Royce cannot hear. The smile on Jennifer's face begins even before her eyes flicker open.

"I have some good news and some bad news," Royce says. "The bad news is we were not able to complete the physician-assisted-suicide as promised."

Jennifer lets out a loopy giggle. She's awake, but not fully conscious.

Royce continues. "The good news, my dear, is that you may no longer be dying." *As long as I can keep this magnet functioning*, he thinks, *she may never die*.

"There's more bad news to share," Royce explains. "Until our engineers can finish creating a miniature-sized magnet to implant in your brain that's capable of generating the same magnetic field as the hybrid magnet, you will have to remain on this table." Jennifer giggles again. It's clear that she can't yet understand the ramifications of what he's saying to her. Her sedative will wear off, but grasping the significance of her new reality may be hard. No one has ever been where Jennifer is now, though he hopes more will follow soon, including the remarkable woman standing next to him.

* * *

The team's engineers go to work that night to develop a tiny replica of the hybrid magnet and strategize about how to dissipate the enormous amount of heat generated by a continuously operating magnet. Royce stalks their progress, veering in and out of their laboratory, his mood swinging from jubilation to fury and back again with each pass. When he's not huddling with the engineers, Royce is watching Jennifer's PET scan from the observation room. He lifts his eyes every so often to watch her as she lies on the table, immobilized, tethered to the magnetic force that's keeping her soul in check and her body alive. *This is no way to live*, he thinks. But the alternative is unacceptable.

Several days and nights tick by, the engineers working around the clock, Royce wearing down the floor between the observation room and the laboratory. He can't remember the last time he felt the cool sheets and soft cushion of his own hospital bed.

As the sun sets on the fourth full day that Jennifer's soul has been harnessed by the magnet, the lead technician greets Royce with a dire look that makes his stomach drop. The magnet has begun to fail. It can no longer generate a 45-Tesla field.

"How long do we have?" Royce asks, thinking about sprinting to the engineer's lab to check their progress.

"We don't know," the technician says plainly. "We've lost 0.5 Tesla in the last two hours. But the loss may accelerate. And we don't know how much lower we can go before—"

"Before the soul cuts loose." Royce finishes the thought.

He finds Alesha, and together, they go to inform Jennifer about what's to come.

Royce feels shame and grief at his failure. He can barely form the words of an explanation to his patient. *I wasn't fast enough. I didn't think hard enough. My best was not enough to save you,* he thinks, as he explains the faltering magnet and what that means for her soul and her life.

A thin river of tears falls from her eyes to the table. She blinks at them, her lips searching for something to say. When she cannot, she rolls her head away from them, her angelic, gold-flecked eyes staring at a horizon beyond the blank wall.

Royce kisses her on the cheek and retreats to the observation room. Alesha remains next to Jennifer, stroking her soft curls.

On the bright screen, Royce watches as the magnetic field wanes and Jennifer's soul passes. Fifty-five minutes later, so does her life.

The moment her life expires, Royce is overtaken by a sudden and overwhelming exhaustion. For a moment, he wonders if his own life is draining too. The observation room empties out as the technicians file into the treatment room to perform Jennifer's post-mortem assessments. Royce is momentarily alone, so disoriented by his sudden fatigue that he can't find the door. As his legs begin to give out beneath him, an arm slips around his waist.

"Let's get you to bed." Alesha leads him gently out of the observation room. They walk slowly the long hallway to the elevator, riding in silence to the floor that houses his suite. He wants to protest, feels ashamed that this cancer patient is practically carrying him. But he's too tired. Alesha helps him into bed, where he falls into a deep sleep.

In his dream, Amanda stands in the doorway of his med school apartment, wearing his favorite Lobos sweatshirt, her curly hair wild and unkempt after a night of sex followed by argument. She's trying to look angry, but Mike Royce can see what she really wants is for him to stop her from leaving. He can't. He won't. It's late, and he's got an anatomy lab exam in two days. They've been going in circles all night. She wants to know what they all want to know: why can't he open up, why won't he let her in. He explains, over and over, "I'm already open, you know me, this is *me*." *Is there supposed to be something else, something more*, he wonders to himself.

"You're broken, and you break things," she tells him, her eyes glaring, showing him that she wants her words to hurt and that she means what she says. "Just because you can't admit it doesn't mean it's not real."

CHAPTER 21

"Dr. Royce, we need you in here."

The call from Nurse Santiago comes at him before he can even put his bag down. Judging from the tone of Susan Santiago's voice, this morning's ER shift is getting off to an intense start. He wishes he weren't on shift this morning. Upright and in his clinical element, he's still feeling the pull of sleep determined to drag him back into that dark, powerful, dream-filled abyss. But Greg Sanchez has done him a solid, keeping him off the ER rotation as much as possible. Royce feels bound to do his part. He needs to free his mind from those murky waters and get through the day.

What he encounters when he arrives at Susan Santiago's side does more than wake him up; it knocks him cold. Royce opens the trauma room door and comes face to face with death, bitter and unforgiving.

The ten-year-old girl who lies motionless on the gurney is exquisitely beautiful, a pure innocent. Her blank eyes are half-mast, and her skin is taking on a blue-purple tint. She is dead. By Royce's estimation, she's been dead for at least thirty minutes.

The technician is about to begin CPR again, but Royce waves him off. As he listens to Nurse Santiago explain the patient's history, passed along by the paramedics who brought her in, Royce gazes into the child's empty eyes, trying and failing to force down the painful lump in his throat. Her parents told the paramedics the girl was well when she went to bed last night. When she didn't come down for breakfast at her usual time, they attempted to wake her, and she wouldn't come around.

Royce's exam of the child's body is slow and deliberate; sadly, there is no reason to rush his work. Nurse Santiago is at his side, and sorrow looms between them like a dark web, holding them close. Searching carefully for any evidence of trauma, he trains a penlight on her vacant eyes, pupils dilating. He looks inside her mouth, nose, and ears. He picks up each limp hand and examines her fingers, palms, and wrists. He does the same with her feet, toes, and ankles. He gently rolls the girl on her side. In a sudden, dark explosion, blood hurls from the child's mouth, splashing Nurse Santiago's white sneakers and flooding the floor around her.

"Oh my god," the nurse screams. She catches herself and instantly apologizes for being spooked.

"It's okay." Royce gives her a long look to let her know she's not the only one feeling unnerved. "You okay?"

The nurse nods and Royce resumes his exam.

He parts the hair at the nape of the girl's neck to inspect the upper cervical spine and he notices a purple patch of flesh, darker than the rest of her skin. Royce feels his stomach drop.

"Get an X-ray tech in here, please."

Life in the ER contains endless surprises. But it's the constants, the acts of horror that show up again and again, that often deliver the most wrenching gut punches. The X-ray shot of the girl's cervical spine reveals her cause of death. Royce is staring at a second cervical vertebra that's been crushed from blunt trauma. "Where are the parents now?" he asks Nurse Santiago.

"In the private waiting room." She turns away, unable to look at the image of the child's shattered spine for another second.

Royce takes a last look at the girl, who could almost be mistaken for sleeping peacefully, if it weren't for her blood splattered on the floor below the gurney. Then he makes a beeline to the unit secretary's desk. He hands her the girl's chart and nods in the direction of the family waiting room. "Call the police."

The nurse winces and lets out a here-we-go-again sigh. The constants take their toll on everyone.

As fast as his long strides will carry him, Royce walks to the break room. Closes the door behind him. Only when he's alone does he allow himself to weep, a flood of frustrated, defeated tears.

The rest of Royce's shift unfolds in a blur. The next thing he knows, it's three-thirty, and his phone is pinging. His heart is instantly in his throat, a cold dread rising fast in his body. Alesha is upstairs, an inpatient again after experiencing spasms of unbearable pain. Her most recent PET scan showed new metastases; this time tumors on her spine.

When he sees the name flash across the screen, his heart retreats and the icy wave of fear recedes, replaced with a sudden burst of anticipation. It's Rudy, now the lead engineer on the research team.

"What's the word?" Royce asks.

"It's in."

Hallelujah, Royce thinks. He needed this news.

"I'll be right up."

Royce takes the stairs two at a time up several flights to the lab, barely breaking a sweat, a gasping Lucy trailing behind him. The first patient has received the implant of the new, miniature magnet. The implanted magnet is a tiny, more powerful version of the hybrid magnet that held Jennifer's soul for four days.

The patient—Hudson Minette, Royce confirms after a quick glance at his chart—rests on the table in the induction room. His lethal injection is scheduled for five p.m. The observation room is crowded with research staff, all gathered for this seminal event, all staring at the PET scan images, anxiously awaiting the appearance of the hot spots. Royce watches as a nurse stands at Hudson's side and thinks of Alesha. Her illness has diminished her role on the research team, but she's been indefatigable in her determination to stay involved despite the exhausting rigors of her treatment and the painful, gutting progression of her disease. In true Alesha form, she's prioritized their patients and attended as many assisted suicides as possible, taking her place at their sides, riding the waves of emotion with them, despite the toll. Her absence at Hudson's bedside feels odd and disconcerting.

Precisely at four, the PET scan shows the hot spots light up behind Hudson's eyes.

"You want to do the honors?" The lead tech asks Royce.

He steps forward, remotely activates the magnet implanted in Hudson's brain, beginning the impossible wait. There's a single question circling unabated his mind right now: Will the magnet hold?

He doesn't have to wait long for an answer. Twenty seconds later, as he's reminding himself to breathe, Royce sees the same low-frequency, to-and-fro motion of the hot spot that he observed on Jennifer's scan.

Seconds later, the motion ceases. The soul is still.

Fifty-nine minutes later at the scheduled time, the nurse pushes the lethal cocktail. As everyone expects, it causes only sedation. As Hudson sleeps off his drug-induced slumber, his heartbeat remains strong.

The observation room erupts in celebration. Someone hands Royce a paper cup of champagne. But amid the techs and engineers and research fellows hugging and cheering, Royce feels like an island unto himself. He's worked so hard and waited so long for this moment. He's devoted his entire being to getting here, and only now does he realize that a part of him never thought it would happen. Having done what he set out to do, what nobody believed was possible, he finds himself in a strange, suspended animation.

It's only hours later, waiting at Hudson's bedside for the patient to regain consciousness, that Royce settles back into his body, and an excitement he's never felt before ignites every cell.

Hudson's eyes flutter, and Royce greets him with a jubilant smile.

"You're here, buddy," he says.

Royce then explains what was, until a few hours ago, unexplainable: as long as this implant remains functional, he, Hudson Minette, may truly be immortal.

To his surprise, the man looks more concerned than elated.

"Does that mean my multiple sclerosis is gone? Is the pain gone now, for good?"

Dr. Royce drops his head. It's a good question with no good answer. He tells Hudson the truth: he doesn't know if the man's suffering will be any less than it was before the implant. Royce can see in Hudson's eyes what the man's next question will be. It's a request he cannot let the man utter.

"Please, please. Just give me some time. I know it's all scary and strange, but let's see what happens—let's see how you do—before we make any decisions about whether to continue."

Hudson is firm. "I don't care about living forever—hell, I don't care about living for another month—if I have to live in that kind of pain."

Together, they come to an agreement: if Hudson's condition is not significantly improved in the next sixty days, Royce will turn off the magnet and help him die a peaceful death on his terms.

With the implant working successfully to hold the hot spot, the study's protocols will change once more. From here on out, there will be two new treatment groups. The first group will receive implants. The second group will have their souls held in place by individual exposure to electromagnetic fields using a plasma-tube resonator based on the Rife-Bare device.

No patients in either treatment group will receive lethal injections. For the first time, his patients have a chance to live. Perhaps to live indefinitely. They didn't get here in time to save Jennifer. But they're here now in time to save others. *Including Alesha*, Royce hopes with an evangelical fervor.

CHAPTER 22

"I couldn't breathe. It was pitch-black . . . all around, except for a . . . tiny sliver of moonlight creeping through a gap . . . in the window curtains. But I couldn't turn my head . . . to see if anyone was in the room . . . with me . . . and I couldn't utter a sound . . . or cry, or moan . . . for help. There I was . . . trapped in my body . . . suffocating."

The patient, Ivan Fornier, takes a gasping breath and releases it slowly, savoring the luxury of lungs filled with air. He's describing a dream that took him back to one of the most terrifying moments in his journey with ALS, a night when his tracheostomy tube somehow became disconnected, leaving him lying prone and unable to adequately oxygenate on his own.

Telling the story of his dream takes painstaking effort, as Ivan pauses between words, allowing his trach tube to fill his lungs with air. The fact that he's able to speak at all is a medical miracle. A month ago, Ivan was reliant on a speech-generating device.

Around the room, patients nod and murmur in solidarity. Every one of Royce's patients has a story like this to tell.

"How did you feel when you woke up?" The question comes from Alesha.

"Disoriented . . . relieved to be awake. Confused . . . it felt so real . . . like it was happening again for the . . . first time. Happy . . . as hell . . . to have this magnet in my . . . head."

Laughs ripple around the room.

Over the past thirty days, thirty-five patients have received magnet implants. For the first time since his research began, Royce is helping patients live, not die. To his profound joy, if not surprise, all patients in both the magnet and plasma-tube resonator groups are alive. And remarkably, these patients are doing more than just surviving on a gurney. In the past month the team has observed no side effects in patients from either treatment group. And every single clinical indicator reveals that their patients are genuinely healthier. Patients in both the implanted magnet group and the group exposed to electromagnetic waves via the plasma tube all talk about feeling full of energy and experiencing less pain. Some of the elderly patients have noticed their wrinkles receding. Others, like Ivan, are regaining function. Patients' lab work confirms their extraordinary rebound: across the board, their vital signs and disease-related laboratory abnormalities have improved.

For Royce, it is a profound delight, like no other he's known, to see his patients feeling more physically vigorous and less shackled by pain with each passing day. There is only one shadow clouding this bright landscape. Among patients in both treatment groups, a confounding, disturbing pattern has surfaced. Every one of his patients is now dreaming intensely and vividly, and often, they're having nightmares. The dreams seem to have an escalating, progressive quality: the patients who've had their implants the longest are experiencing the most intense, incessant dreams. And, as patient after patient explains to Royce and the researchers, the dreams don't really feel like dreams at all.

His patients come from wildly diverse backgrounds. The oldest among them in their eighties; the youngest barely in their twenties. They're bound by a shared reality of terminal disease. But otherwise, there's little that's uniformly similar about them, in experience or education or outlook or psychological disposition. And yet, they're all having an eerily similar experience in their dreamscapes, of revisiting the major events of their lives.

Another patient chimes in. "I had a horrifying—I mean truly terrifying dream where I relived the day my heart stopped," the patient says. "And then, the next night, I dreamed about the last time I had sex with my wife, before I got too weak. That was a good dream, I gotta say."

"I've had some of those, too," says a middle-aged woman across the room. "Not the sex part, though I wouldn't mind," she snorts a laugh, "but some really beautiful dreams of being with my kids, playing with them like I did when I was healthy. Last night, I had a dream about playing soccer with my best friend from grade school that made me feel total joy, like I was an actual kid again." Her smile is wistful. "It was hard to wake up from, honestly. But the bad dreams are . . ." She shudders, the smile wiped from her face. ". . . really bad."

More nods of empathy and understanding ripple across the room. Many patients report feeling joy and bliss at reliving beautiful moments from their lives. But the return to the dark, harrowing moments of their past brings them fresh rounds of pain, grief, and sometimes terror. And they are all disturbed by the genuineness of the re-experiences that fill their dreamscapes.

· · ·

As the days post-implantation go by and as patients stories accumulate, it becomes clear to Royce and Alesha: the patients in their treatment arms are reliving their pasts in reverse order. The most recent events are being visited soon after implantation. Each day thereafter, an event is being recalled that occurred earlier in their lifetime.

"My own experience, Mike, is that these dreams seem to be helping me resolve past traumas from my life." Alesha and Royce are taking a walk along the residence hallway, long after the other patients have returned to their rooms. Royce saw that the implantable magnet helped Hudson stay alive without adverse effects, even providing relief from his MS symptoms. Royce began lobbying Alesha to receive an implant. She'd been resistant at first. She wanted to give her treatment, a combination of conventional chemotherapy, radiation, and the Eastern medicinal practices she'd brought into her treatment plan in consultation with her oncologist, a chance to work. And she was determined to keep working on the study. After a lot of prodding from Royce, his promise to keep her on the research team, and a reminder of the sobering prognosis that she'd received from her oncologist, Alesha agreed. She'd been the tenth patient to have a magnet implanted.

"The first dreams I had were about the cancer coming back— no surprise there. It was horrible to relive it all—discovering the recurrence, the sepsis, the cancer spreading and not responding to treatment, feeling so sick and so weak. And being so scared." Alesha pauses, and Royce sees for an instant the fear reignited in her eyes.

"But after a while, I felt a lightness about it all, a sort of peace and freedom. And that's when my dreams started progressing backward. Like, last night, I was dreaming about being with you in the ER, when we had those school shooting victims come in. Remember?"

He does. But she's got him thinking about another ER dream. His own recurring dream that's plagued him for so many months now. He's never told Alesha about the ER shooting nightmare. But it all comes out now, in a flood of description: the slain boy on the gurney, the swarm of angry, hooded young men spreading out in the trauma room like violent flies, the awful instant of staring into the barrel of the gun, the terrible shredding of his own flesh, the blackening of his world into nothingness.

"I re-dream it," Royce says, feeling puzzled and defeated. "It's like I'm stuck there."

Alesha reaches out a hand to grab his. "Maybe it's too traumatic. You keep repeating it and you can't get through to the rest of your past."

"But, Alesha, it's not like your dreams or the other patients' nightmares. Mine never actually happened. It's a déjà vu, an illusion of memory, not the real thing. And its reference feels—I don't know, infantile? Like, somehow, it's my first and last trauma—my only trauma. How does that make any sense?"

"It could be, absolutely. Like a cumulative, symbolic representation of your traumas. An uber-dream, maybe?" Alesha looks thoughtful. "In terms of our patients, I do think these dreams could be restorative, even curative for them. They may be essential to not only the psychological healing process, but to their physical healing, too."

Royce can't deny that their patients seem to be thriving, and undergoing some sort of profound biological rejuvenation or recovery that he doesn't yet understand. It's true for Alesha as well. She's due for another round of scans soon. But she's out of bed more often than she was a month ago. She's not in pain, and her physical strength seems to be coming back. She and Royce have fallen into the habit of taking long walks around the study's residence floor at night. And in the past week, she's been able to return to work on the research project. But Royce remains fixated and ever-alert to her changed body, with its frail appearance and unsteady movements.

"We're going to want to develop some methodology for tracking how these dreams interact with our patients' health trajectories." She pauses before continuing, as if spooked by the pure, absolute uncertainty of what lays ahead for the study patients and for her. "And their longevity."

"Agreed."

Royce is still not sure what to make of the dreams or how to manage them. For now, he's prepared to continue along with the current program.

His decision to maintain the status quo doesn't last long. Over the next month, the patients are dreaming more and more. They're now spending approximately sixteen hours per day in a dream state. As they re-experience seminal events from their past, they're physically acting out the events that are taking place in their dreams. Royce watches a patient tackle a research tech to the ground, reliving a nighttime robbery on the street. A woman screams obscenities at the patient next to her, convinced he's her abusive father. A twenty-one-year-old man sobs in the lap of a seventy-year-old fellow patient, begging her not to leave, as he dreams of his high-school sweetheart breaking up with him. To Royce, it seems as if these patients are psychotic for two-thirds of every day, unaware of their current reality and incapable of functioning in the present.

And then, like clockwork, the strange, inexplicable storm of dreaming stops. And for the remaining eight hours of the day, his patients are conscious and lucid, thriving with energy and vitality, happy to be alive while still taunted and tormented by recollections of their time spent in their dream world.

It's a fascinating, confounding daily cycle to observe. Royce himself cycles through feelings of excitement, concern, and pity for his patients, who are somehow simultaneously privileged beyond measure, free of the shackles of mortality, and imprisoned within the hospital and their own minds.

When he and a tech are barely able to stop a patient from leaping out a window in the midst of a dream of a childhood house fire, Royce calls an emergency meeting of the research team, bringing a sleep specialist in to consult with them. The team agrees that the patients are becoming a danger to themselves and to others. For their safety, the residence ward will be locked down, and 24/7 staff and security will be on-site to keep patients from hurting themselves and each other.

"I wonder if maybe the resonance is being strengthened by having so many patients in such close proximity to each other." Royce and Alesha are taking their late-night stroll along the residence floor. Their evening chats have become a high point of Royce's day. He looks forward to them especially now that Evelyn no longer wants to see him. Their regular evening get-togethers stopped abruptly, to his dismay and concern. The only reason he can think of for her behavior is that her condition has grown worse. But he's in the dark; her assistant has not returned any of his calls.

"And that's creating the wild dreaming? Maybe so," Alesha muses.

He takes her arm and guides her out of the path of a pair of oncoming technicians. She's distracted, and he knows she's preoccupied with her own distressing dream from the night before. But she won't tell him what it was about. It's impossible for Royce not to wonder whether it involves him.

"Maybe if we separate them, or at least create smaller pods of patients that interact." The magnet-participants and plasma-tube resonators are currently isolated on two separate floors, intermingled with unidentified control-group participants. Patients in the control group are receiving no treatment, no exposure to magnetic resonance. Yet they are dreaming, too.

The more he thinks about it, the more he thinks it may be necessary for each patient to have their own Faraday space, to protect them from one another's individual electromagnetic fields. Right now, it's impossible to gauge each patient's EMF exposure.

He's got to find a way to send a message to Evelyn. They're going to need more space and more money.

Over the next few weeks, Royce is relieved to see a new and tentative calm settle over the residence ward. Patients are still dreaming wildly, but the intensity and duration of their dreams seems to have plateaued. Sixteen hours in a relentless dream state, and eight hours of consciousness and lucidity. They tend to act out verbally and physically in their dreams, but the security precautions have kept everyone safe.

As they reach the two-month mark after magnet implantation, Royce decides it's time to re-image the implant patients with the PET scanner. The invigorating health of his patients and the relative stability of the residence ward has freed up his curiosity; he wants to investigate the state of the hot spots, being held so seemingly steadfast by the magnets.

One by one, he brings each of the thirty-five implant patients to the PET scan. Their brain scans take him by surprise. There are no hot spots to be seen anywhere in the brain. The soul energy has vanished.

Royce jumps into rationalizing the startling scans. His patients are no longer at the brink of death. It's logical, then, that the hot spots disappear. After all, he recalls, from the first time they identified the hot spot, this soul energy was never visible until sixty minutes before death. Alone in the lab, Royce concludes that magnetism doesn't so much hold the hot spot in place as it allows energy to flow. But what does that mean? However logical this conclusion is, it doesn't satisfy Royce. He can't explain the source of dreaming. He can't explain the disappearance of the hot spot. He feels like he's charting a ship through coal-black waters. It's maddening not to understand what's happening to the soul energy.

He's exhausted, and the strange g-force of sleep is tugging at him. But he can't rest until he knows more. He brings one of the patients back to the PET scanner. Georgia Wheeler, a sixty-seven-year-old woman with pancreatic cancer, looks worried when he asks her to come back with him for a second scan. Royce reassures her that there's nothing amiss with her initial results.

"I can ask someone else if you'd prefer," he says, hoping to allay her concerns. "This is purely informational for me—you'd be doing me a favor, really."

Georgia's concern turns to enthusiasm; she's suddenly eager to help.

With her comfortably settled, Royce begins scanning Georgia's brain. As before, he sees no hot spot. He scans her neck and continues down her body.

When he sees the hot spot at her navel, his heart skips a beat. He stares in wonder as he watches the soul energy crawls slowly downward.

With a rush of insight that makes him lightheaded, it all makes sense.

* * *

"I can't believe we were so short-sighted," Royce is practically screaming as he walks with Alesha's arm in his down the residence hall.

Alesha shushes him; it's close to the witching hour, and some of the patients are already falling into their sixteen-hour slumber.

Royce drops his voice, but his tone remains manic. "We assumed that the soul suddenly appears behind the eyes sixty minutes before death. When, in fact, *the hot spot is in the body all the time*—it just doesn't reach the head until the sixty-minute mark."

Alesha's face lights up with questions, but she can't get a word in before Royce launches into his new hypothesis.

"It must be that when life begins, the soul starts out somewhere in the lower portion of the body. As life goes on and a person comes closer to death, the soul moves upward, until it leaves and the person dies."

He stops in the middle of the hallway and turns to her, feeling the white-hot fire of discovery running through his blood. "Don't you see? This explains the dreams."

"How do you mean?"

"The magnets have forced the soul downward toward its origin—"

Alesha's own eyes catch fire as she realizes the significance of Royce's discovery. "And as the soul travels backward—" She's practically shouting now herself. "—so, too, does the patient live their life—backward."

Royce's mind is awash with new questions. "How far back do you think it can go, the soul? Surely, it's got to stop at the beginning of the person's life. And where does the soul go when it leaves? And where is the soul just before it is present in a newborn?" In all his obsessive efforts to keep death at bay, he's shocked to discover how little he's thought about the natural life of the soul.

"Let's go back to the lab, what do you say?" No sooner than he utters the words, he's hit with a wave of fatigue so intense it makes him stop in his tracks and throw a hand up against the wall. These long days, and these giant, magnificent questions, have him reeling, he thinks. "Maybe I ought to get you back to your room in the ward," he says to Alesha, looking sheepish.

"How about I get you to your room? You're not looking long for this world."

Alesha walks him directly to his bed, where he feels the bliss of his body hit the soft mattress, barely hearing the door lock turn as Alesha slips out before he tumbles into sleep.

CHAPTER 23

"God, save this soul," Royce whispers under his breath. Nothing in his residency training, almost nothing in his decade of experience on the ER floor, had prepared Dr. Royce for a sight such as this. If ever there were a place in medicine for taking an individual out of his misery with a bullet to the brain, this is it, he thinks.

The bloodied creature being wheeled into the trauma room in front of him only somewhat resembles a person. Only the agonizing, ceaseless moaning coming from what remains of this once intact human confirms that this is indeed a human. The paramedic struggles to speak as he describes what happened. It doesn't take long. A train hit this thirteen-year-old boy, who'd been riding his bike along the tracks. The traumatized train engineer told EMS that the boy's front wheel got stuck.

Steeling himself, Royce takes stock of the boy. The impact of the train partially decapitated the right side of his head. It also tore off most of the entire right side of his body.

The trauma surgeon, Dr. Alan Sterling, arrives promptly on

Royce's heels. The nurse, speaking through tears as she holds the child's remaining wrist, informs them that the patient no longer has a palpable pulse. But the child's barely audible death rattle, a wet, gargling moan, reveals that the patient still clings to life. Royce feels a wave of nausea riding up in his throat. He cannot fathom what to do, and he cannot abide doing nothing.

"You've got to get this kid's chest open, now." His command to the surgeon comes out as a scream.

The surgeon gives Royce a withering look. "He's pulseless, and half his body is gone from blunt trauma," Dr. Sterling shouts back at him. "Cracking his chest open is futile—and contraindicated. There's nothing left to save, Dr. Royce."

Royce knows the literature as well as his colleague. But he can't stand by and watch the boy suffer. He grabs a ten-blade and, starting at the sternum, begins to carve a deep incision into the mangled remains of the patient's chest. He proceeds to cut all the way around the left side of the boy's chest until his blade cuts into the table.

Filled with futile rage, Royce throws the scalpel on the floor. As he reaches for the rib spreaders, he spots the laceration on his finger. Consumed with anger, he hadn't felt the pain when the scalpel cut him; he still can't feel it now. He quickly rips off his torn gloves, wipes the blood from his hand, and cranks open the boy's chest. And there, among the ruined, partial organs that comprise what's left of this boy's torso, Royce is confronted with the irrefutable evidence. The boy's heart, miraculously intact, beats feebly, once every five seconds. There is nothing else to do for this child, no procedure or drug that will save this boy's life.

"Satisfied, Dr. Royce?" The trauma surgeon tosses his hands up in disgust.

Royce gives him a blank stare, and the trauma surgeon stalks out of the room. Royce turns his attention back to the boy, whose heart is beating slower and less vigorously, his moans of pain all but gone, now. Royce looks into the boy's eyes, and he knows this child is still suffering.

"Twelve of morphine," he barks to the nurse, without tearing his eyes away from the child. This will slow down the patient's respiration and help him die faster and with less pain. But Royce can't be sure the boy isn't still feeling some amount of torture. The seconds turn into minutes that feel endless as he waits by the child's side for him to die. He imagines the boy's soul hovering behind his eyes, and he wills it to flee the body, to find release and relief, to migrate into whatever waits for it in the great unknown beyond this life. Nothing, not even nothingness itself, could be worse than another moment, another second, in this body that lies before him.

At long last, the monitor flatlines and Royce gently closes the boy's eyes.

Royce slowly opens his eyes, reluctant to leave the liminal space between wakefulness and sleep. He'd been afraid to sleep, worried that the smashed, half-gone body of the boy would taunt him throughout the night. He'd had no power to stop himself from sleeping, in the end; slumber takes hold of him by force now, pushing him down into its dark, turbulent waters. But last night, by some grace, those dark waters were still.

Still working to shake yesterday's brutal trauma from his mind, he brings his left hand to his face to inspect the laceration he suffered, from his own haste and carelessness. Royce's eyes go wide. He bolts upright.

The cut on his hand is gone. Not so much as a scab or scar left behind.

He leaps from bed and runs to the sink, where he squeezes each one of his fingers from one end to the other, as though he were massaging an almost empty tube of toothpaste.

He turns on the water and watches it drip from his hands; there's not a speck of blood to be seen.

Thoughts of the mangled boy recede, replaced by confusion and disbelief. He holds his hands to his head, then down in front of his face, then back to his head in a gesture of being overwhelmed. The laceration had been unmistakably there. He remembered wiping the blood away before he dove fruitlessly back into the boy's chest. He remembered how the cut throbbed as he walked back to his hospital room after his shift, struggling to stay awake until he reached his always inviting bed.

His mind races in circles looking to land on an explanation. He wonders if this strange, supercharged healing is related to the magnets. Is it possible that being around such large magnetic fields for prolonged periods of time could in some way enhance his immune system? He's tempted to run it by Alesha, but a vague sense of caution pulls him back; he decides it's wisest not share this information with anyone else, even Alesha, at least for now.

Royce heads first to the lab; after running into Rudy in the hallway they walk together, the engineer catching Royce up on the latest bug fixes to their computer program. After grabbing a set of keys from the lab, Royce heads to the locked ward, which now holds fifty patients. He enters quietly, padding along like a monk, even though he knows he could stomp in with a marching band and his patients wouldn't wake. Scanning the room, his eyes land for a moment on each patient, lying on a gurney, and a smile creeps across his face. They're like sleeping marionettes come to life. Their bodies are prone, but their hands and bodies move as if they're active and alert. There's a cacophony of murmured sounds in the ward; many of the patients are speaking aloud as if in conversation. Watching them so deeply engaged with their dreams, he wonders where they are in reimagining their lives. Surveying the room, he sees a spectrum of pleasure and pain. And then his eyes come upon a single patient lying on his gurney, utterly still.

Royce presses the intercom and calls for a technician to help him get this patient to the PET scanner immediately. His hands shaking with panic, Royce injects the radioactive dye himself, and begins scanning the patient in search of his soul. After a few agonizing minutes, he visualizes the hot spot, deep in the man's pelvis. It appears to be motionless, idling rather than in the slow, constant migration that Royce has seen before. For a full thirty minutes, Royce continues the scan and watches the hot spot, to be certain that this soul is no longer in motion. *What does this mean*, he wonders. *Has this soul reached its end? Or perhaps, its beginning? What happens to a patient whose soul stops running the slow, circular track of a hot spot held by a magnet?*

He casts his scientific curiosity aside. Royce isn't prepared to wait and see what a stalled-out soul will do. He calls the lead technician and demands that she come to the lab immediately. His every cell is screaming at him: this patient's magnet must be turned off, right away. The technician arrives and deactivates the magnetic field. Royce stares at the PET scan and watches with a mixture of relief and dread as the hot spot begins moving again, migrating upward. Without the implanted magnet holding it back, the soul will soon leave the patient's body, and the patient will die.

When the soul reaches the top of the spinal cord, the patient's eyes flutter and open, zigzagging wildly. Royce, seeing the patient's body seize in panic, moves quickly to hold the man's shoulders as he tries to fling himself off the table.

Royce sees recognition, and then a powerful, heartbreaking relief flicker in the patient's eyes. The man tries unsuccessfully to speak. Royce fills a cup with water and helps the patient sit upright enough to take a drink.

"You're safe," Royce says gently.

The patient looks terrified once again. He shakes his head violently as the words pour out in a desperate, agonized outburst.

"Please, no, you don't understand. Please don't do that to me again." The man can't stop shaking his head.

"What don't I understand? Tell me what happened."

The patient stops moving and looks at Royce with a bitter, almost hateful gaze. "It was nothing. Just nothing. The absence of nothing, even. The blackest black, no air, no weight, no—just nothing there at all." His breathing is rapid and harsh as he searches for the words to describe his experience. "Death can't be that terrifying. Death—no matter what death feels like, can't be worse than that. It was like being alive, but—but—" The man is overcome with sobs. "It was like being trapped alive in death."

Royce feels a shudder run up his spine.

"I am so sorry. I promise; I won't ever let this happen to you again."

The man's eyes go wild again with fear. "No, you don't understand. I can't stay here anymore, like this. I can't go through that again. Please, please, can you help me die?" He grabs Royce's arm with a strength that shocks Royce. Even after a month with the magnet implanted, this patient is still frail and rail-thin, his body assaulted by years of cancer treatments. He's holding onto Royce's arm with the strength of a powerlifter in their prime.

Royce apologizes profusely once more. As the patient protests, he assures the man that nothing like this will ever happen again to him or any other patient.

"I promise, you're safe here. You're alive, and well, and getting better."

"But—you don't understand—I cannot bear that again—"

Royce wrests his arm free of the man's iron grip. Ignoring the man's desperate cries, he returns to the observation room, where he instructs the lead technician to turn the patient's magnet back on.

That night, on their evening stroll around the residential ward, Royce tells Alesha about what happened. To a shocked, horrified Alesha, Royce describes the patient's wild, panicked reaction and the man's description of the void he entered when the soul stopped moving. He does not tell Alesha about how the patient begged to be allowed to die. *The patient wasn't in his right mind*, Royce thinks to himself. He couldn't be expected to make an informed decision about whether to continue with the study or not. He's not sure Alesha will see it that way.

As they walk, Alesha wonders aloud. "The patient reached a condition similar to birth but maybe the opposite—like un-birthing—nullifying his existence, as though it—he—hadn't happened in the first place. That would surely be as anxiety-causing as dying, maybe more so."

Royce shudders again, this time at the memory of the man's description. *Like being trapped alive in death.*

Alesha continues to speculate on the soul's circular journey when held by the magnet in the body. "In a sense, their time is going backward like an erasure, stomping out feelings, leaving them milquetoast-like. Like my mama used to say, as flat and boring as a fileted fish."

Royce has been thinking much the same thing. It seems that the soul must keep moving for the individual to continue to experience life. When the soul reaches its origin in the body, it can go no further, and the person experiences something that no human being was meant to endure: the inability to experience.

Alesha stops and looks up at him. Her eyes radiate uncertainty. "We've got a few straight answers, along with a sack full of paradoxes, contradictions, anomalies, and plain old mysteries. I've got to ask: are we leading this research, or is it leading us?"

Royce feels himself bristle at her words, and the implication that things are out of control. "Time seems to move backward in our project. Why shouldn't leadership?" Royce asks. "There's so much we can't know about what's going on here, except through what we see experientially in our patients. Think about it. We're using electromagnetic waves to manipulate a subtler quantum energy—the hydrogen protons and maybe subtler energies not measurable by physics and maybe outside of physics, unknowable but undeniable.

"We know the equations that can measure forces applied on particles in electric and magnetic fields. The strength of the field, its direction, the speed of mass and its location in fields are determinable. It's complicated math, but we have it at our disposal. But this only tells us the effects of the fields on the mass within them. What about the fields themselves? What is a field?"

Alesha nods, falling right in sync with his line of thought. "Right. We can ask the same question about gravity and time.

Aside from its effect on its contents, we don't know what it is. No one knows what gravity is, just what it seems to do."

Her voice crackles with curiosity as she continues. "And what about quanta? All we've got are probabilities, right? No actual relationships? And the energy that underlies our work is finer than even that craziness."

Royce feels his mind sinking deeper into big theoretical questions; it's like wading through spectacular muck. "About energy. What about the energy that causes the vibration that initiates the electrical and magnetic fields that force atoms together and apart. What is that primal vibration?"

Royce watches with delight as Alesha marvels at the question, and counters with her own. "And how can it be primal—as in not preceded by another cause? How can something cause itself? In the end all we've got are questions. What do we actually know?"

Royce responds to Alesha, but he's aware that he's trying to steady himself. "Questions arise when something is missing. They show us what we're lacking, and where to go next."

"Where's that?" Alesha asks, her tone one of pure, genuine wonderment.

"I don't know. But we're not stopping."

Over the next month, Dr. Royce spends hours each day, every day, monitoring the progression of each patient's soul. He discovers that by calculating the rate of descent of the soul, he can calculate the time and date that the soul will reach its origin.

From there, he plots a simple course of action to keep the soul in motion: when the soul nears its origin point, they will turn off the patient's magnet. Without the magnet pulling on the soul, the hot spot rises to the visual cortex within an hour. When the magnet or plasma tube resonator is re-started, the months-long descent of the soul begins again. It is a "reset" designed to keep patients from touching down into the void of non-being.

Royce considers stamping each person's wrist with the date and time their soul will reach its origin point. He quickly reconsiders after images of Nazi concentration camp prisoners flash through his mind. He decides to stamp their right wrists with the expected date of their next reset, using ink that can only be visualized with black light. Each night, two hours before he retires to his own room, Royce checks his master list to see which souls will be reaching their origin before the end of the night. After he reviews the list, he walks through the ward, checking each wrist with a black light. All patients with matching dates then have their magnets deactivated for thirty-five minutes, the time it takes for the souls to return to the visual cortex.

Royce is compulsive about his nightly routine. He was willing to take away his pleading patient's wish to die. But he's vowed never to let another person suffer the emptiness of being trapped alive in the void of non-existence.

CHAPTER 24

"You doing okay, boss?"

Greg Sanchez looks tired. He's got deep lines on his face that Royce doesn't remember being so prominent the last time they saw each other. He's sprouting new gray hair, and his eyes look more sunken than Royce has ever seen. Royce wonders what's up, seems like his boss isn't taking care of himself like usual. *When was the last time I looked in the mirror?* His own self-care routine lately consists of running his fingers through his hair and remembering to shave every couple of days. He probably shouldn't judge Sanchez's suddenly aging looks.

Dr. Sanchez laughs, but there's no mirth in the good-natured man's chuckle. "I'm fine, Mike. I'm just fine." He pauses and a strange sadness clouds his eyes. "How are you doing, buddy?"

Royce shrugs off what sounds oddly like pity in Greg's tone. "I'm pretty excited about what we're doing here today."

Royce and Sanchez are meeting to finalize an arrangement to set up a PET scanner in the ER, specifically to monitor patients' souls. Their intent is not to use the soul monitoring innovation to prevent death. But rather to help the ER triage and handle critical cases effectively. Tracking the disappearance of hot spots will help medical staff discern when life-saving efforts will no longer be useful. If the soul is seen departing, there is no reason to waste energy, time, and money performing a heroic resuscitation that is doomed to fail. Royce hopes one day soon his soul-stop technology will have a place in his ER and in hospitals around the world. Still, this is a giant first step that feels incredibly validating for Royce, like coming home after making it big out in the world.

It took some time to bring Greg Sanchez around to the idea. Sure, he's been guardedly supportive of Royce's work from a distance. But tracking souls in his own emergency department was another matter altogether. "Feels like a big risk," he'd said in their initial meeting. "What if the patient has a shot once the scan goes dark?"

"They don't, Greg," Royce had replied. "They never do."

Ultimately, Sanchez was won over by Royce's compelling, overwhelming data, and assented to a trial run.

"So, we're setting up in trauma room three, right? I'll meet you there to help get everyone up to speed." Royce wants to leap out of his seat right now.

Sanchez shifts awkwardly in his chair, eyes darting as if looking for an escape hatch from his own office. "Thanks, Mike, but I think we've got it covered. A couple of your techs are going to show our staff what to look for."

Two hours later, Royce strolls into trauma room three, whistling a tune. It's Mary Watson's song. He's never quite been able to shake it. It's a sad, haunting song but Royce's rendition today gives it a light, almost happy lilt. There's no way he's going to miss watching his soul-tracking innovation get liftoff in the ER.

"—the most critical patient on the floor will have a PET scan." Greg Sanchez is explaining to the nurse manager how the new ER protocol will work. Susan Santiago is standing in front of the PET scan image screen, speaking in low tones with one of Royce's research techs. A few other ER staffers and members of the research team are consulting over the manual Royce developed.

"Hello, all," Royce says, tossing a wave.

The room goes silent. Everyone stops what they're doing and turns to look at him. He smiles widely, still feeling rollicking, exuberant waves of pride. "Anybody have any questions for me?"

One of the techs starts to walk toward him. Royce sees Greg Sanchez put a steadying hand on the woman's arm. "Like I said, Dr. Royce, I think we've got this."

The hair on the back of Royce's neck stands at attention. Sanchez is definitely giving him the brush-off. Allene, one of the department's longest serving nurse managers, an unflappable presence in the most chaotic ER shifts, stares at him, speechless, the whites of her eyes gleaming as though she's seen a ghost.

Why is everyone gawking at me as if I have two heads?

Nurse Santiago breaks the silence. "It's good to see you, Mike." She looks at him almost helplessly, as if struggling to know what to say next. Something has happened to make his colleagues treat him like a patient loose from the psych ward. Royce wracks his brain, trying to think of how he might've offended or alienated these people he's worked in the trenches with for years.

To break the awkwardness, Royce excuses himself and slips out the door. In the staff restroom, he casts a look at himself in the mirror. He doesn't look disheveled. In fact, his eyes are bright, his hair is thick and shiny, his skin is practically glowing, all despite his minimal attention to his appearance lately. He gazes down at his body—scrubs are clean, toilet paper isn't stuck to his shoe. He feels great and he looks perfectly normal. Whatever's going on, it has nothing to do with his appearance.

Heading back to trauma room three, Royce passes the general surgeon, Dr. Sterling, in the hall. He winces, thinking about the thirteen-year-old mangled by a train and the screaming match the two had over the battered boy's care. To Royce, it's all bygones, and he expects as much from Sterling. He offers the surgeon an amiable "Hello" and is surprised when the man returns his greeting with a frozen look and the drop of a jaw. *Whatever the fuck is happening has gotten to him, too*, Royce thinks. He wonders if his research colleagues have been complaining about his temper in the lab.

Royce distracts his mind from the troubling question by looking up at the patient board. It's instinct, really; he's not on shift, but he can't help surveying the current caseload as if it's his own. A man with facial lacerations, a woman with a diabetic emergency, a couple of guys with abdominal pain. He feels a surge of adrenaline when he sees that Paul Bryson has just been placed in trauma room three, designating him the most critical patient on the ward.

Manny slides up to the admit desk and picks up Bryson's chart.

"What's he in for?" Royce asks, peering over Manny's shoulder. Manny jumps as if he's about to leap out of his own skin. "Jeez, buddy. Didn't mean to startle you."

Manny laughs a little nervously. "Hey, didn't see you there." Manny tells him that the patient in trauma three is being treated for an acute myocardial infarction.

"Dr. Walters, we need you please!" Royce just catches sight of the back of Susan Santiago's head as she drops back into trauma room three. Manny races toward the room, and without hesitation, Royce close on his heels. It looks like Royce himself will get to be the one to perform the first soul-searching PET scan in the ER.

Royce watches as Manny begins chest compressions and calls to Nurse Santiago for a defibrillator. After a round of CPR the patient remains in ventricular fibrillation, an abnormal heart rhythm which is not compatible with life.

Royce can't stand on the sidelines any longer. He brushes the research tech aside, steps to the gurney to inject the radioactive dye, and begins searching the brain for the patient's soul.

He finds nothing. One scan, then two of the patient's brain. The soul has either already departed, and Paul Bryson is soon to die, or the hot spot is farther down in his body and this man isn't even close to death. He relays his findings to Manny, who has intubated the patient and administered a dose of lidocaine.

At last, the abnormal heart rhythm is terminated, and the patient converts to a normal sinus rhythm. Manny steps back as Paul Bryson opens his eyes. Before the man can speak, Manny cautions him to remain still and not to talk, while he removes the tube that's inserted in his throat.

"Oh my god, thank god . . ." The man's breath is ragged, his voice a throaty whisper.

Manny smiles at him. "Took a minute, but we got your heart back on track. Now, we're going to—"

"No, you don't understand," the patient hisses. "I was up there." He points to the ceiling above the gurney. "I watched the whole thing."

Royce steps over to the gurney and the two physicians trade knowing glances. This patient is far from the first to recount an out-of-body experience in the ER. Neither Manny nor Royce have ever put much stock in their claims. But Royce now couldn't be keener to understand what's just happened.

"You," Paul Bryson points to Susan Santiago, "ran over there and shouted for the doctor. And I heard you, doc, ask her for a fibrillat—no, a *de*fibrillator. "I heard that guy," he points to the research tech, "say 'Excuse me,' and you" he points to Royce, "sort of knocked him out of the way and gave me some other drug or something into my arm." Bryson lifts his right arm, which holds his IV tube. "And I saw a bright light coming from over there." He points to a high, far corner of the room. Royce and Manny listen in silence, both familiar with the patient's tale. These claims of out-of-body experiences used to be easy for Royce to dismiss. But even in his most skeptical days, he's always been struck by how meticulously alike the patients' stories are.

And then, Bryson's story takes a turn, one Royce has never heard before.

"Someone—something? I don't know, an entity of some kind—started talking to me from the other side of the light. They didn't talk to me, exactly. But I could hear them—understand them, every single word."

Royce leaps at the chance for more information. "What did the entity say?" Royce asks. Manny shoots him a look like, *What are you getting us into, man.* But Royce wants to know every detail. Bryson's soul didn't depart his body. But he may have come into contact with an entity that engages with souls in another physical, temporal realm.

"Most of it made no sense," the man says, his eyes full of wonder and confusion. "They were talking to me about being a teacher, how I'd steered all these students into purposeful lives, gotten some others out of some really bad situations at home." Bryson knits his brows. "I'm not a teacher—I sell insurance.

"They were going into all this detail about me and my younger brothers—all the things we did together as kids, sports and fishing and stuff, and trips we took together as adults—and how these were, like, the bedrock relationships in my life. But I don't have brothers. I have a half-sister who's, like, fifteen years younger than me. I see her maybe once every few years."

Royce feels Manny shuffling his feet beside him. He's probably had about enough of this man's strange tale. Before his colleague can shut things down, Royce jumps in again.

"Did the entity tell you anything else? What it wanted from you, where you were going?"

Manny stifles a sigh. "Dr. Royce, I don't think this is appropriate for right—"

"No, nothing like that." Bryson seems to need to talk about what's just happened to him. "It did want me to know how much I'd been loved by some girl—Julia something or other—who they thought I'd been involved with in college. I didn't go to college. I went to seminary right after high school, dropped out before I was ordained." The patient snorts. "No Julias there. And I'm gay."

Bryson sighs. "It was bizarre. And then it stopped telling me stuff, but I could still feel it there, just beyond the light." He again points to the corner of the room, where Royce only sees a worn ceiling panel and a small security camera. "Somehow—I don't know how I did it—I told this . . . this . . . thing that I wasn't who they thought I was. But without actually talking, you know?" Bryson closes his eyes and braces his body on the gurney as if it were a sled speeding down a hill. "And then in the next second, I was back in my body, opening my eyes."

Manny has checked out from the man's tale; he's looking over the patient's vitals and conferring with Nurse Santiago about moving him up to the cath lab. Royce is still by the man's bedside, momentarily frozen by the realization that just hit him like a rogue ocean wave.

Then his feet are moving almost before he knows why. He races back to the admit desk and stares up at the chart. The man with facial lacerations is gone. There's a kid in room two with an asthma attack and a baby in room four, vomiting with a high fever. The elderly woman with high blood sugar is still in room five. Royce narrows his eyes as he stares at the names of the two men admitted for abdominal pain. Frank Giulia is having sharp pains in his lower back and side. Gordon Reynolds is being evaluated for upper abdominal and lower chest pain. Royce grabs Reynolds's chart. The initial assessment is that the patient's pain does not seem cardiac related. *Guy probably ate too much greasy food for lunch*, Royce thinks.

Royce spins around and races into room six. Lying on the gurney, Frank Giulia looks pale and terrified.

"Mr. Giulia, are you a teacher?"

The man stares at him for one single, puzzled instant before answering. "Yeah, high school history."

"You like to hunt and fish with your brothers growing up?"

The man's puzzlement blooms into hostility. "What's this all about? I don't have any brothers. Why does it—"

"A doctor will be in to see you shortly," Royce calls, sprinting out the door.

Royce stalks into room nine. Gordon Reynolds is alone, lying on the gurney, looking pale and clutching his chest. He presses the call button for a nurse and leans in close to the man's ear.

"You remember Julia from college?" Royce whispers.

Reynolds's eyes fly wide open with shock. ". . . the love of my life," he whispers, wincing at the effort it takes to speak.

Royce feels his own heart twist in sadness. "She felt the same way, buddy."

He throws open the door just as the nurse arrives. "We need space in trauma three," he shouts down the hall. He turns back to the patient. "Mr. Reynolds, we're going to move you to the next room for a PET scan."

The man's words come out in a painful wheeze. "Name's not Reynolds."

Royce stares at him. "What is your name, sir?" he asks.

"Paul Bryson."

Royce feels the ground buckle under his feet. As he pulls the gurney into the hallway, he looks again at the patient board. Trauma room three is assigned to Paul Bryson, who Royce just discovered in trauma room nine. Royce scans the board. Room nine has been assigned to a Gordon Reynolds. He feels irritation burn inside his chest. Had the ER techs mixed up these two patients and put them into the wrong rooms?

As Royce and the nurse wheel Reynolds down the hall, Royce sees the man he—and apparently the entity—thought was Paul Bryson being quickly moved out of room three, craning his neck to catch a look at the incoming patient.

"Gordon," Royce calls out, and waits.

The patient's head swivels in Royce's direction. Gordon Reynolds recognizes Royce and lifts his hand in a weak, tired wave.

"I'll be here when you get back." Royce gives him a reassuring smile. *That confirms the mistake*, thinks Royce, who is both seething at the human error and intensely intrigued at the heavenly one. But there's no time to dwell on either, with the real Paul Bryson in front of him now.

Royce fires up the PET scanner in time to visualize Paul Bryson's soul just before it disappears from his brain. An ER doc Royce doesn't recognize rushes into the room with a nurse and the pair go to work assessing the patient.

"It won't matter," Royce mutters under his breath. Bryson doesn't need to hear that, not from him. But the ER staff does. Royce goes in search of Greg Sanchez to inform him that his new PET scan protocol has identified its first fatality.

One hour later, Paul Bryson has a cardiac arrest.

No resuscitation is performed. The patient dies.

Royce can hardly wait for Gordon Reynolds to come back from the cardiac catheterization lab. He wants to pick every detail from the man's brain before he loses them to the fickleness of memory. Was there an earthly connection between these two men that gave Reynolds's subconscious the details about Paul Bryson's life, or did he really speak with an entity from beyond this life? Had Bryson had his life temporarily removed from his body, only to be returned after the entity realized its own error?

To his dismay, as the clock nears eight p.m., Reynolds has not returned. Royce can't wait any longer. Before sleep comes upon him, he needs to get upstairs to check his patients' soul origination dates in preparation for resetting their hot spots to repeat their cycles through the body.

Royce enters the locked-down ward to check the patients' wrists. He's looking for three patients with the date of May 25 stamped on their right wrists. He takes the black light and holds it over each patient's wrist. Patient seventeen has a stamp that reads 5/25, 2300 hours. It's now eight p.m., or 2000 hours; the patient has three more hours before his soul reaches its origin. Patient forty's stamp reads 5/25, 2400 hours. He quietly wanders the rows of patients preparing for sleep, greeting some of them and searching for the third patient with a 5/25 date for soul origination. Once, and then again, he looks at every patient's wrist. Puzzled, he heads back to his office to check charts. It's possible there are only two patients who need their souls reset before the end of the day. But he's got to be certain. It's harmless to terminate the soul's descent early, but it's cruel to wait until the soul reaches its starting point. That sentences the soul and the person that soul inhabits, to a fate worse than death: consciously dwelling in a state of non-existence.

CHAPTER 25

The sun is almost set, but it hits his face like a hot, flaring flame, its brightness momentarily blinding to his eyes. His whole body feels assaulted by the merciless Albuquerque heat. Sweat instantly pours from Royce's body, soaking his scrubs.

His vision still spotty, he darts into the narrow V of a corner in the hospital's meandering outside wall, squinting back in the direction of the main entrance, where seconds ago, a security guard was racing toward him, weapon drawn, shouting at him to freeze.

He cannot fathom what this is all about.

Instinct takes over, and Royce makes a dash down the ramp toward the physician parking garage. With reprieve from the blinding sun, his vision adjusts, and he ducks and darts between cars in the darkened space, praying that his car will be in its designated space. When was the last time he drove? He cannot recall.

The familiar lines of the low-slung, black Audi beckon him like a lifeboat, and for an instant, his bewildered spirits lift. He punches in the keycode and slips into the driver's seat. The air inside is thick and putrid, a thin layer of dust covers the console he once kept glossy and pristine. He takes a deep breath, closes his eyes, and prays for the second time in as many minutes. He doesn't open his eyes until after he pops open the glove box.

It's there.

He grabs the key fob and does a double take when he sees his cell phone. Royce snatches it as if someone is about to take it away from him. He tries to turn it on, but it's dead; no surprise. He fishes out his emergency car charger and plugs it into the dashboard USB.

I need one more thing to go my way. God, please.

He presses the brake and pushes the start button.

The long-sleeping engine rumbles to life.

He jerks the car into gear and zips the Audi out of the underground garage, back into the blinding, fast-receding sunlight.

Constantly glancing in his rearview mirror, he drives cautiously along the downtown streets. He has no destination in mind; he only knows he must keep moving. He has no idea where to go and no earthly clue why he's being chased in the first place.

Fifteen minutes ago, he'd been heading down the residence hallway to his office to double check his patients' charts. When he saw Rudy, the lead engineer, coming toward him from the other end of the hall, Royce waved.

That's when things got weird. To his complete bewilderment, without so much as a word, Rudy grabbed Royce's arm and tried to turn him around back in the direction of his hospital room.

"What the fuck are you doing, man?" Royce barked, prying loose Rudy's strong grip and shoving the man's hand off his forearm.

"Time to get some rest, doc."

Royce watched in confusion as Rudy pulled a two-way radio from his pocket. The static of the radio crackled as the engineer spoke urgently to a voice Royce didn't recognize on the other end.

"I'm on twelve. Need help now. Royce is out and angry."

Angry? Hell yes, angry about being manhandled. *What the hell is happening?*

"Dr. Royce, please come with me." Rudy's voice sounds soothing, placating, suspiciously calm. "Can we go over some new programming before you head for bed?"

Royce hovers in a moment of limbo, wondering if this is his own mind playing tricks on him or some sort of bizarre misunderstanding. Then he notices Rudy's right hand quietly digging into his pocket. He watches the engineer slip a syringe into his palm.

Royce raises a leg and thrusts it square into Rudy's torso, sending the man sprawling backward off his feet. Royce is sprinting as soon as his foot hits the ground, throwing his body down into the stairwell. His feet take him without thinking to Evelyn's office. His patron, his benefactor, his advocate, his friend. Now, he can only hope she will be his protector, at least until he can sort out whatever this madness is about.

Royce bursts into the foyer of her sprawling executive office, holding up a hand to her assistant before he can object to his unscheduled visit.

"Dominic, I need just a minute with her—"

He hears a woman's voice shout a protest behind him as he pushes open the double doors to Evelyn's office. The room is dark and stately. Floor-to-ceiling mahogany bookshelves line the far wall, abstract art canvases hang under recessed lights, and a thick Turkish carpet blankets the floor. Royce spots a model sailing ship in a glass box. It's practically a movie version of an executive's suite.

But it's not Evelyn's.

"Can I help you?" The bald, bespectacled man behind the desk stands halfway from his chair. "Dr. Royce?" The man looks as bewildered as Royce feels.

"Where is she? Where's Eve—Mrs. Price? I need to speak with her."

Royce watches the man's face fall into a mixture of pity and alarm. A tingle of recognition hits Royce like a dart. He remembers seeing this man, a little less bald, at the hospital board meeting when he pitched his research. This is one of Evelyn's bean counters.

"Dr. Royce, Evelyn isn't here. This isn't her office anymore."

Royce feels the ground shifting ominously under his feet again. There's only one thing that could have made Evelyn leave her position at the hospital without telling him. He feels grief ripping through his chest.

"When did she die?"

The man looks startled. "She's not dead, Dr. Royce," he says, as if stating the obvious.

"Where is she then?"

"She's upstairs. In your laboratory."

Royce grips the steering wheel, his mind threatening to run off its rails as he replays the last twenty minutes of insanity. He's disoriented being out of the hospital. Driving a car feels alien, the streets familiar but new again. He checks his phone. It's got a small bit of battery life. He scrolls through his contacts and pulls up Alesha's number. Then he remembers. Alesha is out of town. Her father died, and she went to Montana for the funeral. It's the longest they've gone without speaking since . . . Well, since a very long time. It feels like he hasn't seen her in weeks. But that can't be right. It's only been a few days. Long days, he thinks, without her by his side in the lab, walking together at night, unpacking all the big, mysterious ideas their study has unleashed.

He taps out Manny's number.

Thank god, he thinks, when Manny answers. "Jesus, Manny, you gotta help me out . . . Something is totally screwed up. I just got roughed up by one of my engineers and a security guard pulled a fucking gun on me. I need you to call Greg Sanchez and—"

"Mike, where are you right now?"

There it is again. That tone of deliberate, placating calm. Royce feels his heart ripping apart, as it hits him: his best friend is part of whatever madness is going down.

"Manny, don't bullshit me right now. What the fuck is happening? Why am I being hunted like a criminal?"

"Mike, I can't help you unless I know where you are." Manny's stilted, manufactured tone cracks, and Royce hears the anguish underneath the veneer of calm. "You're not a criminal, buddy, you're anything but that. I think you need to come back to the hospital and get some sleep, man."

Royce cuts off the call.

Time to get some sleep. That's what Rudy, in a less than gentle manner, insisted he do. Now, Manny. *Why would people be chasing him around and insisting he go to sleep?* Before the question is fully formed in his mind, a wave of exhaustion washes over him. It's almost as if the mention of sleep conjured the sensation.

Sleep is exactly what can't afford right now. He opens the windows and blasts the radio.

He thinks about the past several months of incredible rigor in the lab, and of how quickly and powerfully sleep has overcome him at the end of each day. It usually happens around nine or ten p.m. Royce checks his watch; it's eight-fifty-five. He recalls that he's often been so tired, Alesha has walked him to his room before heading to her own bed in the patients' residence wing. It feels like forever since he's seen her smiling, soulful eyes. Her eyes were the last thing he saw each night before he dropped like a stone into sleep.

Royce slams on the brakes, almost causing a pileup. Alesha's eyes are the last thing he sees before sleep. But there's something else that happens every night, right before he lapses into unconsciousness. He hears the click as Alesha closes his door.

His skin crawling cold up his back, he remembers that last night, he heard the click, just as he was careening into slumber. Alesha is fifteen-hundred miles away.

Who was in his room with him when he fell asleep last night?

Panicked and confused, he shakes his head violently to ward off the swells of somnolence hitting him like giant, crashing waves. Alesha is gone, Manny is working against him, who knows about Greg or his other ER colleagues. And Evelyn—Evelyn is his patient, somehow. His memory gaps have at times felt cavernous, but it's not possible that he could have somehow had Evelyn's admission into the study swallowed into the black hole of time that plagues him. Is it?

Not knowing whom to turn to or where to go next, he pulls his car into the first open parking space he sees. Scanning the streets as he slips out of his car, he sees several police cars circling the area. *Are they looking for me*, he wonders. The sun is setting now, and a neon sign flashing a martini glass catches his eye. He races into the nightclub, grateful to find music blaring and the room filled with hundreds of people. Nobody could find him here.

"Stamp," the hostess says as he starts to pass her by. He dutifully holds out his arm as she presses a stamp onto his left hand. Royce goes directly to the bar and orders two shots of tequila, pounding them down like a college bro at a frat party. The booze fills him with warmth but does nothing to calm his nerves or restore his composure. He's at a loss for his next move. Royce paces the club, checking his watch repeatedly. It's still nine-thirty, just like it was fifteen seconds earlier. When he grows too fidgety and panicked to stay in the club any longer, he heads for the door.

Suddenly he feels a jolt like a spike through his head and images of the ER begin floating through his mind. His hands are wading inside a patient's bloody, cracked open chest, searching for a bullet. He's intubating a tree worker with a branch impaled six inches deep through one eye. He shakes his head vigorously to keep himself awake, and marvels that he could start dreaming while he's upright and walking around.

"Check your stamp," the hostess says as he reaches the door.

He slides his right hand under the black light.

"Looks like a stamp from another bar," she says. "Other hand, please."

"I haven't been to any other bars," Royce says with impatience. He looks down at the stamp on his right hand. He nearly falls over at her feet as his confusion and his insight clash like twin titans.

He reads the stamp aloud to himself. "5/25/2200."

His feet barely keep him upright as he reels toward his car.

"You okay, man?" A pair of twentysomethings walk by him. "Too many pinot grigios, old guy?"

He hears their laughter as he jumps in his car. Their jeers bounce off him like toy arrows. He's been struck in the heart by a betrayal that he doesn't understand but feels bleeding like a chest wound. He takes a long breath as he starts this car. This time, he's got a destination in mind. He can't believe he didn't think of going there first.

In the whole chaotic mess of this night, with all its unanswered questions, only one detail matters. The stamp on his hand, identifying him as a patient. A patient whose soul is about to reach its nadir.

He's barely put the car in his usual spot when he's running up the driveway. He turns the knob. The door is locked. That makes sense, at least; his mother would make a habit of locking her door after dark. He knocks and bounces back and forth on the balls of his feet, cycling between a dizzy, lightheaded horror and ever-growing swells of exhaustion.

A middle-aged man opens the door, and Royce uses all his strength to stay calm and not lunge at the stranger. He asks where Mrs. Royce is.

The man looks confused. "I think you have the wrong house. There's no Mrs. Royce here."

A rage of confusion sweeps through his mind, almost knocking him off his feet. "This is my mother's house."

The man casts a glance behind Royce and takes a wary step back from the threshold. "My wife and I have lived here for about a year." The stranger closes the door in Royce's stunned, anguished face.

Royce remembers, then, how Dr. Radapathya offered him condolences on his mother's death. As best that Royce can recall, that was about a year ago. But hadn't Alesha stepped in to say that it was Dr. Rice's mother who died? Royce feels betrayal burning inside him like a brush fire. Is Alesha a part of this madness, whatever it may be, to condemn and deceive and humiliate him? The thought of it makes his stomach churn. Suddenly, he's back in the ER, performing a cricothyrotomy on a woman whose botched suicide attempted cost her half her face. His eyes are fluttering, threatening sleep yet again. He smacks his temples with closed fists to make the visions stop.

His mother is dead; this much he knows. And with her death, the last physical remnant of his childhood, his childhood home, has been erased, now in the possession of strangers who have no idea what intimate events transpired there. Memories of his youth float like fragile bubbles across his mind. But it's like watching the childhood of a stranger. A stranger who looks like him, who lived all the moments he lived, growing up in this house. But Royce feels utterly untethered from any emotional connection to the child he was, to those memories now bobbing and breaking in his mind. It's not his childhood anymore. It could be anyone's he's watching unfold. He feels his own mind coming unmoored. He's floating in a relentless sea of images that once were memories but are no longer.

The memory that tickles a connection comes without pictures, as though a gray mist. He's three, maybe four years old, right at the age where memories begin to form. He, baby boy Mike Royce, is crying. No, wailing, a primal wail. Like a swirling cloud, the mist takes him rolling down the narrow hall toward his little room in the corner of their house: arms and legs are thrashing, angry words thundering, a pair of cruel eyes and the smell of dirty socks stalk the room. The mist transports him to a place he will one day call home: a hospital emergency room, his dad on a gurney.

Royce can't see the memory but his long-buried knowledge is now filling in scenes left empty for decades. Some kind of infantile apocalypse—what was it?—like a storm with a terrible thunderclap, then later, at the hospital eyes staring at him. *Why me? What do they want?* Kind people wishing him well. "So sorry, kid." Heads shaking.

Then silence. Silence in his child-mind, which buries the terror. Silence in that childhood home, Mom retreating to her room down the dark narrow hall. For years afterward. Only a moaning sound late at night, every night, from down the narrow hall, broke the silence that lived under their conversations, that walled off the dark world of grief beneath their day-to-day, get-along, keep-going, *do your best, your best is enough.* Royce hooks as if with a child's finger the memory that his own father was murdered: strong-armed, tattooed marauders flooding his house dark as sewer water, swarming into his little room, him under the bed, hiding, his father suddenly in the doorway, drawing the men away from him, paying for his fatherly devotion with his life. He's been hiding ever since, denying it all.

Until now. Indeed, he has been through it all before. *This,* he thinks, *this is the first trauma, the uber-trauma, of his existence.* The ER dream, the swarm of hooded figures, the gun pointed at him. Is this his déjà vu unmasked? Was his ER dream built like a rickety lean-to adjacent to this grand, horrible mansion of a memory?

No wonder he couldn't get closer than arm's-length to anything or anyone. Little surprise he's spent a lifetime in a frenzy of action to distract from his profound non-involvement. Better to dodge the gunfire than feel the bullet.

Until now. Now he is sinking into the muddy trail of his own memory up to his eyeballs. How could it have seemed he was chasing anyone else's soul? He's been chasing his own tail all this time.

There's something else. He feels it like a pulse in his chest.

He doesn't want to know, but he has to find out. He pushes his tie aside and feels under his white button-down shirt for his lucky, don't-die-around-me T-shirt. His fingers press the worn cotton weave, searching more closely than his eyes sometimes see, especially when he doesn't want to see. And he feels it. It's there, unmistakably. A rough-knitted knot. Someone mended the hole from the twenty-two at his heart.

Royce strikes his head again with his fists. He ran from the only place that can save him. And he's got to go back. He jumps in his car and speeds back toward the hospital. As he expected, the moment he walks through the main entrance a huddle of security guards give chase. Months of sprinting the stairwells pays off. He dashes up the ten flights, rushing down the hallway to the locked ward. He feels the thick steps before he hears them; looking up, he sees the determined Rudy trundling toward him. He picks up his pace.

The wheelchair sits just a little too deep into the hallway; Royce takes just a little too long to take his eyes off Rudy up ahead. His left foot catches the wheel bottom, and his upper body goes flying forward, his head striking the admit desk on the way crashing down.

He fights to stay conscious as his hand reflexively reaches toward his head wound. His finger probes deeply inside the large laceration at his scalp, and there it is, the edge of a small piece of metal. Losing his sight and his battle to stay alert, he senses rather than sees Rudy standing over him. His watch beeps its ten p.m. alarm.

All at once, sheets of emptiness and loneliness encircle him like a whirlpool, holding him aloft. Then, just as suddenly, the emptiness fades. And his consciousness slips intact into a cavern of nothingness, a wasteland of nonexistence.

CHAPTER 26

"Male, eighteen, gunshot to the chest, en route, three minutes out."

Royce is just coming off treating a stab wound to the back in a young man who managed to slice the face of his attacker before collapsing when the staccato voice of the paramedic relays the ER's next incoming trauma. *Another gang-related incident*, he thinks, *and it's not even ten p.m.* He takes a quick swig of water and heads toward the ambulance bay when the crying stops him in his tracks. There's a commotion somewhere on the floor. He can hear shouting, pleading, muffled and intense. Someone is pleading for their life, not angry, but desperate. He can barely make out the words: *Let me go*. But he can't tell where it's coming from. Every noise around him suddenly sounds like it's traveling through thick glass.

Out of nowhere, he feels his head swivel back and forth. He's not doing the moving. He's being manipulated like a marionette on strings. Standing in the middle of the ER, his head swiveling back and forth, listening to these anguished cries for mercy, he is certain his eyes are already open.

Then he opens his eyes.

His vision is blurry. He can barely focus on the lines of the ceiling tiles looming overhead. He is lying on a gurney. For a single instant, his mind is wrapped in confusion like an infant swaddled in a blanket. It's all he can do to stare at the square tiles above him. Then her soft, mournful cries alert him to her presence.

Royce turns his head, on his own this time.

Alesha is lying on the gurney next to him.

The sight of her brings his every cell to life, grounding him in his body and lighting his heart with joy. Her tear-stained face reflects so many layers of emotion, he can barely unpack them.

"You're back from Montana. Thank god."

She looks at him with the saddest eyes he's ever seen. "I haven't been to Montana in two years, since my dad died."

Royce feels the quaking of fragmented time, shifting his reality like tectonic plates colliding in the earth beneath him. "What's going on? What are we doing here?"

Alesha meets his questions with a fresh round of sobs that tear at his heart. Between sobs, her breath is ragged, but she manages to unravel for Dr. Royce the mystery which he himself initiated.

"Do you remember getting shot last year?" Her hand touches her own chest, right at the place where Royce felt the stitched-up knot in his T-shirt. "It was the gang guys coming after that kid with the punctured lung."

The memories flash through his mind like snippets of film: the nurse screaming and dropping to the floor. The dark, round muzzles of guns held side by side, stalking toward him in unison, the boy behind him their target. His foolish hands shoved out at them as though he could stop them. The fire in his chest, the dark curtain of fog descending. He looks Alesha in the eyes, needing to understand.

"I think I remember . . ." His voice sounds strange, less deep and assured than he's imagined himself to sound. ". . . Why do I feel like it's about to happen again?"

He sees it there, the pitiful heartbreak in her eyes, which tells him what he needs to know before her words do.

"Because it's going to happen again." The anguish in her voice is bigger than life, bigger than her life and his life combined.

He props himself up on his elbows, scanning the room for the first time. He's never seen the locked-down ward from this vantage point, not that he remembers. The rows of gurneys with patients performing their sleeping pantomimes as their souls carry them back through the dreaming re-creations of their lives. His heart twists in his chest when, several beds down, he sees Evelyn's bony hand wrapped into a fist; he imagines her shaking her cane at something enraging her: something inane, something slow-witted.

In this one way, he is not an observer in his own life. In this one, single way, his devotion to non-involvement has been a fantasy and a delusion.

He is one of them.

And last night, his soul ran its course.

Rudy turned off his magnet, Alesha tells him, just as his soul reached its origin. *Just as I dropped into that hellscape of less than nothingness*, he thinks.

"It's the sixth time, Mike."

Royce does the figuring in an instant: he has re-lived the significant events in his life five times.

"Have I done anything but lie here for a year?" His voice sounds pitiful to his own ears. "Is any of it real?"

Alesha rolls her body to one side and reaches out a hand to touch his arm. Having her skin on his feels exquisite. Every day at three o'clock in the afternoon, she tells him, he becomes lucid. He functions in the present until about nine o'clock, when his soul wakes and continues its journey. "They needed you so badly, Mike," she whispers. "You were the only one who could keep the project going." He was locked in his room every night until his soul rested, and he awakened to the present.

Royce feels his eyes grow cold and distant as he works to comprehend these horrible truths, this reality of his that he's been denying for a year. When he tried to steer Royce back to bed like a child, Rudy had been doing his job. The humiliation creeps through Royce like a virus.

"I haven't been in the ER at all?"

Alesha shakes her head. "Not as a doctor, not since the night you were shot."

Royce thinks about the battered girl, the boy split in two by a train, the drunk assassin-behind-the-wheel. Harry Samuelson, with his deep, gentleman's eyes. What was real? What was his imagination dancing with his psyche? He'll never know. And he struggles to care when it all exists in his mind now, anyway.

The only time he's been to the ER, she explains, is when he was there to help set up the PET scan. No wonder Susan Santiago, Greg Sanchez, Manny, all his colleagues looked at him with such pity and wonderment that day. He was no longer their peer. He was a science-geek-zombie woken from the semi-dead. So, too, with Rick Davies and his endless runaround over the CT scans. Of course Davies couldn't show Royce an image of his brain with the magnet implanted. They've all been in on it, all along, watching him like a circus freak. He's not sure if he's ever felt lonelier. The sting of loneliness transports him back to his newly unearthed memories of his childhood home, a place of violent death and silent, unspoken mourning.

"My mom is gone, isn't she." It's not a question.

"Shortly after you were shot."

Royce thinks about how she had to live through both her son and her husband being shot. The cruelty of it stuns him.

The barrage of information from Alesha has rendered Royce numb. His mind beginning to absorb the weight of what he's learning, a new thought occurs to him. He looks at Alesha. "Where have you been?"

Alesha's eyes are downcast. "For the last three weeks, I've been here." Three weeks ago, she tells him, scans revealed her cancer had metastasized to her liver. None of the litany of chemotherapy drugs she'd been on could hold her cancer in check. Without the magnet implant, she had a month, maybe two. She'd relented at last to joining the study as a patient.

"Mike, I need you to do something for me—two things, actually." Her lip trembles as he watches her summon her courage. He knows what's coming. What else is there to ask of him now?

She breathes out slowly, emptying her lungs of air before she begins. "Please turn off my magnet. I want you to be the one to do it. And I want you to do it today before you go back into your dreams."

Her eyes reveal a dance of agony and delight as she says, "Life is wonderful, but I know this now, and I have no doubts. God meant for us to live in the bodies we were born into once, and only once." Alesha's face is soaked with tears as her fingers interlock with Royce's, their hands now knitted together like a sailor's knot.

He thinks of the patient who begged him to let his soul go. He remembers how easy it was to turn his back on the man, a virtual stranger to him, a piecemeal source of data and little more. Royce cannot fathom letting Alesha go. He knows that he will lose her in their overlapping forever, not once, not twice, but over and again, if he forces her to stay.

"What was the second thing?" he asks.

Alesha squeezes his hand. "Come with me, wherever I'm going. Wherever it is we're all supposed to go." She reaches over and touches his cheek, as if to wipe a tear that isn't there. "We could be together, forever."

It feels like the silence between them itself is waiting for his answer.

Royce looks over Alesha's head, gazing at the observation window beyond which he knows there are techs and physicians listening, watching, busying themselves with their work, his work. *Is it time to let my body go, as God intended, or should I ride this cycle again*, he thinks to himself. He did not know until now how irritating it is to face a window you can't see through. "The day we spent taking pictures together—did that happen? Or was that a conjured dream?"

Alesha smiles at him. "It was real. At least, as far as I can tell. Or maybe we conjured that dream together. Two consciousnesses seemingly separate but bobbing on a common wave."

"If so, it was a wonderful wave." Royce brings his eyes back to Alesha. "That wave feels more believable to me than the reality of our physical separation in two bodies." As he gestures to the open space between the two of them, he sees in Alesha's eyes hope flaring that maybe he will set his soul free with hers.

"I call that wave, love." Alesha gives him a wry look. "Another of the fields we can't prove or comprehend."

"Magnetic, gravitational, electrical . . . Love. It's amazing what we don't need to know to survive."

"Maybe some knowledge is better kept out of reach." Alesha ever his challenger, his conscience.

He understands how Alesha could let her body go. For her, it's all about energy, and the wave. It's about something bigger than her or him, something matterless that can't be seen or imagined. His mind touches down on one of their late-night conversations.

"Some of us are all particles, on-off-on." Royce had been aware, even then, that he was describing himself.

"While others of us span the infinity in-between," Alesha had countered. Coming from someone else, it might've sounded like a judgment. From Alesha, it sounded like an invitation.

Royce knows his nature is to understand love as an abstraction, "a field of love," experienced from the outside looking in, like physics fields, where objectivity requires non-involvement. He can think about it like a scientist peering in, but is he ready to live it from the inside out, like Alesha? Is he willing to let go for the chance to fly with her into the infinity in between?

Royce smiles at her, buying himself time to think. "You see right through me to my abstraction, no matter what I do or how I try. Non-involved, even in love. My experience is objective to the core. It's like there's a congenital part of me that's been removed," Royce says with a shrug. Was it his father's violent death that made him this way, before he ever had a change to know anything else?

Alesha's eyes brim with new tears. "It is your great sadness."

"More than sad, it's tragic. Because it's futile. No matter how much I push, I can't get involved enough or detached enough. I'm stuck in between."

Alesha's eyes throw flashes of pity and irritation at him. "We're paired but not matched. This close to touching but can't touch."

In that moment, the burden of failing her becomes too much,

and his resistance crumbles like a tower of sea-soaked sand. "I don't want that to be our fate," he says.

He pulls her to her feet and into a tight embrace. Feeling her heartbeat against his chest, he whispers into her hair. "Are you ready, then?"

She snuggles deeper into his arms. "Yes. Are you?"

"If we're headed into forever, might as well get going." Royce laughs nervously. "I'll tell them to deactivate us. You first, then me. That way I can be with you here, on this side, when you go."

Royce breaks free from their embrace and walks to the observation room to give instructions to the lead tech.

"It's time," he says, returning to Alesha.

Royce lays Alesha on the gurney where he spent most of his last year and stretches his body out next to her. With their hands entwined as one and their faces inches apart, they stare into each other's eyes, soaking up the final moments to gaze at one another as souls within bodies.

"It's done." The lead technician's voice crackles over the intercom. "Godspeed."

At the moment her soul passes from her body, Royce feels a presence drifting over him, then within him, and his body shivers uncontrollably. Alesha's smile becomes knowing in a way he's never seen before, and her eyes take on an otherworldly contentment. Her familiar whisper tickles his ear. "I have always loved you, with all my heart. And I know we'll be together out there. I believe it, Mike."

"So do I, sweetheart." Royce strokes her hair. "You've made me believe it."

Time fades to nothingness for Royce as he stares into Alesha's eyes and watches them grow gradually distant, shifting their focus toward that unseen horizon. He wonders what his own eyes look like to her.

"Almost there, now." He pulls her close, feeling her heartbeat against his chest for what will be the last time.

After fifty-five minutes, when Alesha's body follows her soul's direction, Royce is there to hold her for her final breath.

Still lying next to her, Royce places both hands on Alesha's face and kisses her lips as the fresh tears on her face merge with his own. To the end, they were as they'd always been to each other.

Royce looks toward the observation window but says nothing.

The tech's voice crackles over the intercom. "Dr. Royce, are you ready?"

Royce thinks of the work that he has done in pursuit of immortality and the work that still awaits. Who will keep up the chase for eternal life if he follows Alesha into the unknown? He glances down at Evelyn, still shaking her fists, fighting every moment to stay alive.

"Dr. Royce?" the tech calls again.

For the first time since he awakened on the gurney, Royce's voice sounds familiar to his own ears, confident, in control. "Keep the magnet on."

His exhaustion beckons him like a lover. His backward-advancing soul wants him to return to the ER. Dr. Royce calls for a needle and a chest tube. The gunshot victim will be here soon.

ABOUT THE AUTHOR

Dr. Mark Rosenberg is a former Assistant Chief of Emergency Medicine at Walter Reed Army Medical Center. He currently leads two medical practices in integrative oncology and antiaging. He is also a medical innovator, founder of a pharmaceutical company that develops targeted drugs to treat cancer, and an inventor of a provisionally-patented device designed to stop the "seeding" of cancer cells, designed to convert a systemic disease back into a local disease.

ACKNOWLEDGMENTS

My life has been one protracted race. One of my many idiosyncrasies is my compulsion regarding time. I am always early for every meeting or appointment and I have even had nightmares about being late for important events. Procrastination is not a part of my vocabulary. Although it took me 23 years to complete this novel, I would not change the timing if I could. I have heard that many novels, especially those written by first-time novelists, are somewhat autobiographical. That is certainly the case here, as there is a lot of Dr. Royce in me. This novel is the product of all my years and life lessons; from being an over-achieving child, to dealing with the heartache of losing far too many patients, including my mother and father, to finally coming to peace with the cycle of life and death. I am thankful for those who taught those life lessons to me. I thank my parents, for teaching me love and compassion. I am thankful to my wife and my children, for tolerating my compulsive behavior. I am thankful to all my patients, who have taught me more about life than I ever dreamed of learning. Finally, I am thankful to Stacey Donovan,(and her team, Caitlin Tunney, Ajla Dizdarevic, and Marc Greenwald), for without her input and guidance, this novel would never have been written.

Made in the USA
Monee, IL
25 October 2024

68674376R00164